AWARDS AND ACCOLADES FOR THE
CRITICALLY ACCLAIMED AND BESTSELLING
PASSPORT TO PERIL MYSTERY SERIES

"Maddy Hunter's Passport to Peril series is a first-class ticket to entertainment. *Dutch Me Deadly*, the latest adventure of her endearing heroine and zany Iowan seniors, offers nonstop humor and an engaging plot woven so well into its setting that it could take place only in Holland. Despite the danger, I want to travel with Emily!"—Carrie Bebris, award-winning author of the Mr. & Mrs. Darcy Mystery series

DATE

Alpine for You
An Agatha Award finalist for Best First Novel and a Daphne du Maurier Award nominee

Top o' the Mournin'
An Independent Mystery Booksellers Association bests

Pasta Imperfect
An Independent Mystery Booksellers Association bestseller
A BookSense recommended title

"The easygoing pace [of *G'Day to Die*] leads to a satisfying heroine-in-peril twist ending that should please those in search of a good cozy."—*Publishers Weekly*

"*Norway to Hide* is a fast paced, page-turning, highly entertaining mystery. Long live the Passport to Peril series!"
—OnceUponARomance.net

"I found myself laughing out loud [while reading *Alpine for You*] ..."
—*Deadly Pleasures* Mystery Magazine

"No sophomore jinx here. [*Top o' the Mournin'*] is very funny and full of suspense."—*Romantic Times BOOKclub* Magazine

"Murder, mayhem, and marinara make for a delightfully funny combination [in *Pasta Imperfect*] . . . Emily stumbles upon clues, jumps to hilarious conclusions at each turn, and eventually solves the mystery in a showdown with the killer that is as clever as it is funny."—*Futures Mystery Anthology Magazine*

Dutch Me Deadly

FORTHCOMING BY MADDY HUNTER

Bonnie of Evidence

Dutch Me Deadly

A PASSPORT TO PERIL MYSTREY

maddy
HUNTER

MIDNIGHT INK
WOODBURY, MINNESOTA

FIRST EDITION
First Printing, 2012

Book design by Donna Burch
Cover design by Adrienne W. Zimiga
Cover illustration © Anne Wertheim
Editing by Connie Hill

Midnight Ink, an imprint of Llewellyn Worldwide Ltd.

Library of Congress Cataloging-in-Publication Data

Hunter, Maddy.
  Dutch me deadly / Maddy Hunter. — 1st ed.
      p.   cm. — (A passport to peril mystery)
    ISBN 978-0-7387-2704-2
  1. Andrew, Emily (Fictitious character)—Fiction. 2. Tour guides (Persons)—
  Fiction. 3. Older people—Travel—Fiction. 4. Americans—Netherlands—
  Fiction. 5. Class reunions—Fiction. 6. Amsterdam (Netherlands)—Fiction.
  I. Title.
    PS3608.U5944D88   2012
    813'.6--dc23   2011037363

Midnight Ink
Llewellyn Worldwide Ltd.
2143 Wooddale Drive
Woodbury, MN 55125-2989
www.midnightinkbooks.com

Printed in the United States of America

In memory of Alice "Dunc" Martin, who honored us with her friendship, dazzled us with her dinner parties, and spoiled us with her kindness. We miss you so much.

—mmh

ONE

HOLLAND IN SPRINGTIME IS a feast for the eyes. Just look at the travel brochures that promise sweeps of tulips radiating toward picturesque windmills. Fields of tulips bordering narrow canals. Crates of tulips glutting flower markets. Gardens of tulips brightening parks. Vases of tulips adorning hotel lobbies.

Holland in springtime offers tourists the most spectacular display of color on the planet.

Unfortunately, we were visiting in late autumn and were missing the spectacle, but with the economy in freefall, investment income dwindling, and our town needing to be rebuilt after being leveled by an F4 category tornado, we considered ourselves lucky to be here at all. So even if we weren't booked into five-star hotels, had no plans to dine at five-star restaurants, and could stay only eight days instead of fourteen, we were still excited about exploring Holland. Iowans are a practical lot and understand the meaning of "shoestring budget," which meant I didn't have to worry about anyone in the group having false expectations.

"So where's the gazillions of tulips I saw advertised in the travel brochures?"

Every tour group has its resident bellyacher. Ours is Bernice Zwerg, whose voice is to the human ear what fingernails are to a chalkboard. Cursed with hair like tangled electrical wire and the grace of a horseshoe crab, Bernice is renowned for having the sourest disposition in our hometown of Windsor City, Iowa. Lucky for me, the core members of our travel group pummel her complaints with sunshine almost before the words leave her mouth, so I can stay out of the fray until I hear the sounds of blood vessels popping, at which point I play my tour escort's card, restoring calm and order.

Even at their most volatile, Iowans are extremely respectful of authority.

I wondered how long it would take the gang to pounce on her this time. I peeked at my watch.

Ten seconds... twenty seconds.

I straightened up in my seat and shot a look around the bus, perplexed.

Twenty-five seconds... thirty seconds.

Okay, what was up with this? They should be all over Bernice by now. How come the only thing I was hearing was deafening silence? And a few extraneous clicking sounds.

I glanced across the aisle to find Margi Swanson and Tilly Hovick fiddling with handheld electronic devices: MP3 players, or iPods, or BlackBerries, or something. There were so many gadgets on the market, I couldn't tell one from the other. But the ladies were obviously so preoccupied with their games that they were completely ignoring Bernice.

I caught my breath, my eyes freezing open at the sudden implication. Oh. My. God. No. NO! If everyone ignored Bernice, the only person left to deal with her would be—my windpipe closed in panic—me!

"Don't give me that baloney," Bernice griped aloud to no one in particular. "I paid for tulips so I wanna see tulips, else *someone* won't be finding any happy faces on her evaluation."

The "someone" to whom she referred was me, Emily Andrew-Miceli, official escort for the twelve Iowans on our tour. For several years, I was the travel coordinator for a senior travel club sponsored by our local bank—an absolute dream job that paid great and included free travel abroad. But all that ended when the tornado roared down Main Street, depositing the bank and all its assets in random cornfields throughout eastern Iowa.

In a classic Hollywood twist, however, a devastatingly handsome Swiss police inspector by the name of Etienne Miceli relocated to Windsor City, built a travel agency out of the rubble, and offered me my old job back. We're called Destinations Travel and we serve a niche group, providing escorted tours, both foreign and domestic, for the senior traveler. We occupy a sleek steel and glass building on Main Street, attract busloads of potential clients with our multimedia presentations and all-you-can-eat pig roast buffets, and enjoy outrageous perks like a fully outfitted gym, a rooftop swimming pool that converts to an ice rink in winter, and a soundproof bowling alley in the basement. All this, plus I get to sleep with the handsome ex-police inspector.

It's one of the perks of being Mrs. Miceli.

"What do you mean there aren't any evaluation sheets in our travel packet?" Bernice complained without provocation.

My windpipe stopped closing long enough for me to flash a diabolical smile. Sleeping with the boss had its advantages. When we'd been in the throes of carnal bliss, I'd convinced him to dump the dreaded escort evaluation forms so Bernice could be denied the pleasure of rating my performance with a big fat goose egg.

"I demand an evaluation form," whined Bernice. "It's my constitutional right! Emily's husband did this. See what happens when you let foreigners buy up your prime real estate after a natural disaster? They shred the Constitution. The next thing he'll set his sights on is cutting our senior discounts and setting up death panels. Mark my words. Life as we know it is ending. The old America is going down the tubes. We're in the midst of a socialist plot that's killing the private sector so big government can destroy our freedoms and take over our lives!"

Wow. Bernice must have bought some powerful new hearing aids to be able to regurgitate what she heard on America's most trusted news network so accurately. And her ability to retain it was *really* impressive. If she was taking expensive herbal supplements to improve her memory, they were worth every penny.

"No, I'm not giving up my Medicare card," she snapped in defiance. "Why would I do that? Do you know what my podiatrist charges to cut my toenails? There'd be nothing left of my Social Security check if I had to pay for it out of pocket."

I looked around the bus again, a little creeped out. *Whose* questions was she answering? Why couldn't I hear them? I plugged my finger into my ear and gave it a rattle. Was I suffering from a condition known to plague kitchen floors and ear canals alike?

Uff-da. Was I a victim of waxy buildup?

A toilet *whooshed.*

Well, duh? How come I could hear that?

A few seconds later, the restroom door creaked open, and my grandmother ambled back to the seat beside me.

"Anything excitin' happen while I was goin' potty?"

I leaned close to her ear. "Bernice has been engaged in a weird conversation for the last two minutes."

"That's not excitin', dear. That's normal."

"Not when she's been having the conversation with herself."

"No kiddin'? That don't sound like Bernice. She'd much rather argue with someone else. That way, when she says, 'You're such a moron,' she don't end up insultin' herself. That can get real embarrassin'."

"You're such a moron, Margi!" Bernice sniped. "I don't care if Pills Etcetera offers free toenail cutting on the first Monday of every month. I'm going to the clinic with the *real* doctors. If the bureaucracy pays for me to enjoy the best health care in the world, by God, I'm gonna take advantage of it."

"See what I mean?" I urged. "Why is she getting on Margi's case? Margi didn't say a word."

Nana glanced across the aisle to where Margi was sitting. "Yes, she did, dear. See there? She's textin'. Seein's how you've been so busy with your new husband and buildin' your house, maybe you haven't heard about it. It's all the rage."

"You can't be serious. How can they be texting?"

"These new phones work anywhere in the world, Emily. That's why they call 'em global smartphones. They got Web access, global positionin', e-mail with unlimited accounts, textin', HD video, Wi-Fi, 5X optical zoom, Hulu, Netflix, and a bunch of other stuff I haven't figured out yet. They're like the Swiss Army knife of cellphones. We all bought one. The nice folks at Pills Etcetera give us a volume discount. And they come in several attractive colors."

This was terrible! They'd be texting absurd messages to each other, and I'd have no idea what they were saying or how to fix it.

I pondered that for a half-second before smiling.

On the bright side, they'd be texting absurd messages to each other, and I'd have no idea what they were saying or how to fix it!

"Okay, so why is Bernice talking instead of texting?"

"She's got arthritis in both thumbs, dear, so she don't type real good. Sometimes all she ends up sendin' are punctuation marks and vowels, which don't make no sense to no one. We kinda get the gist of the question marks, but the semicolons has got us all buffaloed."

Nana was born in Brainerd, Minnesota, during the era of the Model T Ford. She won the lottery on the same day Grampa's ice shanty collapsed on top of him, then moved to Windsor City with her millions to be closer to family. She lives in an upscale retirement village that survived the tornado, bankrolled the construction of the senior center water park and reconstruction of Holy Redeemer Church with her investment earnings, and never met a computer she couldn't hack into. She stands four feet ten inches tall, is built like a bullet, and lives in defiance of my mother, who is always trying to manage her life. Her name is Marion Sippel, and even though she boasts only an eighth-grade education, she's the smartest person I know.

"Attention, please! May I have your attention?" Our tour director was a middle-aged Kansan named Charlotte whose round little face was as soft and dimpled as the rest of her. Standing in the front of the bus, in a pea-green Passages Tours blazer with jumbo shoulder pads, she clapped her hands in snappy bursts loud enough to wake even the guests who'd turned off their hearing aids. "Can the boys and gir—" Cutting herself off sharply, she pulled a face and began again. "Can the people in the rear of the bus hear me?"

"You bet!" yelled Dick Teig from the seat behind me.

My guys *always* sat at the back of the bus. It's not that they're thrilled to pass up front seats with stunning vistas and unobstructed views; it's just that when the roads get bumpy, or their water pills kick in unexpectedly, they prefer to be in the "good" seats—the ones strategically located near the bus's only restroom.

"If you can all hear me, I'll ask you to look out the windows on the side of the bus where the exit doors are."

"The right side?" Dick Stolee threw out, obviously worried that the bus might have spontaneously redesigned itself since we'd boarded.

"Right side! Yes!" She clapped enthusiastically. "Who guessed that correctly? Raise your smart little hand so I can see you."

Two rows in front of me, Dick Stolee slunk down in his seat, taking his smart little hand with him.

"I'm quite sure it was someone in the back. Don't be afraid to speak up. Do we have a bashful Bobby sitting by the little boys' room?"

At the sound of muted *tinging*, Nana unsnapped her phone from her pocketbook and checked the display screen. "It's a Tweet from George."

George Farkas had been Nana's main squeeze since our trip to Ireland, where he had shyly dazzled her with his bald head, unerring sense of direction, and versatile wooden leg. He was now an indispensable part of her life, filling the hole that Grampa's passing had left in her heart.

"George knows how to Twitter?" I asked, mortified that I was being shown up by eighty-year-olds wielding cut-rate electronic devices.

"He says sendin' Tweets is like sneakin' notes in class, only without the paper. George was a real wildman in his grade school days."

"Did he send you a love note?" I teased as she read the message.

"Nope. He's tryin' to guess what Charlotte was before she become a tour director."

"Nursery school teacher," I whispered. "Or jail warden."

As a groundswell of whispers rippled through the bus, Charlotte clapped her hands to restore quiet. "Naugh-ty, naugh-ty," she scolded, wagging a finger at us. "Only one person at a time is allowed to talk. That's the golden rule, and I expect you nice boys and—you nice people to follow it."

Uh-oh. This was getting serious. We were apparently set to travel through Holland by way of Sesame Street. I wasn't sure how my group was going to feel about being treated like kindergarteners, but I had a suspicion they weren't going to be too happy.

Ting. Ting. Ting. Ting.

"This Charlotte's got a real knack for rubbin' folks the wrong way," Nana whispered as she opened a sudden flood of incoming messages.

"Now," Charlotte continued, "take a little peek at the embankment flanking the right side of the road. That's one of the many dikes that was built to hold back the waters of the South Sea, or *Zuiderzee* as the Dutch called it, during the time of the Dutch East India Company."

The embankment was gently sloped and grass-covered and not at all what I'd imagined a dike to look like. It looked more like

Civil War earthworks, or an Indian burial mound, which completely contradicted my childhood vision of a brick dam towering over a little Dutch boy who was using his thumb to plug a leak.

"That doggone pesky South Sea flooded the lowlands for centuries, causing tens of thousands of deaths, but in 1932 Dutch engineers cut off its open link to the North Sea by building an enclosure dam. They drained the salty *Zuiderzee* and divided it into two freshwater lakes, the *IJsselmeer* and the *Markermeer*, and save for the tragic North Atlantic storm surge in 1953 that killed eighteen hundred people, Holland has been remarkably flood free."

"How come I'm seeing what looks like ships' masts poking above that embankment?" a woman called out.

"Because on the other side of the dike, there's a marina," said Charlotte.

"A marina?" The woman sounded skeptical. "You mean there's water on the other side of that mound?"

Charlotte's eyebrows flew up like flustered pigeons. "There's a *lake* on the other side. Haven't you heard anything I've said?"

"Does that embankment on the right side of the bus have some significance?" Dick Teig shouted out.

"It's a dike!" Charlotte shrieked, her voice ripping through the bus like cannon fire.

Margi looked up from her phone. "There's a dike here someplace?"

"Not to alarm anyone," Dick Stolee cautioned, "but if the lake is up there, and the road is down here, do you know what that means?"

"There's a lake?" Margi asked, swiveling her head left and right.

"It means the road is below sea level," said Tilly Hovick. Tilly was a retired anthropology professor with so much knowledge crammed into her head that she didn't need to use Google as her homepage.

Helen Teig gasped. "We're below sea level? Isn't that dangerous? What if the dike breaks?"

Bernice let out a sinister cackle. "Then you better grab your water wings."

"Are they stored in the luggage racks?" Margi asked as she eyed the overhead compartments. "Do you think they're sized? If they are, I'll need a medium, unless they run small, in which case I'll need a large. I hope they're not one-size-fits-all. That's such a crock. How can something that's big enough to fit over Dick Teig's head possibly be small enough to fit the rest of—"

"QUIET!"

Tongues stilled. Muscles locked. Thumbs froze.

"If you people in the back can't put a sock in it, I'm going to move you to the front of the bus!"

Move my group away from the restroom? Oh, yah, that would go over big.

I heard a chorus of horrified snorts and gasps, followed by a flurry of clicking sounds.

Tingtingtingtingtingtingtingting.

Nana bobbled her phone as it lit up maniacally.

"Our first stop this morning will be at a windmill a few miles south of our destination town of Volendam," Charlotte said pleasantly, returning to her canned narration. "It's called Molen Katwoude—*molen* is Dutch for mill—and it's a glorious example of a traditional Dutch windmill. Have your cameras ready because it's a real Kodak moment. And I'll give you fair warning. Stay! On! The! Sidewalk! If you wander into the road, you'll be run down by a scooter or a bicycle, and will end up in the morgue, like the pig-headed guest on my last tour. I harped and harped about the dangers, but no one was going to tell Mr. Know-It-All what to do. So he ended up dead. People *never* listen. It's epidemic."

"See, Emily?" Nana encouraged in a grandmotherly undertone. "Charlotte's had her problems, too. So don't go blamin' yourself for them tour guests what croaked while they was travelin' with you. Just about anything can do in us old folks. Hit n' run. Hearin' loss. Stupidity."

But my guests hadn't just dropped dead. They'd been knocked off. In fact, so many had died on tours I'd escorted that the body count was hovering somewhere around the national debt. Which goes to prove something I've suspected for several years: a surprising number of homicidal maniacs treat themselves to really nice holiday tours.

"Enjoy the scenery until we reach the windmill," Charlotte advised, "but when we arrive, *do not* jump out of your seats, trying to push and shove to be first off the bus. You will remain in your seats until I give you further instructions. Do you understand? Show of hands, please."

Uh-oh. She obviously didn't understand how important it was to an eighty-year-old with two hip replacements and a bum knee to be first off the bus. Claiming that honor not only gained the person rock star status, it earned him the kind of respect and awe usually reserved for people who could actually stay awake for events scheduled after luncheon buffets. Charlotte's edict could destroy the whole social dynamic of our group! What was she thinking?

I could sense rebellion brewing when only a few hands crept into the air.

Charlotte twisted her mouth into a pouty contortion. "I see. You're trying to be difficult. Is it any wonder I'm popping anti-anxiety drugs like Tic-Tacs? I just *knew* you people were going to be trouble. Well, put this in your pipes and smoke it: I'm in charge. You're not. So there!"

She flung herself back into her seat. Nana leaned toward me. "You s'pose she forgot there's no smokin' on the bus?"

I hung my head and sighed. Eight whirlwind days in Holland. The trip had sounded so short. Now, I realized, it was going to be way too long.

Oh, God.

TWO

As we sped along the two-lane road that hugged the dike, I realized that Iowa and Holland had a lot in common despite being separated by the North Sea, the Atlantic Ocean, and half a freaking continent. Both places were flat as ironing boards, with acres of level fields stretching as far as the eye could see. But while Iowans grew grain, the Dutch grew hay. While Iowa cornfields were crosshatched with a precise grid of gravel roads, Dutch hayfields were crosshatched with a precise grid of narrow canals. Iowans raised prize-winning hogs that became Blue Plate Specials; the Dutch raised woolly sheep that became winter sweaters. Iowans bought John Deere equipment to cut their grass; the Dutch bought scruffy sheep to eat theirs.

"Wow, look at that house." I pointed out the window at a fairy-tale cottage made of rose-colored brick and trimmed with decorative gingerbread. The roof was a steep pyramid of red tile, the windows were offset with white shutters and window boxes, and the front lawn was a topiary maze surrounded by circular gardens and elegant footbridges. "It's straight out of *Cinderella*."

"Uh-huh," Nana muttered as she studied her phone's display screen.

Two seconds later, we were past it. "You missed it."

"Uh-huh." Her thumbs flitted over her keypad.

I gave her arm a playful nudge. "I hope you realize you're missing all the scenery that you spent an incredible amount of devalued money to see."

"I know, dear. But this is real important. The Dicks wanna start a movement to protest the way Charlotte's handlin' things. They say all our freedoms are bein' threatened, so we need to take back our tour before it's too late."

I tried unsuccessfully to suppress a grin. "By asking you to leave the bus without trampling each other, Charlotte isn't exactly depriving you of *all* your freedoms."

"It's a slippery slope, Emily. She might start by tellin' us we can't be first off the bus, but what'll be next? No more textin' while we're in transit?"

I'd like to suggest that one myself.

"You got any ideas about what we can call ourselves, dear? Teabaggers is already taken. Carpetbaggers don't make no sense now that wall-to-wall is out and hardwood is in. Helen come up with Handbaggers, but the Dicks say they're not gonna join any movement where they gotta carry a purse."

"Way too emasculating," I agreed. "You could go generic and call yourselves anarchists. Then you could eliminate any fashion accessory problems."

Her eyes lit up behind her new glasses. "I like that. Lemme see if it flies with the gang." She poised her thumbs over her keypad. "How do you spell that, dear?"

As I provided the correct spelling, the bus decelerated into the breakdown lane and coasted to a complete stop near a pristine complex of multi-level town homes that boasted steeply pitched roofs and paint jobs in pink and charcoal. Charlotte stepped into the center aisle, her gaze lasering down the length of the bus. "Before we exit to see the windmill, I want you all to synchronize your watches. It is now *precisely* 10:06, so please set your watches. Ten. Oh. Six."

She waited a few beats, looking pleased that everyone seemed to be following instructions and no one was giving her grief. "We're scheduled to be here exactly fifteen minutes, so don't squander your time. Take your photos, then head directly back to the bus so we can continue on to Volendam. We won't wait for stragglers. If you miss the bus, you're on your own."

Hmm. That seemed a bit excessive. I wondered who'd established that policy—the tour company or Charlotte? I bowed my head close to Nana's. "Does your movement have any age requirements?"

"When Dietger opens the front door, I want you all to file out in an orderly fashion," Charlotte announced. "One row at a time. Right side first. And remember what I told you. Stay on the sidewalk!"

The door *shushed* open. Dietger vacated his driver's seat and hustled down the stairs. Charlotte clapped her hands as if she were keeping time to a military march and started herding guests into the aisle and down the stepwell. I fished my new digital camera out of my shoulder bag and slid to the edge of my seat, pumped to hit the pavement.

"Is everyone jazzed to see the windmill?" I asked my guys.

"We're not going, dear," Nana informed me as she poked her keypad with the tip of her forefinger.

I stared at her, nonplussed. "Not going? You *have* to go. It's a windmill. The most iconic symbol in all Holland." Well, besides wooden shoes, tulips, and Hans Brinker's silver skates. I shot to my feet. "Cellphones down! Refusing to participate in the tour experience *should not* be part of your movement. Why are you boycotting the windmill?"

"She lost me at 'synchronize your watches,'" complained Dick Stolee. "I haven't figured out how to adjust mine yet. The counter clerk at Walmart set it for Dutch time when I bought it last week, but it's still off by a few minutes."

I gaped at him. Dick was such an accomplished gearhead that he could have Humpty Dumpty put back together again before any of the King's men ever thought to yell, "Compost heap!" What kind of watch had he bought, besides "on sale" and "dirt cheap"?

"Do you have the instructions handy?" I asked as the seats in front of us began to empty.

"Yup, but I can't read them."

The inability to read the small print on manufacturers' labels was a growing problem among seniors battling cataracts, glaucoma, and macular degeneration. Happily, I'd racked up a perfect score on my last vision test, so small print was my specialty. "My eyes are a little younger, Dick. Do you want me to take a look?"

He held the instruction sheet out to me. "Can you read Chinese?"

"My phone has an app for that!" enthused Margi. "Chinese checkers, Chinese calendar, Chinese—"

"Truth is," Nana piped up, "fifteen minutes is cuttin' it way too close for us, dear. We'd be so pressed for time, we'd be leavin' by the front door and climbin' right back on by the rear. We'd look like we was doin' one a them Chinese fire drills."

Margi let out a sullen breath. "I don't have an app for that."

I knew better than to hassle them when they were fretting over time issues. An Iowan is so genetically hardwired to be punctual that being "on time" to him means being jawdroppingly early, kind of like an early-warning smoke detector that goes off a week before the fire starts. In a recent survey asking what Iowans feared most, 99 percent of respondents said "being late." The remaining 1 percent indicated in order of priority: having my watch stolen, breaking my watch, my alarm clock not going off, dead battery in my watch, and "Dude, none of your f-ing business." Iowa was obviously being overrun by a flood of transplants from North Jersey.

"So what are all of you planning to do while the rest of us are oohing and ahhing over the windmill?" I squeezed past Nana into the center aisle.

"We're going to update our status on our Facebook pages," announced George. "If we don't update on a regular basis, people start thinking we're dead."

"If you don't start participating in the tour, *I'm* going to think you're dead," I threatened. "Let's get with the program, people. Interact. Socialize. Have fun!"

"I thought we *were* having fun," objected Helen.

"Show of hands," insisted Osmond as he rose to his feet, pen and tally sheet at the ready. "How many people are having fun?"

Heaving an exasperated sigh, I hurried down the now empty aisle, appalled that my guys had adapted to the "information age" so well that they'd become mobile-phone junkies. They were as addicted to texting and social networking as Hollywood was to Botox and breast implants. This was terrible. I needed to call Etienne. How could we plan the photo exchange we'd talked about if none of our travelers looked up from their cellphones long enough to take any?

I rushed down the stepwell to find Dietger standing by the door with his hand extended to assist me. "*Dank u,*" I thanked him, testing out my one Dutch phrase as he helped me to the ground.

Dietger was a rough-shaven Belgian with a gruff manner, wild brown hair that needed cutting, and a physique as compact as a brick port-a-potty. He smoked too much, wore horn-rimmed glasses that gave him the appearance of a sixties government employee, and looked as if he might take his morning coffee black, with a beer chaser. I'd yet to see him smile, but he had dour down to a science.

He plucked his cigarette from his mouth and waved it toward the rear of the bus. "And the others?" he snapped. "Are they coming?"

"They're too afraid you'll leave without them, so they're taking preemptive measures by staying on the bus and inventing new ways to antagonize each other."

He took a drag on his cigarette and leered at me through a haze of smoke. "You want to go to bed with me?"

I stared at him numbly. My newly updated *Escort's Manual* had no directive explaining how to deal with sexual solicitation, so unless I could pull something useful out of the erectile dysfunction section, I was pretty much on my own.

Opting for the old standby, I flashed my ring finger at him. "Wouldn't you know? I'm married."

He flashed his ring finger back at me. "So am I married. Four times. So what?"

Hmm. How could I explain monogamy to a serial adulterer in terms he wouldn't find insulting? I mean, I had to interact with this guy for the next eight days, so I had to be careful not to generate any bad blood. If he turned out to be the vengeful type, he could break more bones with his bus than I could with my shoulder bag.

I offered him a perky smile. "Sooo ... I don't think so, but thanks so much for asking." Scooting around the bus, I darted across the highway and onto the narrow sidewalk, falling in line behind the other guests who were making the short trek to the windmill.

Abutting the pedestrian walk was a low concrete barrier that was supposed to prevent people from falling into the canal on the opposite side, but if this was the Dutch idea of a barrier, I imagined that swimming might soon overtake skating as Holland's favorite national sport. The windmill, a spectacular hexagonal structure with four open-grid sails that resembled giant propeller blades, was perched at the foot of the canal, surrounded by open field. The lower third of the building was sided with clapboards painted a dazzling emerald green. The upper two-thirds was overlaid with thatching so meticulously trimmed, it looked as if the building were wearing a mohair sweater.

As I scrambled to keep up, a man wearing a *Bar Harbor, Maine* jacket broke away from the group and ambled into the middle of the street, where he got to enjoy an unobstructed view of the windmill without the clutter of heads in front of him.

Uh-oh. This wasn't good.

Our bucolic ambience was suddenly ripped apart by the shrill blast of a whistle. "Get out of the street!" Charlotte screamed, charging into the street, arms flailing. She punished him with another earsplitting blast. "I told you to stay on the sidewalk! Are you deaf?"

If he wasn't before, he sure was now.

She steamrolled toward him, her expression promising a calamitous confrontation. "I said move! Do you have a death wish?"

Making no attempt to move, the man snapped a picture of the windmill before locking his sights on Charlotte, skewering her with a look so surly, it stopped her dead in her tracks.

She swayed on her heels like an off-balance Weeble wobbling back to vertical, then screwed her face into an indignant contortion that promised instant reprisal. Eyes throwing daggers at him, she stuck her whistle back in her mouth and blew with the explosive power borne of a pair of lungs bursting with hot air.

The whistle shot out of her mouth and skidded onto the street like a skipped rock, bouncing crazily over the pavement until it came to rest at the man's feet.

Wow. Charlotte might not look like a guy, but she could sure spit like one.

The man snatched it off the ground, hefted it in his palm, and with a self-satisfied glint in his eye, hurled it unceremoniously into the canal.

"My whistle!" Charlotte cried. "You're going to replace that, mister!"

He strode past her, leaving her red-faced and fuming as he stepped onto the sidewalk in front of me.

"You—I swear you people are going to be the death of me!" she ranted. "If you refuse to obey the rules, there *will* be conseque—"

She would have continued had a motorcycle not roared down the street at just that moment, seemingly hot to lay rubber down the length of her spine. With a terrified shriek she leaped out of the way, making a megaphone of her hands to yell after him: "Maniac! You should have your license revoked! You're a threat to all mankind! I hope you get arrested for noise pollution!"

"Cussed nuisance," grumbled the guy in the Bar Harbor jacket, giving no indication which nuisance he found more irritating, the motorcyclist or Charlotte.

"My group is starting a movement to protest unfair treatment," I joked as I came up behind him. "They're actively recruiting membership if you'd like to apply."

He stared at me as though trying to figure out who I was and why I was talking to him.

"I'm Emily." I extended my hand in greeting. "I'm the official escort for the group at the back of the bus."

He was all angles and elbows, like a Disney version of Ichabod Crane, with stooped shoulders, a long face, and thinning gray hair. His lips were razor thin and looked as if they had never learned to smile. His eyes were small and guarded, like those of a man struggling to hide a lifetime of secrets behind them. He probably hadn't turned seventy yet, but I figured it wouldn't be long before he did.

He regarded my hand dully before giving it an awkward shake.

"We're the Iowa contingent." I smiled and waited for him to introduce himself.

He narrowed his gaze and eyed me warily.

Okay, so he was a little shy, but I was a whiz with shy people. "There are twelve of us from the little town of Windsor City, in the North-Central part of the state. Have you ever driven through Iowa?"

"Why?"

"No reason. Just … just asking." My smile stiffened on my face. "Lots of corn in Iowa. Do you like corn?"

"No."

"Lots of hogs, too."

He stared at me. "So?"

"So it works out well if you're partial to pork chops. Have you ever eaten an Iowa chop?"

"No."

"Really? That's a shame because they're totally awesome."

"So?"

I could feel my smile crack around the edges and slide off my mouth. There was only one way to deal with people who were this hard to talk to. "It's been fun chatting with you. We'll have to do it again sometime." I waved my camera at him. "Would you like to be in my picture?"

He scowled and turned away.

Guess that was another no.

As the group pushed forward, I lagged behind, feeling as deflated as a week-old birthday balloon. This was just great. I was traveling with Charlotte the Loon, Dietger the Lech, and Oscar the Grouch. I could hardly wait to interact with the other members of the group. If they all turned out to be as sour as Oscar, it might behoove me to dart in front of the windmill's rotating blade right now so I could get knocked senseless. Being in a coma for the rest of the tour would probably ruin my holiday, but on the up side, the ongoing drama might give my guys something to text each other about while they camped out on the bus, ignoring all the sights.

"That's Pete Finnegan," said a woman who stopped beside me on the sidewalk. She was a pretty platinum blonde with straight, shoulder-length hair, skin that had withstood the test of time, and blue eyes that snapped with good humor. "He was the valedictorian of our graduating class. Smart as a whip, but he was never big on conversation. A lot's changed in fifty years. I could hardly believe my eyes when I saw him talking your ear off just now."

I stared at her in disbelief. "He only said a half-dozen words. Most of which were no."

"That's pretty typical. He's a Republican." She offered me a warm smile. "I'm Mary Lou." She tapped the name tag that was pinned to her jacket, drawing my attention to a photo of a teenaged Mary Lou O'Leary, a list of high school activities in which she'd obviously participated, and a name in larger print that read Mary Lou McManus. "It was my idea to design our name tags with our graduation pictures as well as our maiden and married names. I mean, we all know what we looked like five decades ago, but none of us look like that anymore. Except maybe Pete. I would have known him anywhere. Still skinny as a rail and looking like he'd be happy if everyone else in our graduating class would disappear."

"More like everyone in the world," corrected a man who ambled up beside us. He draped his arm around Mary Lou's shoulders and smiled pleasantly. "I'm Mike. Her other half."

"Emily," I said, returning their smiles. Mike's graduation picture showed a bespectacled teen with Bugs Bunny teeth, a buzz cut, a bad complexion, and a blank space where his activities should be listed. "Are you sure that's your photo?" I studied it more closely. "It looks nothing like you."

"Never underestimate the cosmetic benefits of good orthodontics and dermatological treatments. But let me tell you, high school isn't easy on guys who look like trolls and are introverts to boot. It was the worst four years of my life."

"You did *not* look like a troll," Mary Lou teased. "Trolls walk upright. You walked with your head down in a constant slouch, like a human question mark."

"I was trying to make myself invisible. It worked, didn't it? The only female who ever noticed me was you."

"That's because I knew there was a prince hiding somewhere behind your Mr. Slouchy impersonation."

He laughed, squeezing her shoulder affectionately. "You and my mother."

"And Sister Margaret Mary. Remember how she'd clap her hands on your shoulders and tell you to stand up straight when you went to the library?"

He winced. "More ignominy."

Mike McManus certainly had improved with age. He was now a lean six-footer with great posture, a golden tan, and silver hair that could earn him millions in shampoo endorsements. His eyes were intelligent, his gaze direct, and his body language that of a man whose confidence level was off the charts. High school might have been the worst four years of his life, but he looked as if every year after that had been nothing short of spectacular.

"So the two of you, and Pete, and everyone else who arrived late last night are graduates of the same high school class?" I asked them.

"St. Francis Xavier High School in Bangor, Maine," Mary Lou announced. "I thought we should pull out all the stops for our fiftieth reunion, so I cooked this up. Our granddaughter planned a destination wedding, so I thought, why not a destination class reunion? The planning committee all agreed, so here we are."

"Mary Lou was always something of a visionary," Mike said proudly.

"Of course, not everyone could join us. Some classmates are rehabbing from hip or knee replacement, and others had family obligations pending, but we signed up a good cross-section of our graduating class."

"If our flight hadn't been delayed by weather at Logan, we might have made the welcome reception last night," Mike lamented, "but by the time we arrived, we were all too tired for socializing."

"You didn't miss anything," I assured him. "Since your group wasn't there, the rest of us scarfed down an early-bird meal and packed it in for the night." I gave them the abridged version of who we were and where we came from. "I was back in my room by seven."

The sidewalk had emptied as guests reached the windmill and spread out over the grounds to take their photos. I checked my watch. "If we want photos, we'd better do it now before Charlotte starts herding us back to the bus."

"How does a woman with such a foul disposition get hired as a tour director?" Mary Lou asked as we hurried to catch up with the other guests.

"By lying on her personality test," joked Mike. "She probably claimed she had one."

"She reminds me of Paula Peavey." Mary Lou lowered her voice. "Remember what a sourpuss she was all through school? She'd as soon bite your head off as look at you."

"She's standing right over there," said Mike. "Why don't you ask her if she's changed?"

"I'm not going anywhere near her. She was just too hateful for words."

"Why was she so hateful?" I asked as I paused to snap a quick shot.

"I don't know why." Mary Lou lowered her voice another decibel. "She just was. Her favorite pastime was making people cry, which she did on a daily basis. I'll never forgive her for some of the hurtful things she said to me."

"C'mon, hon," Mike cajoled. "That was fifty years ago. Let it go."

"*You* let it go!"

"So what did she say that has any bearing on who you are today?"

"I might not be able to recall exactly what she said, but I remember how it made me feel." Her tone grew prickly. "And it'll remain with me until I die."

"One of the mean girls, huh?" I asked. We'd had mean girls in my high school. They'd squeeze around the same table in the cafeteria and gaze with disdain at the rest of the student population, sniggering importantly as they called us dorks and losers. They usually spent their high school years on academic probation, campaigned to be elected Corn Queen at Homecoming, and married guys whose main goal in life was to buy a three-quarter-ton pickup with a built-in beer cooler and move to the Big City, like Muscatine or Dubuque.

"Mean?" Mary Lou's eyes drained of humor. "Dogs can be mean. Paula fit into a whole other category. She was pathologically mean. *Serial killer* mean."

I froze in place. Like I needed to hear that. "Which one is Paula?" I asked, my voice cracking midsentence.

"Sweetheart," Mike admonished. "You're scaring Emily." He handed me his camera. "Would you mind taking a picture of us in front of the windmill?"

I framed the shot and clicked. "So if the two of you had such bad experiences in high school, why did you sign up for the reunion?"

A funny look passed between them before Mike shrugged. "Old-fashioned curiosity, I guess."

"And not all my experiences were bad," confessed Mary Lou. "I joined a lot of activities and had lots of friends. In fact, my high school years would have been fantastic if I could have found a way to avoid Paula, but she sat behind me in every single class, so it was pretty much a death sentence."

"Time's up!" yelled Charlotte. She did the hand clapping thing again for emphasis. "Back to the bus! We're on a schedule. Quickie quickie!"

"See that guy in the light blue University of Maine sweatshirt?" Mike asked me as people started heading for the sidewalk. "He was the class clown. What a character. Always had a clever comeback for everything. He was the only guy who fit into every social strata. Popular kids. Unpopular kids. Who doesn't want to hang out with

27

the guy who makes you laugh? I guess laughter is the universal equalizer."

"And see the couple holding hands and making moon eyes at each other? The guy is wearing a St. Francis Xavier letter jacket." Mary Lou pointed them out discreetly. "He was the football quarterback and she was the head cheerleader. We were all so envious of them. They had everything we didn't have. Good looks. Athletic ability. Popularity. We would have sold our souls to be them."

My eyes widened. The man was bald, had no neck, and was built like a side-by-side refrigerator. The woman was equally large, with a helmet of dyed black hair teased into a bouffant with pink bows clipped above each temple. A health specialist might advise him to lose the weight. A beauty specialist would advise her to lose the bows.

"They married right out of high school," Mary Lou continued. "It was the second biggest social event of the year."

Which prompted me to ask, "What was the first?"

"The wedding of the basketball captain and the girl who was elected class president four years in a row," said Mike. "Football was popular in Bangor, but basketball was king. And the girl hailed from one of Bangor's 'elite' families, so everyone who was anyone received an invitation."

Mary Lou chuckled. "There was a big flap between the two girls about wedding dates, churches, and reception halls. I can't remember the details, but all of us 'outies' would get together to giggle about the latest earth-shattering news in the dueling divas drama."

"Outies?" I regarded her oddly. "You belonged to a club for students with protruding bellybuttons?"

She and Mike fell against each other with laughter. "Outies," she repeated. "Students outside the inner circle, as opposed to 'innies,' the ones who wield all the power. The 'in' crowd. You probably called it something else when you were in school."

"Speak of the devil," Mike said under his breath, wrapping his arm around his wife to form a close semicircle around me.

A man and woman brushed by them on the walkway—he, tall and well-dressed, she, petite and well-kept. They projected an air of prosperity, as if they'd be more comfortable riding in a Lincoln than in a Dodge, more satisfied eating at the country club than at a restaurant, more relaxed living in a mansion than in a townhouse. They strolled hand in hand, their fingers intertwined tightly, as if by clinging to each other, they could keep all their good fortune to themselves. Their nametags proclaimed them Gary and Sheila Bouchard.

"Looks like they've fared well," I commented when they'd passed.

"Not half as well as Laura LaPierre," said Mary Lou in a voice that oozed disbelief. "She looks thirty years younger than everyone else. She's drop-dead gorgeous. We used to be such good friends, but you know how it goes. You lose touch. Have you seen her, Mike?"

"How could I miss her?" Then to me, "If you think my graduation picture doesn't look like me, wait'll you get a load of Laura's. She used to be so drab and shy that the 'innies' poked fun of her by nicknaming her Minnie Mouse, which was only one of their many put-downs. Now she looks like the mouse that roared. I wouldn't mind getting the name of her plastic surgeon."

There was only one woman among the dispersing crowd whom I'd classify as drop-dead gorgeous, and that was a shapely blonde wearing skinny jeans and a form-fitting jacket that accented her small waist and impressive bustline. Her hair was tied back in a simple ponytail. Her only accessories appeared to be small pearl earrings and a thousand-watt smile that caused her face to glow with healthy exuberance. She was chatting up a couple of other guests, her hands flying in wide, animated gestures. "If you're talking about the blonde with the ponytail, not only is she pretty. She looks really friendly. And extroverted." In fact, besides Mike and Mary Lou, she was the only person in the Maine contingent who was smiling.

"That's Laura. Do you suppose she's had a chemical peel or a facelift?" Mary Lou wondered aloud as she ran her fingertips over her own jaw line. "She's lived in California for years, with access to all the plastic surgeons of the stars. God, she really does look good."

"Sweet revenge for all the years she spent being the butt of 'dog-faced girl' jokes." Mike swept his arm toward the bus. "Shall we, ladies?"

As we trekked back to the bus, I realized how much I admired Laura LaPierre's ability to treat her former antagonists with such good humor, because if a bunch of insensitive creeps had called me dog-faced for four years, I'd want to do something more diabolical than simply smile at them.

Like an avenging angel in a Lifetime channel movie of the week, I'd probably want to kill them.

THREE

"You're absolutely going to love Volendam," Charlotte gushed as we passed a sign announcing its city limits. "This is the one place in Holland where you'll sometimes see residents dressed in traditional Dutch costumes—men in baggy pantaloons and striped vests, and women in long skirts and white caps with wings. And naturally, they're all tromping around in those god-awful clogs and making enough noise to wake the dead."

To my right, the white-capped Markermeer stretched toward infinity, becoming a smudge of blue-gray haze where lake met sky. Powerboats, sailboats, and barges dotted the horizon, while closer to shore, a two-masted schooner scudded through the chop, the sun drenching its billowing sails with light so searingly white, it made my eyes smart.

"There are shops up and down the main street that cater to tourists wanting to have their pictures taken in traditional costume," Charlotte continued, "so if that appeals to you, do it first thing, because we're not going to be here very long." She gave us one of her patented schoolmarm looks and said in an annoying singsong, "And you know what'll happen if you're not sitting in your seats when it's time to leave."

Low, irritated groans rumbled through the bus. I hoped this was an indication of spontaneous indigestion rather than impending mutiny.

Dietger nosed down a street so glutted with traffic, we were forced to slow to a crawl. Sidewalk cafes lined both sides of the street—festively appointed enclosures with overhead canopies, hanging plants, potted plants, and marquee-size letters advertising Heineken and Amstel beers. T-shirts filled the windows of souvenir shops. Outside tables displayed painted wooden shoes, miniature windmills, decorative tiles, and souvenir dolls. Dutch flags fluttered above doorways, and tasteful blue signs invited visitors to part with their Euros in eight different languages.

"Once we leave you at the car park, you'll be on your own for two hours, so if you're hungry, I suggest you try the smoked eel. It's a Volendam specialty, although if you suffer from ulcers or acid reflux, you might want to pop a few antacid tablets before pigging out. For those of you who'd prefer to explore, stroll down the side alleys. They'll lead you to a lovely maze of narrow streets and canals with little wooden houses and footbridges, but if you get lost, don't expect anyone to go looking for you. We're on far too tight a schedule." She smiled sweetly. "Have a wonderful time, but wherever you go or whatever you do, remember this." Her voice rose to a near screech. "Stay on the sidewalk!"

We pulled into a "Tour Busses Only" lot that flanked the dike at the far end of town. When Dietger killed the engine, I regarded

Nana sternly. "I hope you're going to tell me that you're ready to ditch your cellphone in favor of smoked eel and antacid tablets."

She cradled her phone possessively to her chest. "What'll happen if I'm not?"

I knew of only one threat scary enough to have any effect on her.

Digging my own cellphone out of my shoulder bag, I clutched it in my fist and poised my forefinger over the keypad. "Then I'm calling Mom."

She sucked in her breath so hard, I thought she'd swallow her uppers. "You wouldn't."

I smiled. "Try me."

"This is blackmail." She narrowed her eyes. "Or is it extortion? I always get them two mixed up."

"I'm pretty sure it's extortion. So what's it to be? Drinking in the sights of Volendam"—I waved the phone at her—"or a long dose of Mom?"

She shoved her cellphone into her pocketbook and stood up. "Anyone feel like taggin' along while I find one a them shops that takes souvenir photos of tourists dressed up like the little Dutch boy?"

"I'll go," said George, popping out of his seat.

"Me, too," said Tilly. "My thumbs are locking up."

Osmond boosted himself to his feet. "Show of hands: how many are in favor of having a group photo taken in dorky costumes?"

All hands went up.

"The yeas have it in a landslide."

"I want to amend my vote." Bernice stood up. "I don't want to be in a group photo. I want to have my picture taken all by myself so I can add it to my portfolio"—she fluttered her stubby lashes—"just in case Hollywood comes to town wanting to film *Twister 2*."

"Or *Night of the Living Dead*," sniggered Dick Teig.

She whipped her head around to drill him with an evil look. "I heard that." A thousand years ago, Bernice had worked as a magazine model, and "comeback" was never far from her mind.

The doors of the bus *whooshed* open, prompting my guys to gather up their jackets and cameras and scramble toward the rear exit.

"No exiting out the rear door!" shouted Charlotte. "You have to leave by the front. Get away from that door!" she yelled at the Dicks. "Honestly, you people are going to be the death of me!"

Sensing blood pressures rising and excitement waning, I made a quick decision. "Bite your tongues and do as she says," I cautioned under my breath. "I'll have a heart-to-heart with her when I can get her alone. Maybe I can convince her to lighten up."

"I'm so excited to try on one of those white caps with the wings," Margi enthused as we shuffled down the aisle single file. "Do you suppose it'll look like the one the flying nun used to wear on that TV show? I wouldn't mind flying around like she used to, but I have a few pounds on her, so I'd probably need a bigger hat."

"I've located the nearest photo shop on my GPS," Tilly called out. "When you step off the bus, take a right and head due northwest."

Iowans are renowned for their remarkable senses of direction. Some people say it's a learned skill, but I think we're just born that way. My dad claims if Moses had been from Iowa, he'd have led the Jews through the desert in way under forty years, even with the inevitable delays for sandstorms and potty breaks.

They hit the ground running. "Be back by two!" I yelled after them. Nana gave me a quick thumbs-up before overtaking Bernice in a footrace to the main street. The reunion people splintered into

34

smaller groups and loitered in the parking lot awhile before following Nana's lead toward the street. Dietger escaped across the lot to join a couple of uniformed bus drivers whose heads were engulfed in cigarette smoke, but Charlotte seemed to have disappeared into thin air.

Noticing Mike and Mary Lou McManus in a small group still lingering by the bus, I hurried over to them. "Did anyone happen to see which way Charlotte went?"

"Didn't see her leave," said the guy Mike had pointed out as the class clown, "but I hope the hell she never comes back." He was small and wiry, with a fringe of white hair circling his head at ear level, a mustache like a whisk broom, and a nametag that identified him as Chip Soucy. "Geez, what a pill. Reminds me of that nun you girls were always complaining about back in school. The one who got drunk on her own power when she was principal. What did you call her? Sister Hippo?"

Mary Lou exchanged smiles with two female classmates. "Sister Hip-PO-ly-tus," they chimed in unison. "The Hippo didn't refer to her size," Mary Lou explained to me. "We weren't that mean. It was short for hypocrite."

"She wore makeup," accused one woman whose photo showed her younger self in a pageboy and bangs, "and we were supposed to act like we didn't notice. I mean, no one's cheeks are that red. Not even if they're spray painted."

"She was so vindictive," said the second classmate, a heavyset woman with a tight perm. "She hated me, but the feeling was mutual. I heard she lost her position after we graduated and got demoted to housekeeping duties at the rectory. A lot of important people filed complaints about her to the diocese, so she got the shaft. And atheists say there is no God. Huh!"

"Did you know there was a massive turnover in the teaching staff after we left?" asked Mike. "Keeping us in line for four years wore them all down."

"We didn't wear them down," corrected Mary Lou. "We kept them on their toes. Our standardized test scores showed that we were a bright class. That's not bragging. It's the truth."

"The only reason you girls did so well was because you didn't have us boys in class to distract you," teased Chip.

"Wait a sec," I interrupted. "You all went to the same school, but you didn't have co-ed classes?"

Mike nodded. "Boys on one side of the building, girls on the other, with a big auditorium in the middle to keep us separated. The brothers taught the boys and the nuns taught the girls, with a sprinkling of lay teachers thrown in for local color."

"Remember Mr. Albert?" Mary Lou asked the group. Then to me, "He taught algebra and geometry to both sides, but he was so shy, he could never look us in the eye. He'd explain theorems while he looked out the window or stared at his shoes. Poor man. Paula Peavey mouthed off to him continually, but he was too embarrassed to punish her. The boys were always playing practical jokes on him, like sticking imbecilic signs on his suit coat or gluing his desk drawers shut. Pete Finnegan thought he was smarter than Mr. Albert, so he never missed a chance to argue with him over the simplest math problems. We made a nervous wreck out of the poor guy. We antagonized him so much, I honestly think he grew afraid of us."

"He never threw chalk at me," said Chip, "so I liked him."

I frowned. "Why would he throw chalk at you?"

"The brothers always fired chalk across the room at us if we gave them wrong answers," said Mike. "And they nailed us every time.

The Xaverian brothers had exceptional throwing arms. I wouldn't be surprised if a few of them left the brotherhood for more lucrative careers in the major leagues."

The heavyset woman beside Mary Lou sighed. "Just think. They're probably all dead by now. That's a little depressing."

"On the other hand," Mike announced in a booming voice, "the rest of us are very much alive, so let's celebrate that." He gestured toward me. "By the way, this lovely young woman is Emily."

I waved a quick hello.

Mike continued with enthusiasm. "Would you believe, Emily, that not only were we the brightest class to walk the hallowed halls of Francis Xavier High, we were apparently the healthiest and least accident prone? Not one person in our graduating class has died."

Chip cranked his mouth to the side and gave his jaw a thoughtful scratch. "Well, that's not exactly true. What about Bob Guerrette?"

Smiles stiffened. Limbs froze. Exuberance dissolved into sudden silence.

"He never graduated," said the lady with the pageboy picture, "Remember? So he really shouldn't be included."

"Why didn't he graduate?" I asked.

"He died," Mike admitted uncomfortably.

"We *assume* he died," corrected Chip.

"Everyone assumes he died," said Mike, "but I wish we knew for sure. It's tough not knowing. Every time the evening news airs a story about a backcountry hiker in Maine tripping over a decomposed body in the woods, I always wonder if it could be Bobby's remains."

Chip shook his head. "Poor bastard. I've often thought about how much he missed in life—marriage, kids, Super Bowl I—"

"Vietnam," said Mike.

"Colonoscopies," added Chip.

"Has anyone seen my husband?" asked the lady with the tight perm as she surveyed the near-empty parking lot.

"What does he look like?" asked Mike.

"He has hair. Does that narrow it down enough for you?"

The sound of screeching tires and blaring horns suddenly filled the air. I fired a glance toward the main street, my heart stopping in my chest as I replayed an image of Nana sprinting in front of Bernice to be first out of the parking lot.

"What do you suppose all that ruckus is about?" asked Mary Lou.

Shouts. Echoing cries of distress. A cacophony of car horns.

"S'cuse me." Overwhelmed by a surge of panic, I raced toward the street as if I were wearing tennis shoes instead of leather ankle boots with four-inch heels. Traffic had slowed to a standstill. Drivers were stepping out of their cars and rubbernecking to identify the cause of the holdup. Turning the corner, I saw an ever-widening circle of pedestrians gathered on the sidewalk, their eyes riveted on the street.

Oh, God.

What if my guys had been texting each other while they were crossing the street? What if—

I saw legions of tourists on the perimeter of the crowd, but no Nana, no Tilly, no George.

Oh, God!

Spying a familiar face, I ran toward him. "Do you know what happened?" I asked Pete Finnegan.

He regarded me, stone-faced. "Dunno."

I stood on my tiptoes, unable to see over the bystanders' heads, but I wasn't about to let that stop me. Squeezing around a baby

38

carriage, I created a tiny opening and excused my way through the crowd until I reached the curb, where I stared in numb horror at the scene before me.

The tortured wreck of a bicycle lay on its side, surrounded by loose Brussels sprouts, a smattering of broken eggs, and a woman's walking shoe. The cyclist was curled in a fetal position nearby, his trousers ripped, his face and hands bloody, being attended by several people who were yelling desperately into cellphones.

A dozen feet away, in a swirl of diesel and exhaust fumes, a woman in a pea-green blazer with jumbo shoulder pads lay face-down on the pavement, seemingly unaware of both the foul air and the people who were hovering over her. Her legs were twisted into impossible angles. Her shoeless foot hung limply from her ankle. She neither coughed, nor groaned, nor moved.

She was still. Absolutely still.

"I know that woman!" I cried, hoping that someone who spoke English would understand me. "Her name is Charlotte."

The cyclist fought to sit upright. Propping his elbows on his bent knees, he braced his head in his hands and threw an anguished look at Charlotte's lifeless body. He let out a tormented sob, then wailed something in a language I couldn't understand.

It was gut wrenching. The poor man was so beside himself with grief that I felt guilty bearing witness to his heartache. I blinked away tears as I turned to the woman standing beside me. "Do you know what he's saying?"

"*Ja*. He says, 'Damn these tourists. They're going to be the death of me.'"

FOUR

IF THE CELLPHONE RECEPTION in our Amsterdam hotel lobby had been subpar, my conversation with Etienne might have been reduced to a few minutes of frustrating static, but aided by a profusion of cell towers in the area, I was able to recount the tale of our most recent tribulation with landline clarity.

"So the bus driver dropped us off at our hotel about a half hour ago, and we're supposed to leave again in twenty minutes for a dinner cruise on the canal. Not that anyone can think about food right now. But our driver informed us, and I quote, that 'the show must go on.' Why are Europeans so fond of American clichés? Don't they have any of their own?"

I waited a beat for him to answer. When he didn't, I figured the call had been dropped despite the good reception. "Hello? Etienne? Are you there?"

"Your tour director is dead?"

I winced. This wasn't exactly the kind of event we could high-light in our travel brochure. "She warned us about the bicycles, but she apparently forgot to heed her own warning."

"Your tour is one day old, and already you've transported a body to the morgue?"

"C'mon, sweetie. You've visited Holland. You know what bicy-cle traffic is like around here. An accident like that could happen to anyone." I paused. "I guess."

He muttered something in French, or Swiss-German, or Ital-ian. I couldn't tell which.

"Here's the thing," I explained. "Charlotte was a terrible tour director. No one liked her. Actually, that's an understatement. Ev-eryone *hated* her. She was controlling, and petulant, and treated us like children."

"So you think the accident happened on purpose?"

"You bet I do." Etienne had hung up his Swiss police inspec-tor's badge only a short time ago, so his law enforcement genes were still easily stimulated.

"Did any eyewitnesses step forward?"

I cupped my hand around my mouth and lowered my voice. "That's the really weird thing. The sidewalk was absolutely choked with tourists, but not one person claimed to have seen anything. How unbelievable is that?"

"Not as unbelievable as you might think, *bella*."

The lobby elevator *dinged* open to reveal the entire Iowa con-tingent staring mindlessly at their cellphones, heads down, shoul-ders hunched, and thumbs flying.

"Any number of crimes can be committed in crowds where peo-ple are preoccupied with window shopping, talking on cellphones, listening to iPods, text messaging. We're allowing crimes to happen in plain sight because we're no longer aware of our surroundings. Too many other distractions vying for our attention."

I rolled my eyes as the elevator door slid shut with my guys still crammed inside. "Ya think?"

"Do you know if the police are continuing to investigate the incident?"

"According to the woman who was translating the blow-by-blow for me, the bicyclist involved in the accident swore that Charlotte stumbled into the street right in front of him." The indicator needle over the elevator drifted to the first floor, second floor, third floor... "The police discovered a broken paving stone near the curb, so they put two and two together and decided that she probably tripped over it, stumbled off the curb, and never saw what hit her. Nice, neat, and tidy."

"A reasonable explanation."

"Not if you consider the ill will she'd stirred up with the guests. She'd already had one serious run-in with a grouchy guy from Maine who just happened to be in the vicinity when she took her spill. He conveniently disappeared after the police arrived, but I wouldn't mind getting him alone so I could ask him a few questions. The bicyclist might have thought Charlotte stumbled into the street, but how do we know she wasn't pushed?"

"By the grouchy guy from Maine?"

"Or by some of the other Mainers. They're all old high school classmates, so they could be covering up for each other."

"Do you think they're so fond of each other as to risk becoming accessories to a crime?"

I gnawed my lip as I watched the indicator needle glide back toward the first-floor lobby. "I don't actually know that any of them like each other. In fact, I think the opposite is true. A few of them really despise each other. Or at least, they used to. Popular kids versus nerds and wallflowers. Bruised feelings. Emotional scarring. Youthful insecurities. The whole nine yards."

"I have another call coming in on line one, Emily. Could I trouble you to hold for a moment? I think it's important."

Yeah, but ... my call was important, too, wasn't it?

The elevator *dinged* open again.

"This is the lobby, you morons! Are you going to get off this time?"

"You're standing on my foot!" snapped Margi.

"I can't move until Bernice moves," whined Helen.

"Can anyone see Marion?" George asked desperately.

They were jammed in the car like college kids in a VW Beetle, hips bumping and arms tangling into knots as they struggled to squeeze through the door at the same time.

"Press the button to keep the door open!" yelled Alice.

"I can't see the selector panel," fussed Tilly.

"That's 'cuz Dick's stomach is squashed against it," cried Nana.

Osmond's voice rose to a fever pitch. "Well, yank him outta there before his stomach hits the button for the fourth floor again."

Amid a cacophony of frustrated grunts and grumbles, Dick got catapulted out the door and into the lobby. With the human log jam broken, everyone else staggered into the lobby behind him, massaging the kinks out of their necks and shoulders like the survivors of a train wreck. I shook my head, wondering if I should declare their phones a health hazard and demand they hand them over to me. One inattentive step in Amsterdam and *splat!* They'd either be bobbing in a murky canal with the rest of the swill or flattened on the pavement like Charlotte. But they'd never give them up willingly.

As I watched them bend their heads over their phones again, I made up my mind. If they were to survive Holland, they needed to get rid of the things. I could convince them. I knew I could.

I just had to figure out how.

"Sorry, *bella*." Etienne came back on the line. "That was your mother."

"You ditched me for my mother?"

"She needed to tell me what time she and your father are picking me up in the morning."

Alarm bells began ringing inside my head. "You're going someplace with Mom and Dad?"

"Fishing," he said in a pained voice. "In the wilds of Minnesota. Away from Main Street, cable television, and cellphone towers."

"Fishing?" I paused. "Why?"

"Because your mother set off the sprinkler system when she flambéed lunch for me in the office yesterday, so while the cleaning crew squeegees the water out of the carpet, I'm going fishing with your parents, at their insistence, to help me cope with the stress of the situation."

I sat frozen in place, my stomach sliding to my knees. The sprinkler system? "How much damage did—"

"Another call coming in, Emily. Forgive me."

Outside, our tour bus pulled up by the revolving door at the entrance to the hotel, its engine roaring powerfully enough to rattle the window glass. My guys, however, remained in cellphone comas until they noticed a steady stream of Mainers meandering into the lobby from the stairwell, and then they pounced, approaching the newcomers, engaging them in conversation, acting unnaturally friendly.

Whoa. This was a little weird. My guys never volunteered to break the ice, so what was up with all the spontaneous schmoozing?

"I'm back," said Etienne, "but I can't talk. Our insurance adjustor is on the other line. But tell me quickly. What are the Passages people doing about your tour director issue?"

"The company is sending us a replacement. We're expecting him to arrive either late this evening or early tomorrow morning. He's on holiday at the moment, so he probably won't be too happy about having his vacation interrupted. Keep your fingers crossed that he's not another Charlotte. I don't think any of us could handle an instant replay of that fiasco."

"Promise me you'll contact the authorities if the man from Maine gives you reason to suspect him of something untoward."

"I promise."

He sighed. "I miss you, *bella*."

"I miss you more."

"I'll call you the minute I return to civilization."

"You better! Happy fishing. I love you." I disconnected.

Fishing? Etienne? I shook my head. This could turn out to be an even bigger disaster than the Hindenburg.

"Emil*yyyyyyy*!"

I looked up at a woman so tall, she could have played the lead role in *Attack of the 50 Foot Woman*. Her hair was long and glossy—the kind that men imagine seeing fanned over a satin bed pillow. Her complexion was flawless, her makeup so artfully applied that her face could have hung in the Louvre. She was dressed in a leather skirt the size of a man's handkerchief and a cropped leopard-print jacket that hugged her curves like plastic wrap. A gargantuan designer bag hung over her shoulder—metallic bronze, to match the stiletto-heeled boots that caressed her legs all the way to her thighs. Her name was Jackie Thum. Before she'd acquired breasts and a passion for handbags the size of Delaware, she'd been a guy named Jack Potter, and I'd been married to him.

"Give me a hug!" she squealed, yanking me off the sofa-bench and hoisting me into her arms like a weightlifter executing the clean and jerk. "I thought we'd never get here!"

"Where've you … been?" I choked out as she bear-hugged the air out of me.

"Sitting in Kennedy Airport, waiting for the weather to clear." She set me back on my feet and boxed my shoulders to straighten the lines of my jacket. "I thought we'd never get out of there. And of course, no one met us at the airport this morning, so we had to hire a taxi. Do you know why the Dutch ride bicycles, Emily?"

"I think it's be—"

"Because they can't afford to pay freaking cab fare. I about blew my whole budget to get to the hotel, only to discover that the tour bus had already left for the day. If we'd known you guys were going to skip out without us, we'd have walked from the airport and saved ourselves forty Euros. So we had to wander the streets of Amsterdam by ourselves, sampling the local pastry products."

I scanned the lobby in search of a face. "You keep saying, 'we.' Is Tom here with you?" Following my annulment and her gender reassignment surgery, Jackie had moved to upstate New York, where she married a New Age hair stylist who was fast becoming an industry phenomenon despite one prominent distinction.

He wasn't gay.

"Tom is in Binghamton," she said in a breathy voice, her eyes twinkling with excitement. "I brought someone else." She fisted her hand on her hip and perused the lobby. "If I can find her."

My eyes froze in their sockets. "Her?"

"She's the surprise I e-mailed you about, Emily. Wait 'til you meet her. You're going to love her! I sure do. She's changed my life so much. There she is. Yoo-hoo!" She waved her arm. "We're over here!"

Unh-oh. After two years of marriage, Jack had left me for another man. Now that Jack was Jackie, was she pulling the same stunt and leaving Tom for another woman? Oh, my God. Was my ex-husband a serial home wrecker? Or was she simply crying out for a hormone replacement drug with more active ingredients?

"Here she comes," Jackie tittered, bouncing on her heels in anticipation. "Isn't she adorable?"

I wouldn't have pegged her for Jackie's type at all. She didn't look self-absorbed, ditsy, or flamboyant, but rather gave the impression of being modest and quietly intelligent, the kind of person who'd be happy to give you directions or walk your dog if you were pinched for time. Her eyes were snappy, her makeup tastefully understated, her clothes fashionable without being overly trendy. She was about my height and weight and had hair the same color and length as mine, but hers was sleekly cut into cascading angles that rippled with movement and liquidy shine. I suppressed a twinge of envy. I supposed my hair could look like that, too, if I borrowed someone else's head.

Jackie grabbed the woman's hand and pulled her close. "Emily," she gushed, "this is Beth Ann Oliver. I told her all about you, but I didn't want to tell you anything about her until she and I had set our relationship in stone."

I forced a tentative smile. Not only did Beth Ann and I share the same body type and hair color, we had the same shape face. The same green eyes. The same fair complexion. She extended her hand to shake mine.

Holy crap! We were wearing the same color nail polish! We probably even used the same name-brand concealer and blush. Oh, Lord. This was terrible. The unthinkable had happened.

Jack had fallen in love with me all over again. Only it wasn't the real me. It was a lookalike me! The only difference between us seemed to be our perfume. I smelled like white tea and lemon; she smelled like a funeral parlor. Oil of roses. I hated oil of roses.

"I'm so happy to meet you, Emily," my lookalike effervesced as she gripped my hand with both of hers.

"Me, too." I pumped more energy into my smile. "Imagine. You. Me. Together on the same trip. Wow." The smile remained plastered on my lips. "So, how long have the two of you been, you know…together?"

They exchanged questioning glances. "Has it been two months already?" asked Beth Ann.

"Two months, three days, and"—Jackie checked her watch—"six hours." She lifted one shoulder in a coquettish shrug. "Approximately."

"They've been the most wonderful two months of my life," Beth Ann confessed. "I've never felt so vital, or alive, or—or fulfilled."

Jack used to have that effect on me, too—before he realized he felt more fulfilled in my bikini panties than his boxer shorts. "It's official then?" I asked squeamishly. "The two of you are a couple?"

"I prefer to think of us as a team," Beth Ann corrected. She looked up at Jackie. "What do you think? Does team work for you?"

"Euw, I like that," Jackie tittered. "A team. Like Laurel and Hardy, or Batman and Robin, or Rocky and Bullwink–"

"I was thinking more like Huntley and Brinkley." Beth Ann's voice grew wistful. "My dad always claimed that television wasn't worth watching after they broke up."

"Honey, if he came unglued over Christie Brinkley's breakup, he must have been apoplectic when Brad Pitt ditched Jennifer Aniston for Angelina Jolie. I mean, celebrity breakups can absolutely destroy a fan's sense of wellbeing. It can alter his whole vision of the universe."

Beth Ann regarded Jackie quizzically before breaking into a wide smile. "You're such a kidder."

Sure she was. And I invented the Internet. "So am I correct in assuming that you've booted Tom off the team?"

Beth Ann looked horrified. "Tom's the one who introduced us, so we're not about to boot him anywhere. He guaranteed we'd hit it off, and he sure knew what he was talking about. Look at us! We've been connected at the hip since the day we met."

"It's so freaky, Emily. Who knew Tom would turn out to be such a dynamite matchmaker? I mean, your average guy is usually so wrapped up in himself that he doesn't realize other people *have* emotions."

The voice of experience talking.

"Maybe we should show our appreciation by making Tom an honorary member of our duo," Beth Ann suggested. "Do you think he'd go along with it?"

Jackie gasped with excitement. "Would he ever! The three of us together on the same team? Can you imagine the possibilities? We'd rock!"

So help me, if they became a threesome, Jack could do the honors of explaining *ménage à trois* to Nana.

I startled as a horn blared long and loudly outside the hotel. Jackie peered out the lobby window. "Geesch, what's with the guy in the bus? Why is he laying on the horn like that?"

I followed her gaze. "That would be our driver. Dietger. A real charmer." I checked the time. "He's probably signaling us to board the bus."

"Isn't that the tour director's job?" asked Beth Ann, looking disappointed that someone with an official uniform and striped umbrella wasn't herding us toward the revolving door.

"It usually is," I explained, "but at the moment, we have a vacancy in that department."

"Get out of here," whooped Jackie. "What happened to our tour director?"

I bolstered myself with a deep breath. "She had issues."

"What kind of issues?" asked Beth Ann.

"Personality. M*aaa*jor personality issues. And maybe some trouble with her peripheral vision. And balance problems. And—"

"She's dead, isn't she?" said Jackie.

"As a doornail," I replied.

"Yes!" Jackie pumped both fists in the air, then to Beth Ann, "See what I told you? Emily always ends up with a body count on her tours. This is so exciting. Day one and we already have our first victim!" She grabbed my arm in a pleading gesture. "It was murder, wasn't it? Are we going to investigate? Can Beth and I tail your suspects? Can we wear disguises? *Pleeeeease?* I packed some great outfits that I can wear undercover. No one will ever know it's me."

I responded to her questions by ticking off the answers on my fingers. "I don't know. Maybe. No, and forget it."

Her exuberance drained from her face in slow motion, making me suffer the kind of guilt I sometimes feel when I have to send my nephews to their rooms for shooting peas out their nostrils at the dinner table. She stared at me in disbelief, shoulders slumping, face flooding with disappointment, mouth sliding into a pout. Nuts. Why was I such a pushover for a pathetic look? I could think of only one way to redeem myself.

"Love your boots."

"Really?" She threw off the pout for a pose, angling her foot to show off her stylishly pointed toes and pencil thin heels. "I ordered them online. At Nordstrom's. And are you ready for this? Free shipping!"

My jaw went into freefall. My heart fluttered. My fingertips tingled. There was nothing to get a girl's adrenalin pumping like the prospect of having trendy footwear arrive on her doorstep minus shipping fees and handling.

Dietger laid on the horn again, forcing guests in the lobby to cover their ears to prevent their hearing aids from exploding.

"What is his problem?" Jackie snapped, marching to the window and pounding on the glass to get his attention. "Hey, you! Enough already!" She waved her arms above her head, then made a quick slashing motion across her throat.

51

Dietger bore down on the horn even longer.

"Try a time-out sign," Beth Ann suggested, joining her at the window. "Maybe he's a fan of the NFL."

Okay, I knew I wasn't in charge of the tour, but someone needed to take over before we all went deaf.

I stuck my thumb and forefinger in my mouth and let fly a shrill whistle that cut through the blaring horn and spun every head in the lobby in my direction. "I'm acting in an unofficial capacity," I said in a loud voice, "but that's our bus outside, and Dietger isn't going to lay off the horn until we board it, so will you please exit through the revolving door *now* so we can preserve whatever hearing we have left?"

"I don't recall anyone putting you in charge," a dissenting voice protested.

"I'm not in charge. I'm just hungry."

Everyone else must have realized they were, too, because a current of anticipation suddenly electrified the room as guests looked left and right, sizing up the competition. Bodies shifted. Feet scuffed forward. And in the next instant the floor shook as the entire lobby stampeded toward the door.

"You can't all squeeze through at one time!" I shouted as six guests wedged themselves into a space that was designed for one, forcing the revolving mechanism to jam mid-turn.

I stared at the people shoehorned into the compartment, sighing at the faces crushed against the glass, noses flattened, and lips twisted askew.

Yup. That had gone well.

FIVE

"Melted brie and caramelized onion bruschetta," announced our waiter as he placed the serving platter in the middle of our table.

"*Dank u*," I called out to his quickly retreating back.

We were packed into a glass-enclosed canal boat, enjoying unobstructed views of Amsterdam at twilight. Watercraft flanked both sides of the waterway—houseboats longer than mobile trailer homes, their sliding glass doors opening onto wraparound patios. Derelict schooners with boxcar-shaped dwellings perched on the main deck. Fishing boats converted into two-story, open-air eateries. Powerboats and skiffs, barges and rowboats—all moored in a magnificent clutter against the canal wall, like a floating passenger train. Narrow Dutch buildings lined the streets: centuries-old brick structures with tiers of window glass rising all the way to their decorative gables. Some stood as straight as church steeples, while others looked slightly off kilter, as if they'd tired of perfect posture after six hundred years and decided to slouch. Strings of white lights hung from an array of fairytale bridges, twinkling above us as we tunneled through spaces so confined that I waited for the inevitable shattering *crrrunch* of stone bridge against glass roof.

We'd been directed into booths that accommodated three diners on either side of a table that was bolted to the floor and covered in crisp white linen. I'd hoped to park myself at the same table as grouchy Pete, but the best I could manage was a space directly across the aisle from him, in a booth with two reunion couples and a woman with bulldog jowls and small, inscrutable eyes that were completely devoid of warmth. Her hair was steel-gray and cut painfully short, as if she were more interested in ease of care than style. She wore a long print scarf that showcased every dog known to man, and only when she unfurled it from around her neck did I see her nametag.

I tried unsuccessfully not to wince.

Paula Peavey. St. Francis Xavier's "mean girl." Oh, no. I let fly a quick prayer that the description no longer applied. I mean, wasn't there some natural cycle at play that forced meanies to mellow after fifty years?

She directed a suspicious look at me from across the table. "If I look puzzled, it's because I'm trying to figure out why you're sitting with us. Shouldn't you be at a different table, hanging out with your own group?"

Okay, so maybe she was on a hundred-year cycle.

"Where do you want her to sit?" asked the man beside me. "On the floor? Looks to me as if all the other booths are full."

He was the guy Mike and Mary Lou had pointed out as Xavier's former basketball captain, the well-dressed six-footer who reeked prosperity and country club taste. "Don't pay any attention to Paula," he advised me in a casual tone. "No one else does."

She pulled a face and stuck her tongue out at him.

He ignored her.

"The rest of us are happy to have you join us," he assured me. "I'm Gary Bouchard." He angled his nametag toward me so I could see for myself. "And this is Sheila." He leaned back so I could catch a glimpse of his wife, the four-time class president, who nodded politely, but seemed either unable or unwilling to manage a hello.

"They're married," Paula explained in a sarcastic tone. "To each other."

"So are we," chimed the woman sitting beside Paula—Xavier's former head cheerleader, the woman with the helmet of black hair and pink bows, and her husband, the no-neck bruiser who'd once quarterbacked the football team. "I'm Mindy," she said, joining her hand with her husband's and holding it up to indicate they were together. "And this is Ricky. Hennessy. Two n's, two s's, no e before the y. It's annoying how many people spell it wrong."

Ricky grabbed a bruschetta with his left hand and stuffed it into his mouth, making no attempt to chew before he swallowed it whole. Nice. I could hardly wait to see what he did with a Belgian waffle.

"Emily Andrew," I said with a subdued wave, averting my gaze as Ricky grabbed another bruschetta. "Escort for the Iowa contingent."

"Honestly, Mindy," Sheila protested in disgust. "Fifty years of marriage and he still eats like an animal? Couldn't you at least teach him how to chew?"

"It's no wonder he's the size of the Goodyear blimp," droned Paula. "He probably hasn't digested a scrap of food for decades. What do you say, Rick?" She angled her head in his direction. "Have you chewed anything since those six pepperoni pizzas you devoured on Senior Skip Day? Refresh my memory. How many beers did it take to wash them down?"

A sudden silence fell over the table.

"I distinctly remember you arriving at Cascade Park with a six-pack of Schlitz under each arm," she persisted. "If you drank all of them yourself, it probably would have killed you. So who'd you share with? And why do I keep thinking it was Bobby Guerrette?"

My ears perked up. Bobby Guerrette again? His name was certainly popping up a lot, and the two couples at my table seemed none too happy about it.

Ricky stuck five meaty fingers in the air. "Five pizzas," he snuffled in a spray of caramelized onions. "Three pepperoni. Two sausage with double cheese. Five pizzas, not six."

"That's not the point, genius."

"Do you mind keeping your spittle on your own side of the table?" Sheila griped as she flicked onions off the tablecloth.

"I'm on it." Ricky gave her a sassy grin as he crammed another appetizer into his mouth, his expression changing dramatically when we lurched crazily in the wake of a passing boat. His eyes widened. His face paled. His brow beaded with sweat.

"You're looking a little seasick, Hennessy," Gary needled. "Cruising in the little putt-putt boat too rough on the ole quarterback's system?"

"He gets terribly seasick," Mindy admitted as she fanned his face with her napkin. "And I'll warn you right now, he's descended from a wicked line of hurlers."

"I *told* you I didn't want to sit with them." Sheila thwacked her husband's shoulder. "Move! I'm leaving."

"I have motion sickness pills," I said as I riffled through my shoulder bag.

"If they're whiskey flavored, he'll be happy to down the whole bottle," jibed Paula.

I held up the package. "Orange flavored."

Mindy made a gimme motion with her hand. "I'll take 'em anyway." She tore the box open and popped four pills out of their foil-backed packaging. "Chew on these," she said as she forced them into his mouth.

"There's optimism for you," taunted Sheila. "Maybe you should demonstrate how it's done so he won't be at a complete loss."

My stomach fluttered as we dipped into a trough and rolled sideways on the wake of another boat. Ricky slumped against his wife and groaned.

"There, there," Mindy soothed as she patted his head. "Listen to me, hon. If you feel that sudden urge coming on, aim it at Sheila."

"You better damn well hope I don't get spattered with half-chewed motion sickness pills!" Sheila threatened.

"Or else what?" Mindy challenged, her eyes lengthening to slits. "You'll stick us with the dry cleaning bill?"

"You got that right." Sheila thunked her forearm on the table and wrenched the sleeve of her blouse back and forth in an adult version of show and tell. "See this? It's silk. Silk requires special handling, and it's damn expensive to have laundered."

Mindy thrust out her bottom lip and fused her pencil-blackened eyebrows together in an angry vee over her nose. "So … what are you saying? You think we can't afford to have your crummy blouse cleaned?"

"The thought did enter my mind. Frankly, I'm amazed you're even on this trip. What did you have to do? Mortgage your house?"

Ricky shook free of his wife and planted his elbows on the table, cushioning his chin in the palms of his hands. His eyes were bleary, his words labored. "You guys wanna hear about … the thirty-three-yard touchdown pass I threw in the game we played against—"

"Zip it, Ricky," snapped Mindy, then to Sheila, "Not that it's any of your business, but I'll have you know that a land transportation engineer earns some of the highest wages in Bangor."

"Land transportation engineer?" Sheila crowed with laughter. "He changes oil and rotates tires. He's a grease monkey! Where do you get off calling him an engineer?"

"It was fourth down," Ricky rambled on. "Five ticks left on the clock. Brewer's throwing everything they got at us …"

"Let me tell you whose oil he changes," bellowed Mindy. "He services all the lemons that Gary Bouchard sells at Bouchard Motors. You hear that?" She drilled a menacing look at Gary. "Your cars are crap. And the more dealerships you open, the crappier your cars get. But don't change anything. Ricky's getting rich repairing the defective brake lines and electrical systems in your over-priced clunkers."

"Hennessy scrambles. He fakes." Ricky wishboned his arms over his head. "Touchdown!"

Gary gave him a squinty look. "Homecoming? Senior year? Xavier versus Brewer?"

Ricky nodded.

"You lost the game by thirty points."

Ricky shrugged. "I know. But it was still a great pass."

"And furthermore," Mindy ranted, "if that blouse is made of silk, I'll eat it."

"Why don't you let Ricky eat it?" Paula volunteered. "It might be easier on his digestive system than bruschetta."

Ricky curled his lip into a sneer. "Stuff it, Paula. I'm not eating no cussid blouse."

I wouldn't be able to eat a blouse after downing a whole platter of appetizers either, but before the mudslinging deteriorated into food slinging, I decided to redirect the discussion to a less controversial topic.

"Did anyone actually see what happened to Charlotte today?" I asked off-handedly.

"A bicycle plowed into her," said Gary. "Did you sleepwalk your way through Volendam?"

"I know she was hit by a bicycle. I'm just curious if any of you were nearby when it happened."

"What if we were?" Paula's tone was combative. "What's it to you?"

I offered her my most innocent look as I concocted what I believed to be a credible story. "It's nothing to me personally, but my group is balking at having to cross the street now, so you can imagine how much that's going to slow us down. I figure if I can reassure them that Charlotte died not because a bicyclist was flagrantly reckless, but because she failed to look both ways when she stepped off the curb, they might feel less skittish."

Mindy pointed a stubby, manicured forefinger at me. "Are you with those old geezers who are pestering all of us to become friends with them on Facebook?"

I flashed a clueless smile. "Excuse me?"

"They practically accosted us in the lobby tonight," groused Ricky, looking slightly less gray than he had five minutes earlier. "They were so desperate, they even offered to access our accounts from their cellphones so we could accept their invitations and become friends immediately. Why should I become friends with them? I don't even know them. They've got a lot of nerve wanting to stick their noses in my private Facebook business."

"I'm sure they were just trying to be cordial," I defended. "They're quite respectful of other people's privacy."

"Maybe they'd like to become friends of Bouchard Motors," Gary piped up. "Do they ever travel to Maine? I give senior citizen discounts on year-end models."

"For God's sake, give it a rest," his wife bristled. "Do you always have to be groveling at the feet of complete strangers?"

"There you go again." Paula wagged her finger at Gary. "Acting common. Shame, shame. You know how much it pisses Sheila off when you associate with the little people. She's afraid you'll catch something vulgar. Like poverty."

"Shut up, Paula," snarled Sheila.

I sighed inwardly. Man, trying to keep these people focused was harder than trying to herd cats. I breathed with relief when I saw our waiter heading toward us, balancing a tray with the next course.

"Chinese vegetable soup," he announced as he placed small soup bowls in front of each of us. He removed the empty appetizer platter from the table and hurried off again to someplace where the conversation was probably less hostile, which made me realize that if I was going to tease any information out of these people, I needed to skirt the issue rather than be so direct. Who knew that Chinese vegetable soup would provide the perfect diversion?

"Did anyone get a chance to eat in Volendam today?" I picked up my soup spoon and poised it over my bowl. "I lost my appetite after Charlotte's accident, so I missed lunch."

Mindy stared into space, her eyes crinkling in thought. "Come to think of it, that's where Ricky and me were when Charlotte got creamed. We were waiting in line to get into a little restaurant across the street from the scene of the accident."

"What's this white gunk floating in the soup?" asked Ricky. He nudged it with his spoon. "Looks like a hunk of rubber."

"We only had to wait about five minutes because two women who were sitting at a window table were just finishing up, so the hostess showed us right to their table." She smiled smugly, her voice dripping with entitlement. "It was absolutely the best seat in the house. We saw the ambulance arrive, the bicyclist getting first aid, Charlotte's body being carted off. We didn't miss a trick."

Ricky fished the questionable ingredient out of his soup and dumped it onto a saucer. He poked it with his finger. "What the hell? It *is* a hunk of rubber." He squinted at his wife. "I'm not eating no rubber vegetables."

"You're never up for trying anything new," Mindy complained. "Rubber vegetables are probably the latest trend in Chinese cuisine. I bet they're a delicacy, like grilled scorpions or chicken's feet." She shrugged. "Could be that rubber has more nutritional value."

Gary dipped his spoon into his soup bowl then held it aloft for Ricky to see what he'd retrieved. "It's not rubber, dufus. It's tofu."

"Toe what?"

"Tofu. Unfermented soybean curd. It's the vegetarian version of a T-bone steak."

Ricky snorted derisively. "T-bone steak. Right. You're so full of crap, I'm surprised your eyes haven't turned brown."

Gary shook his head, his voice almost sympathetic. "You haven't changed at all, Hennessy. Still the same mental giant you were fifty years ago."

"Like you're so smart," Mindy fired back. "I didn't see you graduating first in our class. Or second. Or third. I can't imagine how disappointed your daddy must have been when you told him you got beaten out by an orphan, a social misfit, and a girl who was afraid of her own shadow. If Bobby hadn't disappeared from the picture, you wouldn't have even ended up in the top five. That would have killed your daddy, wouldn't it? Hard to show your face around town when your kid's high school career ends up a total bust. No basketball scholarship and no academic awards."

"Ya," Ricky piled on. "You must have been turning cartwheels when Bobby made his exit. Finnegan gets bumped up to valedictorian, Laura gets salutatorian, and you get upgraded to fifth in the class. Pretty convenient if you ask me."

I sat up straight in my seat. Pete Finnegan became valedictorian only after the infamous Bobby Guerrette disappeared? I sidled a glance across the aisle at Pete. Hmm. How interesting was that?

"Are you accusing my Gary of something criminal?" Sheila demanded.

"If the shoe fits," taunted Ricky.

"How come you're not throwing accusations at Pete?" Sheila raved on. "He's the one who benefited most from Bobby's absence."

"And you know damn well I would have earned a basketball scholarship if I hadn't blown my knee that last semester," Gary defended.

"Ouch." I cringed. "Basketball injury?"

"He slipped on a piece of toilet paper in the boys' restroom," Paula said with barely contained humor. "The captain of the basketball team, felled by a square of generic two-ply."

"One-ply," Ricky corrected. "They were too cheap to spring for two-ply."

"Yah, well, if you football lunkheads hadn't been horsing around, it never would have happened," Gary sniped.

"You can't take a joke," accused Ricky. "You never could. Getting rid of all the toilet paper in the restroom was hilarious."

"You and your stupid prank ruined my basketball career," Gary bellowed.

"Ya, he coulda been a contenda," said Paula, aping Marlon Brando.

"Are you blaming me?" Ricky challenged. "Hey, I ain't taking the rap for your accident. Nobody pushed you. You went down all on your own."

"And one of these days *you're* going down, too, Hennessy." Gary's jaw pulsed angrily. "We'll see how you like it."

Mindy gasped. "Is that a threat?"

Paula threw her arms into the air and circled them around her head erratically, like a mime imitating chaos. "Geez-Louise, don't get Mindy in a huff, or she'll make up a derogatory cheer about you. Remember the one she made up about Laura and taught to the whole squad? *Lau-ra, Lau-ra, she's so scary. Looks like a dog, and acts like a ferret.*"

I stared at Paula, horrified. Oh, my Lord. If my schoolmates had been that cruel to me, I'm not sure I would have had the courage to show my face in class again. The Francis Xavier cheerleaders apparently weren't paragons of school spirit and good will.

They were bullies.

I sucked in a deep, calming breath.

I hated bullies.

"Ferret doesn't rhyme with scary," Sheila pointed out.

"No one asked you," spat Mindy.

"Was there anyone on your squad of losers who realized that 'scary' could be rhymed with 'fairy'?" questioned Paula. "Laura acted a hell of a lot more like the good fairy than a rodent."

Mindy skewered her with a look that inspired more fear than the Death Star's going operational. "You would have sold your grandmother's dentures to be on the cheerleading squad, Paula Peavey, so I'm not listening to any of your trash talk. Here's a cheer for you: *Paul-a, Paul-a, can't you see? You're eaten up by jeal-ou-sy.*"

Paula snorted with laughter. "Oh, please. Your glory days have gone to your head." She flashed a snarky grin. "And everything else has gone to your butt."

"Is the Laura you're talking about Laura LaPierre?" I asked, leaping into the fray.

Dead silence, followed by an incredulous look from Mindy. "You know Laura?"

"In a roundabout way," I fibbed. "She's quite the celebrity. Did any of you read the interview she gave to *Fitness Magazine?* It was dynamite. She offered tips on how to stay ultra toned and flab-free past sixty-five. And she should know, because she looks like she has about zero percent body fat." I smiled at Mindy. "She provided statistics on the high correlation between a pissy attitude and the high incidence of halitosis, boils, and rickets." I smiled at Paula. "And she gave pointers on how to turn ordinary business ventures into cash cows. I guess she's an entrepreneurial genius with more money than God." I smiled at Gary. "Have you spoken to her?"

Eyes bulged. Expressions froze. Jaws fell.

"We haven't run into her yet," Mindy finally said in a small, tight voice.

"Well, you might not recognize her because she looks like she graduated last year instead of fifty years ago. What a knockout! You must be thrilled that a member of your class has made such a big name for herself. I think *Vanity Fair* is doing a feature article on her next month, and after that, she'll be on the cover of *Vogue.* You should corner her sometime so you can reminisce about old times. I bet she's dying to thank all of you."

Ricky looked confused. "What's she got to thank us for?"

"For treating her the way you did. If you'd been nice to her, she probably would have stayed in Bangor … and ended up like the rest of you."

The floor tilted as we quartered into a wave. "Oh, jeez," Ricky squawked, grabbing the table with both hands. We slammed into a trough with a *boom* strong enough to shake the table and cause the silverware to jump. Dishes rattled. Soup sloshed onto the table-cloth. And Ricky's head fell forward as if he'd been guillotined.

"Is everyone ready for the next course?" I asked brightly as our waiter strode toward us, seemingly immune to the lurching deck. "Wow. Looks like a week's worth of food. Hope everyone's hungry."

Ricky let out a groan like a wounded animal.

"Would you get him off the table?" Paula exploded. "Unless you expect the waiter to serve the next course around his head."

"Is he going to be sick?" Sheila asked anxiously.

I stuck my nose in the air and sniffed. "Smells like onions, and hot chile oil, and peppercorns, and—"

"Somebody..." Ricky pleaded in a whisper of breath, "shut her up."

"Bang Bang Chicken," our waiter announced as he snapped open his tray jack and set his heavy serving tray atop it. "Very pi-quant." He arched his brows at Ricky's head. "Does der gentleman vish to try der entree?"

"He's feeling a little out of sorts," explained Mindy, "but he wouldn't want his meal to go to waste, seein's as how it's already paid for, so you can give it to me, and I'll just pick on it after I finish mine."

"Give her mine, too," Sheila instructed. "There's no way I can enjoy my meal with Jumbo's head in my lap."

"His head is nowhere near your lap," argued Mindy.

"How would you know what a lap looks like?" railed Sheila. "When's the last time you saw yours?"

Paula laughed. "I doubt she can remember that far back."

"I'll tell you what I *do* remember," Mindy shot back. "I remember who Bobby Guerrette refused to go to Senior Prom with. The girls were supposed to ask the boys. Remember him turning your invitation down flat? He decided to stay home rather than go with you. How'd that make you feel, Paula? Or did it happen too long ago for you to recall?"

"Witch," hissed Paula.

"Bitch," spat Mindy, proving that her rhyming skills had improved appreciably since high school.

"Duck!" cried Sheila, which seemed a lame entry in a name-calling contest, until I realized it wasn't a name.

It was a warning.

"He's ready to blow!"

Which he did, with animation, sound effects, and impressive range.

"Jeesuz, Hennessy!"

"OH MY GOD!!!"

I launched myself out of the booth, escaping across the aisle before my cashmere twinset fell victim to Ricky's malaise. Unfortunately, my dinner companions were less mobile, so they bore the full impact of the assault, their screams and cries attracting the attention of the entire boat.

I regarded them in disbelief. Ugh. They could kiss those clothes good-bye. I couldn't even read their nametags anymore. *Euuuw.*

As the scene escalated into a full-blown shouting match, I realized that even though I'd failed to trick them into coughing up any new details about Charlotte's death, I'd learned two intriguing facts: first, that Pete Finnegan had benefited hugely from the death of a fellow student fifty years ago, and second, if Ricky Hennessy had been able to throw a football half as far as he could hurl, he could have gone pro.

SIX

"Our waiter told us the Bang Bang Chicken was real 'pee-kant,'" Nana confided when we returned to the hotel, "but he didn't say nuthin' about it bein' so dang spicy. Two bites done me in. Feels like I don't got no skin left on my tongue." Peering down the length of her nose, she stuck her tongue out and studied it cross-eyed. "Whath it look like?"

We were loitering in the lobby along with other guests who were reading the schedule on the whiteboard, bugging the front desk clerk for brochures, and queuing up at the elevator. "Skin's still there," I said, wrapping my arm around her shoulder and giving her an affectionate hug. "But I think 'piquant' is restaurant code for hot. Like, 'Yeow, my mouth is on fire' hot."

"No kiddin'?"

"I'm surprised Tilly didn't interpret for you."

"We got split up, so she ate with George and I ate with a fella named Peewee. Awful nice young man. He's one of them reunion folks. He don't live in Maine no more though. He lives in Arizona in one a them retirement communities." She scanned the lobby. "That's him over there by the front desk, gettin' hit on by Bernice."

I found Bernice locked in conversation with a guy who probably had to duck his head when he passed through most doorways—a big bear of a man with shaggy white hair and a jacket that wouldn't zip over his stomach. I laughed aloud. "I see him, but I can't believe his name is Peewee."

"He grew."

"Why is Bernice hitting on him? Is she on the prowl for husband number two?"

"*Psssh.* You see the way she's wavin' her phone around? I bet she's askin' him to be her friend on Facebook. But it won't do her no good because I already asked him, and he said he don't do social networkin'."

A lightbulb slowly brightened over my head. "My dinner companions mentioned that all you guys had been pestering them about Facebook. 'Accosted' was the word one of them used. So why the frantic push to collect more online friends?"

"You can't never have enough, dear." She whipped out her phone and fingered the touchscreen. "What's their names? Maybe I don't got 'em yet."

"You don't. They're not interested in sharing their personal information with strangers from Iowa."

"But I wouldn't be no stranger if we was friends."

I narrowed my eyes at her. "Okay, what's this really about?"

She peeked at me over the tops of her wire-rims, her eyes sheepish, her voice resigned. "It's on account've Bernice. She's been so obnoxious braggin' about how many Facebook friends she's got that

69

the rest of us decided to one-up her. So it's kinda turned into a competition."

I regarded her sternly. "That's why you're pestering the other guests? You're trying to sign up more friends than Bernice on Facebook?"

She nodded contritely. "Yup."

I gave her confession a moment's thought. "I like it! So how are you doing so far?"

She snapped back into action like a brand new rubber band. "We got a lot a catchin' up to do, but we been gainin' on her." She quickly consulted her screen. "I got forty-eight friends so far. Tilly's got fifty-two. George has thirty-five."

"And how many does Bernice have?"

She swept her forefinger across her screen. "Six hundred eighty."

"WHAT?"

"Ain't that somethin'? Bernice don't got no friends except me, and sometimes even I'm on the fence, so how'd she come up with six hundred?" Her phone chimed. "Oh, boy. Incomin' text message." She read the screen. "It's from Margi. She says everyone's starvin', so we're gonna get some dessert. You wanna join us, dear?"

Even though I hadn't gotten beyond the Chinese vegetable soup course, I wasn't ready to face any more food this evening, not with Ricky Hennessy's command performance still so fresh in my mind. "I'm looking forward to a long soak in a hot bath, and then I'm going to hit the sack." I looked beyond the lobby proper to the French doors of the dining room. "Is the hotel dining room open for dessert?"

"Just a sec." She typed my question and sent it off, then stayed focused on the screen as she waited patiently for a reply. "Margi's good about gettin' right back to me."

"Where is she?"

"Right behind you."

I turned around to find Margi standing by the revolving door, less than ten feet away, typing a message into her phone.

"She says the dinin' room's closed, so we gotta go someplace else." Nana's phone chimed again. "We're s'posed to meet by the front door in two minutes."

I glanced around the room. "That shouldn't be too hard, considering you're all standing within ten feet of the door already."

"It's nice to have a little cushion, dear. Takes some of the pressure off."

As I ushered Nana toward the front entrance, Jackie pushed her way through the revolving door and swooped into the lobby like a rock star in search of an entourage, heels clacking and eyes gleaming.

"Well, would you look at that," said Nana. "It's that nice girl what you was married to."

"Mrs. S!" cried Jackie, smothering her in a rib-crushing hug that pushed her wirerims off her nose and flattened her hair. "I waved to you at dinner." She readjusted Nana's glasses and fluffed her hair. "But you had your back to me, so you probably didn't see me. So what did you think of the meal? Pretty awesome Asian fusion, huh?"

Nana gave her teeth a thoughtful suck. "Osmond said the rubber in the soup was a bit salty. Margi ate one a them slices a toast with the onions and said it bit back. And Bernice said cat food

71

woulda tasted better. Don't know if she was talkin' about canned or dry."

"But the Bang Bang Chicken, Mrs. S. Wasn't it the best?"

"It burned the skin off my tongue."

"Mine too!"

"And I don't got no feelin' in my lips."

"Me either!"

"So what'd you like about it so much?"

Jackie paused, looking suddenly bewildered. "That it burned the skin off my tongue and left me with no feeling in my lips. I thought that's what made it so good."

Nana peered up at her, smiling indulgently. "You're very tall, aren't you, dear?"

"What did you do with Beth Ann?" I inquired when "lookalike Emily" failed to follow Jackie through the door.

Jackie tittered excitedly. "If all goes according to plan, she should be negotiating with the people from Maine right now."

"About what?" asked Nana.

She bowed her head and cupped her hand over her mouth, her voice low and conspiratorial. "Our dinner companions expressed a keen interest in seeing the Red Light District at night, so they've offered Dietger a really big tip to take them on an unauthorized field trip. Beth Ann and I are trying to get in on the action."

Nana's jaw dropped to her navel. "*The* Red Light District? The real one? The place where ladies of the evenin' earn high-yieldin' investment capital by boinkin' complete strangers in storefront windows?"

Jackie nodded. "Impressive, isn't it? The Dutch are so enter-prising."

72

"Are you guys nuts?" I looked from one to the other. "According to the guidebooks, the Red Light District is a seamy cesspool of perversion, pot, porn, and prostitutes. It's overrun with sex shops, opium dens, live nude revues, junkies, drug dealers, brothels—"

Nana held up her hand. "You don't need to say no more, dear. I get the picture." She stared up at Jackie with an imploring look. "Can I go, too?"

"Nana!" I cried. "What are you thinking? It's too dangerous! You—you could get mugged, or—or drugged—or kidnapped at knife-point and sold into white slavery."

Her face lit up. "No kiddin'?"

I rolled my eyes. "Do you know how much hot water I'd be in if Mom discovered I'd encouraged you to wander around the Red Light District in the company of perverts and prostitutes?"

"I wasn't plannin' to tell her, dear."

"Aw, c'mon, Emily, lighten up." Jackie patted the crown of Nana's head as if she were a favorite pet. "She'll be with me and Beth Ann and all the people from Maine. What could possibly happen to her?"

Oh, yeah. That was reassuring. "Which would you prefer to hear first? Best-case scenario or worst-case scenario?"

"Who's Beth Ann?" asked Nana.

"Oh!" Jackie gushed. "I need to introduce you! Beth Ann is my—"

I clapped my hands over Nana's ears.

Jackie fired me a narrow look. "She's going to have a *really* hard time hearing me with your mitts covering her ears."

"I know."

Nana tapped the back of my hand. "What'd she say?"

I shook my head and mouthed, "Noth-ing."

"Marion!" Dick Stolee hurried over to us, his thumb resting on the button of his stop watch. "What's the holdup here? We're thirty seconds behind schedule. Time's a wastin'."

Nana squinted hard at his face. "WHAT'D HE SAY?"

I dropped my hands. "He says it's time to go. Have a good time." I scooted her toward him. "Eat hearty. Stay on the main thoroughfares. Don't wander down any dark alleys."

"Where are you guys headed?" asked Jackie.

"We're going out for dessert," said Dick, "but we don't know where yet because Osmond is still tallying the votes." He lowered his voice to an exasperated whisper. "Grace and Helen's phones are out of juice, so he's insisting on secret ballots."

"Stop the balloting!" cried Jackie. "Have I got a place for you." Grabbing Dick's arm, she aimed him toward the front door. "Exit the building. Turn right. Walk two blocks, and it's on the left-hand side of the street. A delicious little pastry shop with all kinds of scrumptious chocolate cakes and fruit tarts in the display cases. To *die* for." She turned to Nana. "Trust me, Mrs. S, I guarantee you'll be happier gorging yourself on chocolate than checking out the nightlife."

"You think?" she said, not looking entirely convinced. "Well, maybe me and George can share somethin'. We love whipped cream and chocolate sauce." She grinned wickedly. "Sometimes we even put 'em in a bowl."

I hung my head. *Oh, God.*

She looked up at Jackie. "If I give you my spare camera, would you take a few pictures? We're studyin' the seven deadly sins at the Legion of Mary this month, and they're handin' out door prizes

74

for photos what capture the best nonliteral interpretation of the featured sin. Last week we done sloth." A beatific smile split her face. "Next week, it's lust."

Jackie squeaked out a sound like a faulty vacuum cleaner leaking air. "There's absolutely *no* picture-taking in the Red Light District, Mrs. S. None. *Nada.* Forget it. Show up with a camera anywhere in that part of the city at night and you could be flirting with serious consequences."

"Red Light District?" hooted Dick. "Hell, I vote we cancel dessert. I didn't know we had another choice."

"You don't got no other choice," Nana informed him as she dragged him toward the waiting group. "You're married to Grace."

"Call me when you're done eating to let me know you're all back safely," I called after her.

Jackie splayed her hand over her heart and smiled. "She handles disappointment so well. She's an inspiration to us all." She leveled her gaze on me, brows arched and sparks flying in her eyes. "So, would you care to explain?"

Even though we'd been husband and wife only briefly, we still retained the ability to discuss serious issues like veterans of a much longer marriage. "I have no idea what you're talking about."

"The earmuff business?"

"Oh, that."

I looked to see who was within earshot, then motioned her to an isolated corner of the room. "Okay, Jack, here's the deal. If I have to explain your flip-flops to Nana *yet again*, I'll probably overload her circuits and cause her to have a stroke. Or acid reflux. Or something equally life altering."

"Flip-flops?" She stuck out her foot. "Hel-looo? I'm wearing boots."

"Flip-flops, Jack. You've developed a pattern. When you were a he, you married me but ran off with another guy. When you became a she, you married a guy, but now you've run off with another woman. What *is* it with you? Back and forth and back and forth. Can't you just make up your mind and live with it?"

"Emily Andrew! Are you accusing me of leaving my adoring husband to engage in a tawdry affair with—with?" She paused, elongating her eyes to tiny slits. "Refresh my memory. Who have I run away with?"

"Duh? Beth Ann Oliver?"

"What?"

"Maybe you can't help it, Jack. Maybe your brain chemistry is so out of whack that it's caused an irreparable tear in your moral fabric."

She circled her hand around her throat as if trying to hold together the fabric that hadn't already split apart. "Oh, my God. This sounds serious." She grew silent, then perked up again, as if her brain were rebooting itself. "Wait a minute. My moral fabric isn't coming apart at the seams. You know why? Because I'm not cheating on my husband. You know why? Because Beth Ann isn't my girlfriend."

"Then who is she?"

"My client."

"What kind of client tags along with you on a European vacation?"

"The kind who pays me to give her advice on a daily basis!"

I blinked my surprise. "You mean, like Dear Abby?"

"Oh, please. I blow Abby out of the water with all the services I offer. I'm available to accompany my clients to any location in the world. My advice is individual and immediate. I'm equipped to handle any problem from what book you should read next, to how to prevent yourself from falling apart when you smudge a fresh manicure. And as a special bonus, I offer professional fashion advice, lessons in makeup application, and best of all, free foot massages. I'd like to see Abby top that."

"So, you're like a globetrotting Dear Abby?"

She fisted her hand on her hip. "What I am, Emily, is an honest to goodness, card-carrying, board-certified … life coach!"

"Wow."

"Isn't that awesome?"

"Awesome. What's a life coach?"

She groaned in disgust. "Have you people in the Midwest ever heard about *any* popular trend before it became passé?"

"Mom says we were ahead of the curve with the hula hoop."

"Being a life coach is *only* the most thrilling job I've ever had, Emily. Better than acting off-Broadway. Better than caulking bathroom and kitchen tile. Better than writing a romance novel. People *pay* me to tell them what to do. And they don't snarl at me to butt out or get lost. They *want* me to make decisions for them. It's the dream job of every control freak. It's like—like being a parent, with financial benefits!"

Or a psychologist without a license. "Did you say you were actually certified to do this?"

"I most certainly am. It usually takes six months to complete the course work, but I took the accelerated course on the Web, so I was certified in two short weeks!"

I shuddered with terror. Jack telling people how they should live their lives was like Donald Trump telling men how to style their hair. "Two weeks and *bam*—a whole new career. I'm—I'm speechless."

"I know. Isn't it amazing? Internet training allows just about anyone to hang out a shingle these days."

"How many clients do you have?"

"Well, only one so far, but I'll probably have to beat them off with a stick when word gets out how good I am."

"How did Beth Ann find you?"

"She read the ad I stuck up on the bulletin board at the salon. She asked Tom for particulars, he said he thought we'd hit it off, and here we are."

I glanced across the room to find Beth Ann chatting with Mike and Mary Lou McManus and several other Mainers. "Actually, I'm surprised she responded to your ad. She seems so together. It's hard to believe she needs help making everyday decisions."

Jackie flicked her hand back and forth at the wrist. "Honey, the poor girl is a mess. Tom has done her hair for years, so he's gotten an earful. Her husband left her. She got laid off from her job. Her father died. She might look cool, calm, and confident, but trust me, she's being held together by piano wire."

"She doesn't seem to have any trouble mingling with people."

"That's because she's on special assignment. If we're going to nail the killer, we have to infiltrate the enemy camp, so she's practicing her infiltration techniques—smiles, flattery, and a wad of Euros to defray the cost of Dietger's tip. Money always talks."

"Whoa! I never said anything about a killer."

"You didn't have to. Our dinner companions told us all about Charlotte's dictatorship, so it was pretty obvious. Take it from me, there's a killer. And since you have such a lousy record for apprehending criminals, I've decided you need more boots on the ground to assist with the investigation, so Beth Ann and I are teaming up to help you."

Oh, God. Just what I needed. Scooby-Doo and friend turning my subtle fact-finding mission into an afternoon soap opera.

"So …" she leaned over close to my ear, "who do we think did it?"

Was I starting to question my own suspicions? Or was I simply afraid what Pete Finnegan might do if he found himself being stalked by a six-foot transsexual with a penchant for playing dress-up?

One thing was for sure though. If I refused Jackie's help, she'd find a way to play detective anyway, so if I couldn't talk her out of it, I'd be better off giving her my blessing to get into it … with a few guidelines. "Okay, Jack, you and Beth are in, but you need to follow the ground rules."

"Yes! I love ground rules!"

"You hate ground rules."

She sighed. "I know. I'm in denial."

"Three things." I waved a trio of digits in her face. "These folks from Maine aren't cream puffs; they're pretty tough hombres. So whatever you do, don't bug them. Stay out of their personal space. And don't ask them stupid questions."

"How am I supposed to know if a question is stupid or not?"

"As a general rule? Anything out of your mouth that contains the words 'Did you kill the tour director?' is a stupid question."

She looked confused. "Why is that stupid?"

"It's a go," Beth Ann announced as she joined us, "but it's costing us twenty Euros apiece for the honor. Is twenty too much? Do you

79

think I should have haggled the price down to ten?" She compressed her head between her hands and squeezed. "Did I do the right thing? I think I screwed up." She gave Jackie a beseeching look. "I'll die if I screwed up. Really. I'll just open a vein, lie down, and die."

Yup. Jackie had called that one. Beth Ann's cool, calm, and confident demeanor was all window dressing, which meant that despite Jackie's wanting to play Nancy Drew, her hands were going to be so full addressing Beth Ann's insecurities that she'd have precious little time to derail my investigation.

I smiled impishly. *Thank you, Jesus!*

"Twenty Euros is a fair price," Jackie reassured her. "You think twenty Euros is fair, don't you, Emily?"

Twenty Euros was highway robbery, but Beth Ann didn't need to hear that, especially if she was carrying sharp objects in her shoulder bag. "Sounds good to me."

Beth Ann gasped with relief. "Ehh! I was really sweating it." She fanned her face at warp speed. "We can leave as soon as two couples and a female guest change their clothes. They were sitting in the booth where the guy got seasick and blew his cookies all over his table companions. I'm surprised they're coming with us. Word on the grapevine is that the aggrieved guests are so incensed, there could be an old-fashioned rumble."

"How very *West Side Story* of them," cooed Jackie. Then to me, "Do we need to cover that?"

"Consider all guests in the Maine contingent persons of interest," I suggested. "You can judge for yourself what you want and don't want to cover."

"I don't want to cover a rumble," she said with an admiring glance at her hands. "I just had my nails done."

Figuring my influence here was about spent, I spotted some-one standing by herself near the front door and realized there was one more thing I needed to do. "Stay out of trouble," I cautioned Jackie and Beth Ann before making my way across the lobby to the pretty blonde in the skinny jeans and ponytail. "I'm sorry to bother you," I said by way of greeting, "but my name is Emily, and I have a confession to make."

"Don't we all," she said, laughing. "Glad to meet you, Emily. I'm Laura, and if you have something to confess, I'm all ears." Her smile was magnetic, her eyes warm and lively. She looked like the type of person who could coax a cat out of a tree or a child out of a tantrum. I liked her already.

"You're going to think this is pretty weird, especially since you don't know me, but I took the liberty of inventing a personality profile for you at dinner tonight."

Her smile widened. "Did you make me sound good?"

"I made you rock. You are now as financially savvy as Oprah and as physically fit as Wonder Woman."

She threw her head back with laughter. "Fantastic! Do I wear hot pants and a brass bra?"

"You're wealthy enough to wear whatever you want. You've al-ready done an interview for *Fitness Magazine* with tips on how to remain flab-free, optimistic, and disgustingly rich throughout re-tirement, and next month, you'll be doing a feature article for *Van-ity Fair* and a cover shoot for *Vogue*." I shrugged. "Just a few minor events in your life."

"*Vogue*? Boy, have I come up in the world. I may have to drag out my curling iron and rethink my makeup. So, tell me, what ne-cessitated the grand fiction?"

I opened my mouth, then snapped it shut. Hold it. I couldn't tell her all the hurtful things her classmates had said. The idea was to stick up for her, not rip the scab off an old wound. I stared at her stupidly, hoping the ground would open up beneath my feet so I could disappear into it.

"Ouch. That bad, hunh?" She smiled sympathetically. "Maybe I can make this a little easier for you. Who did you eat with this evening?"

"The Hennessys—two n's, two s's, no e before the y—the Bouchards, and Paula—"

"Peavey," she finished for me. "Say no more. I get the picture. I guess they made it clear that I was the butt of their jokes for four years. I'm so sorry you had to sit there and be exposed to their negative energy. Did Paula recite the twisted rhyme they made up about me? *Lau-ra, Lau-ra, she's so scary. Looks like a—*"

I held up my hand. "Hearing it once was more than enough. It was really mean, not to mention it didn't even rhyme."

"I know. And Mindy, being the master of iambic pentameter that she was, never figured out that 'ferret' didn't rhyme with 'scary.' 'Fairy' would have been a better choice. Even I knew that. I'm surprised her grades were even good enough to graduate with the rest of us, but she was already planning her wedding senior year, with a bun in the oven, so Sister Hippolytus probably wanted to get rid of her as soon as possible. Not the kind of image our high school wanted to promote, especially back then."

I shook my head. "How were you able to handle the humiliation for so many years without cracking?"

"I knew myself better than they knew me. I might have been painfully shy and geeky, but I knew that there was an attractive extrovert hiding somewhere inside me, so I just kept my mouth shut and my nose in my books and bided my time until I could head off to college."

"Has anyone nominated you for sainthood yet?"

"Don't get me wrong, I did my fair share of crying over having my feelings hurt, but I thought they were a bunch of loud-mouthed idiots who probably wouldn't amount to much, so that kept me going." Her eyes sparkled with sudden tears. "And I had a protector who always came to my defense when something derogatory was said about me. I wish I could have been so brave, but I took the coward's way out. I simply told myself that the meanies were living the best years of their lives in high school, while I was looking ahead to bigger and better things. And see? I was right. I'm going to be on the cover of *Vogue!*"

"Boy, how do you resist wanting to pay them back for all the misery they put you through?"

"Believe it or not, I've forgiven them."

"You're kidding."

"It was either forgive them or let the experience weigh me down for the rest of my life. So I chose forgiveness. It was very liberating. I highly recommend it. And it's allowed me to direct my energy and talents toward something *con*structive rather than *de*structive. Revenge is such a downer. If you feed it enough negative emotion, it can eat you alive."

She took my arm and navigated me away from the door as Dietger stormed into the lobby like a prize bull stampeding through the streets of Pamplona. "Geesch. He walks the same way he drives," she scoffed. "Like a maniac. I'm glad we're going on foot tonight. The only thing we'll have to dodge is bicycles. Are you coming with us? We'll probably be treated to quite the spectacle for a measly five Euros."

"Five Euros? Not twenty?"

"It's probably worth five. No way is it worth twenty."

Oh, God. I hope no one mentioned that to Beth Ann. We could be looking at a total nuclear meltdown.

"So, what do you say?" asked Laura. "Can I twist your arm? I think you and I have great friendship potential."

"Thanks for the invite, but I'm forcing myself to do the responsible thing tonight by waiting for my group to return from their outing. They want their independence, but I need peace of mind."

"Fair enough. I'll catch you later then. And I can't thank you enough for pumping up my brand at dinner. That was really sweet. I owe you."

"No problem. It was worth the fib to see the shock on their faces. I wish I'd thought to take a picture." As Dietger blared out orders to the assembled group, I was relieved that my guys would be safely ensconced in a pastry shop this evening while everyone else explored Amsterdam's hellhole of live porn and illicit sex. Thank God. One less thing to worry about.

Laura scanned the crowd. "I'm trying to decide who I should hang out with on our field trip. My old friend Mary Lou or the guy who was the class clown?"

I was struck with a sudden thought. "Why don't you hang out with your high school protector. Is he here?"

"I wish." Sadness flooded her face. A faraway look filled her eyes. "There's so much I'd like to thank him for. So much I—" Her voice cracked. She shook her head. "He's not here. Bobby disappeared over a lifetime ago."

I waited a beat. "Bobby?"

She nodded. "My protector. Bobby Guerrette."

———

As investigations went, I was discovering precious little about Charlotte but practically everything about Bobby Guerrette. Too bad Bobby hadn't been our tour director. I'd gathered so much background information on him, I'd have the case cracked by now.

Once back in my room, I soaked in the tub for a half hour, slipped into something comfy, then curled up on the bed with a book and my phone. On a whim I tried Etienne at home, but when he didn't answer, I had to satisfy myself by leaving him flirtatious kissy sounds on the answering machine.

He'd know it was me. We had caller ID, which made it impossible to make lewd phone calls anonymously anymore.

I turned the television on to an international business channel, opened my Dutch/English dictionary, slunk into a cozy cocoon of pillows and blankets, and began to peruse the section on what to order in a restaurant.

It was the last thing I remembered...until the phone woke me up.

Jackie's voice. High and screechy. In full-blown panic. "You've gotta get down here, Emily! I've rounded up everyone else, but I've lost the Dicks!"

SEVEN

"How can they be lost?" I ranted at Jackie forty minutes later. "What happened to the pastry shop? The chocolate cake? The anticipated sugar highs?"

"Oh, the rest of them are high, all right," she shot back hysterically. "But it ain't from sugar."

The taxi driver had dropped me off at an unlit alleyway with instructions to head toward the neon lights at the end of the alley and cross the footbridge over the canal. "Der place you're looking for vill be right in front of you."

"You can't take me right to the door?" I objected.

He'd snorted with laughter and driven away.

I understood the laughter now, because there were so many people jammed into the strip of real estate between the city's two oldest canals that the street had morphed into a pedestrian mall. The Red Light District was apparently closed off to vehicular traffic to accommodate the hordes of curiosity seekers who were too mesmerized by the mind-numbing debauchery to take notice of the occasional car speeding straight at them.

I'd found Jackie pacing in front of a corner building called the Café Bar de Stoof—a luminous white structure whose enormous windows were set up on a grid as precise as an Iowa street map. Music screamed into the night from every opened door. Lights blazed like electric rainbows—flood lights, strobe lights, flashing lights, street lights. Graffiti defiled every staircase and door stoop. Whistles vied with cat calls. Onlookers lingered in boisterous circles, crowded the hoods of parked cars, and hung from the railings of staircases and balconies, chanting and singing with drunken abandon. A carnival atmosphere prevailed, reminding me of the annual Windsor City Hog Festival, only without the Tilt-A-Whirl or the hog.

"Define 'high,'" I asked Jackie as a tattooed guy with spiked purple hair and anchor chains dangling from his nose sauntered up to us. He swayed slightly as he eyeballed Jackie's boots.

"Niiiice," he slurred, sticking his tongue out as if to lick them. "My girl would look *sooo* hot in them. How about you slip 'em off and hand 'em over."

Jackie stared him straight in the eye and lowered her voice to a deep basso. "How about you get lost before I rip that tongue ornament out of your head and use it to pierce what's left of your brain?"

He turned abruptly on his heel and staggered back into the crowd, proving one of those axioms of human nature: it was mind-numbingly scary to be threatened by a six-foot Barbie doll with Darth Vader's voice.

"Pervert," Jackie sniped. Wheeling around, she motioned for me to follow her down the alleyway behind us.

"Where are we going?" I asked as I chased after her.

She stopped in front of a gaggle of seniors who were huddled near a brick building, making strange animal noises and laughing giddily at each other. Jackie swept her arm toward them. "I did what I could. They're all yours now."

I did a sudden double-take. Oh, my God! It was them! I took a quick head count. Onetwothreefour—

"Look, everyone," giggled Margi as she pointed at me. "It's— You know. Her. The girl who's on the tour with us." She swayed against Tilly in super-slow motion and giggled some more.

Fivesixseveneight. EIGHT? That couldn't be right. Onetwothreefour—

"Are we on a tour?" Bernice twirled in a slow circle, head back and mouth open, as if she were trying to catch snowflakes on her tongue. "I was wondering what we were doing here."

Fivesixseven . . . eight. Nuts!

"*Ewwww*," said Alice, hugging George's prosthetic leg to her chest and gazing skyward. "Look at the pretty colors."

"Who's missing?" I cried at them.

Osmond raised his hand. "I am."

I looked left. I looked right. No Dick Teig. No Dick Stolee. No—. My heart stopped in panic. "Where's Nana?"

They regarded me stupidly with their glassy eyes and goofy smiles.

"Why is there a bird sitting on your head?" asked Helen, tilting her head to view it from another angle.

Eh! Somewhere between the hotel and here, Helen had apparently lost both her eyebrows and replaced them with adhesive bandages that she'd colored with permanent black marker. Not the best fix, but in comparison to what everyone else around here looked like, it was actually quite attractive.

Tilly stared trancelike at my bare head. "That's *Pteroglossus torquatus*," she whispered in awe, "found only in the tropical rainforests of Belize, Guatemala, Honduras—"

"*Ewwww*," cooed Alice, eyeing me in a similar manner. "Look at the pretty feathers."

"—Nicaragua, Costa Rica, Panama, Colombia—"

"There is no bird on my head," I shouted.

"—Equador, Venezuela." Tilly swung her walking stick into the air. "Do you want me to knock the damn thing onto its keister?"

"No!" I ducked as her cane whirled toward my head.

"Why is the pavement shaking?" asked Grace, squatting low and riding out the tremor like a surfer riding a wave. "*Weeeeee!*"

"That's enough!" I yelled. "Grace, stand up. There's no earthquake. Alice, give George back his leg." I narrowed my gaze as my brain caught up to my eyes. "Alice, why are you holding George's leg?"

Jackie snatched Tilly's walking stick off the ground and handed it to me. "They decided to play croquet," she said under her breath. "George's leg was the mallet. Alice was supposed to be up next."

My jaw came unhinged. "What were they using for balls?"

She shook her head. "You don't wanna know."

Oh, God. "Eyes on me, everyone! One last time. Where? Is? Nana?"

"I had to go potty," she called out as she shuffled up behind me in her little size-5 sneakers.

I exhaled the breath I'd been holding and wrapped my arms around her. "Stop doing that! You scared the bejeebers out of me."

"Emily, dear, what a nice surprise. I wasn't expectin' to see you here. Listen, everyone," she enthused as she turned to the group. "If anyone's gotta go potty, I found a real nice one in that corner buildin' over there. Only thing is, I think I was in the wrong section 'cause a fella poked his hand under the partition while I was sittin' there doin' my business. He didn't speak no English, but I figured he didn't have no toilet paper, so I helped him out and give him a big wad. Poor fella. God only knows how long he'd been holed up in that stall before I come along."

I hung my head. Maybe it was time for me to switch careers to something less stressful—like, say, bomb defuser.

"Where's that bird, Helen?" Margi squinted in my direction. "I can't see it anymore. I think there's something wrong with my glasses."

Osmond removed his wire rims. "Here, try mine."

"Stop that!" I scolded. "You can't wear each other's glasses."

Nana's shoulders slumped as if weighted by concrete shoulder pads. "You don't know the half of it, dear."

Why did I *not* want to know what that meant?

"Everyone is here except for Dick Teig and Dick Stolee," I said, raising my voice several decibels. "Does anyone know where they are?"

Jackie snorted. "Good luck with that one."

"My Dick is missing?" Helen studied the faces around her with sudden interest. "When did that happen?"

Yup. It was going to be a long night. I rephrased my question. "When is the last time you saw the two Dicks?"

"September twenty-first, nineteen-fifty-nine," said George.

Osmond raised his hand. "Why is Helen missing her dick? Did she have a sex change?"

"See what I mean?" taunted Jackie.

"What is *wrong* with all of you?" I cried.

"It's on account a the chocolate cake," Nana blurted out. "The pastry shop what Jackie sent us to was closed, so we found another one. But while we was sittin' there, eatin' our pastries, everyone's eyes started goin' berserk."

I frowned. "Define berserk."

"Well, the Dicks was complainin' about lightnin' bolts flashin' in front of their eyes. George swore he seen giant flies attackin' him. And Bernice said she could make me look a whole lot more like Winston Churchill if I'd let her move my nose closer to my eyebrows."

"Hmm. Ocular migraines can cause symptoms like that, but I don't understand why all of you started suffering the same effects at the same time. That's really weird." I tilted Nana's chin up so I could examine her eyes. "Are you seeing anything unusual?"

"I seen Dick Stolee pull out his wallet to pay the taxi. That was pretty unusual."

"So, everyone's eyes went berserk except yours?"

She nodded glumly. "It was pretty disappointin'. Everyone else was seein' fireworks and insects. All I got to see was George swattin' kamikaze flies."

I shook my head. "Why do you suppose you were the only person not affected?"

"I think it's 'cause I didn't eat no chocolate cake. They run out by the time I give 'em my order, so I got a poppyseed muffin instead and it tasted so bad, I give it to the Dicks. They didn't notice it tasted funny on account of they eat so fast, they don't know what they're chewin' half the time."

"So everyone who ate the cake displayed symptoms?" This was becoming less of a medical enigma and more of a no-brainer. "Are you absolutely sure you went to a pastry shop?"

"It wasn't a pastry shop," Tilly called out. "It was a coffeeshop."

I sucked in my breath with horror. "A coffeeshop? You were supposed to *avoid* coffeeshops. Remember? I told you at all three group meetings. I handed out special memos. I made a notation on the bottom of your itineraries."

"We knew you talked about 'em," Nana confessed. "We just couldn't remember what you said."

"To reiterate," I announced pointedly, "Dutch cafes serve light meals. Dutch *coffeeshops* serve bakery items laced with marijuana and God only knows what other drugs!"

They exchanged sheepish looks with each other before dissolving into giggles again.

I eyed them accusingly. "You're all high as kites, aren't you?"

"Congratulations for just figuring that out," quipped Jackie.

Tilly swayed against George, circling her arm around his neck for support. "I haven't felt this good since I chewed root bark with the Pygmies forty years ago."

"I haven't felt this good … ever," slurred Margi.

Nana looked up at me imploringly. "You s'pose we could stop by that coffeeshop again on the way home, dear? I know where it is."

"No! Has anyone tried phoning the Dicks?"

They gaped at me. They gaped at each other. Helen whipped out her cellphone and stared at it in confusion. "Hey, who replaced my phone with a remote control?"

"I have one, too," marveled Osmond as he studied his screen. "I wonder how many channels I get?"

No doubt about it. A career change was looking more appealing all the time.

Nana punched a key on her cell and waited. "I'm gettin' nuthin' but dead air on Dick Teig's line, Emily."

"What about Dick Stolee?"

She repeated the process. "Nuthin' there neither."

Unh-oh. This wasn't good. "Are you a hundred percent positive you didn't leave them back at the coffeeshop?" I mean, with everyone acting so batty, anything was possible. The Dicks could be sitting in the coffeeshop, wondering where everyone went.

"They was the ones what suggested we come down here, dear. They was the first ones into the taxis."

"And then what?"

"The taxis left us off on some side street and we followed the noise 'til we found where the action was. We all kinda huddled together, wonderin' what to see first, but the Dicks took off before Osmond could even ask for a show of hands." She cupped her hand around her mouth and lowered her voice. "Last I seen of 'em, they was headed for someplace called the Moulin Rouge."

I brightened a little. "Like the famous cabaret in Paris?"

"What's that one look like?"

"It has a big red windmill and a marquee touting its musical revue and can-can girls."

She shook her head. "Don't think it's the same franchise. This one's got a sign toutin' itself as an Erotic Nightclub and Live Sex Theater."

Oh, God. I inhaled a fortifying breath. I was Catholic. This was outside my comfort zone. "Okay, which way do I go?"

"Hang a left at the end of the alley and keep walkin.'"

"Does anyone have a spare leg I can use?" George called out. "Alice won't give mine back to me."

"Not until I have my turn!" she protested. "Everyone had a turn except me. It's not fair."

"Life's not fair," Jackie sympathized. Then with more enthusiasm, "Which is exactly why each and every one of you would benefit from the services of your own personal life coach! I have business cards. Anyone want one?"

Before Jackie could turn what remained of the evening into a private infomercial, I caught Nana's eye. "Would you be a peach and dial up Alice's cellphone for me?"

She punched her speed dial and handed me her phone.

Alice cocked her head as a muffled ring tone chimed nearby. "*Shhhh*, everyone. Listen. That's my phone!" Unable to answer it with her arms full, she heaved George's leg at him. With her hands free, she riffled through her pocketbook for her phone. "Hello?" she said breathlessly.

"Thank you for returning George's leg," I said before disconnecting. "Okay, everyone, listen up. I'm calling a couple of taxis to get you out of here. You will join hands and *not let go* of each other until you are safely inside the cabs. Jackie has volunteered to escort you back to the hotel—"

"I have?"

"—where she will entertain you with a short presentation about her new business venture until you're feeling more normal."

Groans. Razzberries. "Borrr-ing," crabbed Bernice.

"Ew." Jackie perked up. "Good idea."

"Keep them in the lobby and do not let them return to their rooms until I get back," I instructed her. "I don't want any of them

94

mistaking their arms for wings and thinking they can paraglide off their window ledges."

Jackie gave her hands a little clap. "This is so exciting. I'm getting butterflies already. My first formal presentation! All right, everyone, let's form a nice, straight line."

"Shortest first?" asked Osmond.

"I'm sick of doing shortest first," complained Bernice. "Marion's always in the lead. Give someone else a chance."

"How about tallest first?" Jackie suggested.

"Then the short people in the back won't be able to see what's up ahead," protested Alice.

"Oldest first?" Jackie said, a little less patiently.

"Age discrimination!" yelled Osmond.

Her voice exploded from her mouth like grapeshot. "WHATEVER! Just get in a damn line!"

I sighed with relief. Their highs were obviously wearing off because they were sounding more like themselves again. I phoned the cab company I'd used earlier, and by the time I finished my call, they were queued up like schoolchildren filing in from recess. Wow. Jackie was a natural at this. It gave me confidence that she'd get the job done.

I hoped.

"You're not comin' with us, dear?" asked Nana.

"Gotta find the boys. If they ate the cake *and* your muffin, they're probably still flying high, so I'm thinking they might be in dire need of rescuing about now."

She flashed me a look somewhere between guilt and regret.

"Don't worry," I soothed. "I'll find them. And please don't feel guilty. It wasn't your fault."

"I'm not frettin' about that, dear. It's just that—if you happen to look for 'em in a little shop called the Erotic Outlet, would you mind pickin' me up a catalog? It'll save me a bundle on postage."

EIGHT

"How old are they?" asked the bouncer at the Moulin Rouge. He was tall and muscle-bound, with gold hoops in both ears, wraparound sunglasses, and a Technicolor serpent tattooed across his shaved skull.

"Early seventies!" I shouted above the music. "One is six-footish, smartly dressed, and wears a very nice toupee. The other one's about a foot shorter and has a head the size of a medicine ball—with hair plugs in the front. Kinda makes him look like a Chia Pet."

"A what?"

The Dutch were obviously spared TV advertising that made salad shooters and leaf-sprouting pottery indispensable holiday gift items. "It's not important. Can I go inside and look for them?"

"Not without paying an admission charge, you can't."

"But I have to find them," I said anxiously. "They're high."

"So's everyone else in this crowd."

"But they don't realize it!"

He peered at me over his sunglasses and rubbed his fingers together. "Thirty-five Euros or they stay there, and you stay here."

I dug my heels in. "Casa Rosso was only going to charge me thirty."

"Casa Rosso doesn't include two free drinks with the price of admission. Make up your mind. There's paying customers lined up behind you."

"Are you sure I—"

"I'm sure. Next!" He waved me away and motioned for the guy behind me to take my place. Discouraged and frustrated, I picked my way back through the crowd toward a narrow bridge where demonstrators in white robes waved signs that were going mostly unread by the hard-core revelers. JESUS SAVES. THE END TIMES ARE HERE. REPENT. THE END IS NEAR. And my personal favorite, WORLD BIBLEFEST 2025! MAKE YOUR RESERVATIONS NOW.

"Emily? Oh, thank God! A friendly face." Beth Ann Oliver latched onto my arm like a tick onto a beagle. "Jackie is going to be so put out with me. I thought I could keep track of everyone after she spotted your group and left, but it was impossible. Some detective I turned out to be. I don't know where anyone is anymore."

I sighed. "Welcome to the club."

"What am I going to do? They all scattered after the big blowup."

That earned her my undivided attention. "Blowup?"

"It was frightening, and pretty embarrassing. Not to state the obvious, but I don't think some of these people from Maine like each other very much."

"Oh, my God. Did the Hennessys and Bouchards actually follow through with their rumble?"

"Just a sec." She dug a mini notebook out of her jacket pocket and flipped to the first page. "Jackie told me to take detailed notes, but I was scribbling so fast, I'm not sure I'll be able to read my own handwriting." She squinted at the page. "I need more light."

I whipped out my super-bright LED pocket flashlight and shined it on her notebook.

"Perfect. Okay, here's what I have. 'Red Leader blazes path through darkest sections of city. Arrives at destination without incident. He suggests we ask for group rate at seamy porn place. Miss Manners reels with indignation and says that going inside wasn't part of the plan. Red Leader asks what the expletive she's doing in this bleeping expletive place if she's not going to see the bleeping shows? Mr. Bulky demands to know if they have other options.'"

What? "I'm sorry. Mr. Bulky? Miss Manners? Are these people on our tour?"

"I don't know who everyone is yet, so I gave everybody a code name. You know, like the Secret Service does with the President and his family." She continued. "'Miss Manners indicates that everyone wants an overall view of the area rather than a visit to a specific hotspot, because no member of a St. Francis Xavier's graduating class would demean themselves by watching lewd acts performed live onstage. Red Leader appears not to give a flip. He grins lecherously and disappears into the building.'"

"I assume Red Leader is Dietger?"

"Right. Him, I know. 'Mr. Bulky grows irate and yells at Miss Manners that she's not the bleeping class president anymore, so she had no bleeping right to speak for everyone else, and how were they supposed to find their way back to the bleeping hotel without Red Leader? Ms. Godzilla, attired in a polka-dot scarf and ballerina length skirt that exposes her thick ankles, cackles with laughter. She tells Miss Manners she's full of horse bleep and is bleeping self-righteous because Ms. Godzilla recalls Miss Manners and Mr. Clean bleeping every time they could find a bleeping horizontal surface back in high school. Godzilla asks if that's a bleeping double standard or plain old run-of-the-mill hypocrisy?'"

Beth Ann paused, frowning at her notes.

"What's wrong?"

"I may have left out a bleep. These Mainers are insanely fond of expletives."

"I'll insert it mentally. So what happened next?"

"'Miss Manners screams at Mr. Clean that if he doesn't shut Godzilla the bleep up, she'll do it herself, to which Mr. Clean asks what the bleep she wants him to do, to which Miss Manners answers, "Bleep her!" Godzilla, who looks happy to have stirred the pot, doesn't bat an eyelash and scoffs that Mr. Clean doesn't have the guts to bleep her.'"

I regarded Beth Ann skeptically. "Reptiles have eyelashes?"

"Literary license." She continued breathlessly. "'From the depths of the crowd, an eerie voice shouts out that he'll bleep her. "So will I!" shouts another. "She's a pimple on the expletive of the world." Mr. Greenjeans, dressed in an attractive Bar Harbor, Maine jacket, saunters over to Godzilla and tells her that he'll do the honors, because he's been wanting to bleep her for fifty years.'"

"Mr. Greenjeans is Pete Finnegan!" I blurted out, wondering if he was on a deranged mission to knock off every woman who didn't see eye to eye with him. Uff-da. Had whacking Charlotte unleashed his appetite for killing?

"I'll make a note," said Beth Ann, looking a little exasperated by the interruption. She inhaled an excited breath. "'Godzilla gets twitchy. The Mainers close in on her. She fends them off with an evil growl, scattering their ranks, then makes an end run around them and vanishes into the crowd. "So what are we supposed to do now that Miss Manners has ruined our evening?" gripes Mr. Bulky. "Have you noticed how she ruins everything?" Mr. Clean suggests Bulky eat bleep. "Don't blame my wife for ruining your bleeping life. You did that yourself. You and Little Lotta!" Everyone who isn't yelling at each other appears discomfited by the exchange.'"

Discomfited? Real people actually said "discomfited"?

"'Little Lotta swears she has a bleeping glandular problem and refers to Mr. Clean as a bleeping expletive. Miss Manners laughs demonically and insists that Lotta would eat a rock if it was covered in buttercream frosting. Mr. Clean doubles his fist. "Let's settle this once and for all, Bulky. Just you and me. No holds barred. A fight to the finish. I'm going to ring your clock so bad, you won't know—" Mr. Greenjeans suddenly rages that no one cares what the bleep they do anymore. He tells them they're bleeping irrelevant and they better get over their bleeping selves because the world didn't revolve around them anymore.'"

Gee. Pete Finnegan was getting absolutely verbose.

"'Someone from the crowd yells that Greenjeans is right. "You bleeping people are has-beens!" Someone else shouts that they should grow up. Hissing ensues, followed by boos. "Let's get out of here!" suggests a woman with a squeaky voice. "We'll only encourage their bad behavior if we stand here watching them. Why should we make them feel important? I say, ignore them! Ignore them like they always ignored us!'"

"A mini revolution!" I marveled. Or a *coup d'etat*. Whichever one featured the ruling elite taking it on the chin for being such snots all their lives.

"'The crowd of onlookers scatter like billiard balls in a desert wind.'"

What?

"'Bulky, Lotta, Mr. Clean, and Miss Manners are left standing by themselves, looking shocked and insignificant. They've just witnessed a changing of the guard, and they obviously don't like it. They look lost and abandoned, dazed and confused. They seem unable to cope with the fact that they've become nobodies. Rather than pound each other into oblivion, Bulky and Mr. Clean take their wives' arms and stumble off in opposite directions. They look depressed enough to want to jump into the nearest canal, which looms a few feet behind me, a seething cesspool of inky blackness.'"

She narrowed her eyes at me. "Do you think Jackie will appreciate my descriptions? I should probably make my notes really cut and dry, but I thought a published author might enjoy my literary efforts. Maybe it'll make up for the fact that I lost everyone."

I smiled stiffly. "I'm sure your prose will stun her. So, were you able to tail anyone after the group broke up?"

She shook her head. "I tried following Mr. Bulky and Lotta for a while, but I got swallowed up by the crowd outside some erotic nightclub and lost them. I don't know how all those Mainers disappeared so completely in such a short time, but they sure left me in the dust."

"Maybe they were anxious to get back to the hotel." I glanced beyond her, eying the red lanterns and floor-to-ceiling windows where women were posing in skimpy satin underwear while texting on hot pink cellphones. "A little of this place goes a long way."

She flipped her notebook shut. "I might as well call it a night and head back, too. Doesn't look as if there's going to be any more action here tonight. You want to walk back with me?"

"I'd love to, but two of my own people are missing, so I need to track them down."

She whistled softly. "Good luck with that. Anything I can do to help?"

"Thanks anyway, but you don't know what they look like, so there's not much you can do."

"Watch yourself, then," she cautioned. "You're not in Kansas anymore, Toto." With a sigh of resignation, she squared her shoulders and plunged back into the mayhem, leaving me alone to decide where I should venture next—The Erotic Cellar or the Video Sexshop? Honestly, if the Dicks weren't so endearing in their own annoying way, I'd want to kill them.

"Je-sus, yes! Porn-o, no!" The demonstrators on the bridge began a rhythmic chant. "Je-sus, yes! Porn-o, no!" Their voices grew louder as they hypered each other into a frenzy, thrusting their signs into the air like peasants brandishing pitchforks and torches. "JE-SUS, YES! PORN-O, NO!" And in the middle of it all stood Mike McManus, eyes slatted and mouth tight, scanning the crowd like a human surveillance camera.

"Mike!" I waved my arm over my head and shouted his name again, but realizing there was no way he was going to hear me, I pushed my way onto the bridge and made a beeline for him before he could pull a disappearing act.

"Gotcha!" I grabbed the sleeve of his jacket.

Startled, he jerked his head around and stared at me blankly before recognition crept into his eyes. "Emily. Jeez, I thought you were some loony."

"Sorry!" I cupped my hand around my mouth and spoke close to his ear. "I called out your name as loud as I could, but I got drowned out by the competition. I'm surprised the protesters haven't fixed you up with a sign yet."

"I could use a sign! Something that says, 'Mary Lou, Where are You?'"

"How long since you've seen her?"

He checked his watch. "About an hour. I was leading her and Laura through the crowd but got a little too far ahead. When I turned around, they were both gone. It was the damnedest thing. They literally vanished into thin air."

"There's a lot of that going around tonight. At least Mary Lou's not alone. She and Laura are pretty cool customers. They're probably making their way back to the hotel even as we speak."

"I dunno." He passed a glance over the crowd again, his face etched with doubt. "There are some serious nut-jobs walking around out there. Gives me the willies to think Mary Lou might be walking around with them. Coming down here was a bad idea. A *really* bad idea. Wait'll I get my hands on that damn Dietger. He's probably laughing all the way to the bank."

"How much longer are you going to wait here?" I questioned.

"As long as it takes. I'm not leaving without her. She's my whole life. I mean, what would I do without her?"

"I'll tell you what, if you're still here when I wrap up looking for my guys, I'll stop by and we can walk back together. Deal?"

"You're missing people as well?"

"My two Dicks. I figured they might have found their way into one of the live sex theaters, but the three classiest places insisted I pay full admission for the privilege of looking for them, so I'm narrowing my search down to less classy establishments, like triple X-rated video shops and tattoo parlors."

"Are your boys wearing the standard issue nametags?"

"Last I knew, they were."

"I'll keep an eye out for them."

"Thanks." I smiled my appreciation. "And if I run into Mary Lou and Laura, I'll stick with them like glue and drag them back with me."

He tried to smile, but there was such anguish in his face, his mouth refused to cooperate. "Sounds good," he said dismally, looking as if his knees were about to buckle beneath the weight of his predicament.

Poor Mike. I sure hoped Mary Lou showed up soon, because if she didn't, he looked as if he might suffer a complete breakdown. This was so weird. At first blush, he'd struck me as the kind of guy who bled confidence, but had I read him correctly? Or was the real Mike McManus still an emotionally stunted sixteen-year-old whose mental health could be derailed by the slightest disruption?

I mulled this over as I rejoined the mob in the street.

Funny thing about people. Old friend or new, they always managed to surprise you.

———

The Dicks weren't here. I'd looked everywhere I could possibly search—darkened doorways, smoky cafes, hotel lounges, dingy cellar shops, erotic bars, erotic clubs, and several erotic outlets where

I picked up a slew of free catalogs for Nana. I gave descriptions to store clerks, waiters, bouncers, and desk clerks, but all I heard was the same old thing: "Haven't seen them."

At two o'clock I called Jackie's cell. "Please, please, *please* tell me the Dicks are back at the hotel."

They weren't. "But everyone else is functioning normally again, except for the double vision, so I made them form a conga line on their way back to their rooms so they could hold onto each other for support. You better get them to a clinic in the morning though. Double vision isn't a good thing for old people to have. I don't want to be an alarmist or anything, but I think it means they're all getting ready to suffer kidney failure."

At 4:20 a.m., discouraged by my failed efforts and unable to keep my eyes open, I decided if I didn't call it a night, Nana might soon be sending out a search party for *me*. Not only did I need to catch forty winks, I needed to regroup.

I passed by the "Come to Jesus" bridge, where the same batch of protestors were warning people to repent, but Mike was gone, so I hoped that was a good omen. Too tired to hoof it back to the hotel, I phoned a cab and began the weary walk to my pick-up point. As I approached the footbridge by the Café Bar de Stoof, I noticed a woman leaning against a van parked by the canal and realized there was a good chance *she* might know more about the Dicks' whereabouts than any other person I'd talked to this evening.

"Excuse me, Officer," I said as I approached her, "could you help me?"

———

I returned to the hotel armed with official police forms that were to be filled out and delivered to the nearest station within twenty-four hours of my reporting the members of my party missing. The policewoman had assured me that most people who went missing in the Red Light District usually turned up embarrassed but deliriously happy the next morning, so I should probably wait a few hours before filing a formal report. "Things like dis happen all der time," she insisted.

Feeling slightly more confident that the situation would have a positive outcome, I headed straight for my room, kicked off my shoes, and collapsed face down on the bed without bothering to brush, floss, or moisturize. I was awakened about six seconds later by a loud and persistent knock on my door.

"God, Emily," Jackie warbled when I let her in, "you look terrible, but you don't have time to do anything about it now. You have five minutes to get downstairs before the breakfast service ends. Our new tour director wants to speak to you, Nana and the gang are running into the furniture in the dining room like it's not even there, and the Dicks never came back last night."

I hung my head tiredly. "Is that all?"

"Nope. Paula Peavey never came back either."

NINE

"Emily?" The man waiting for me at the entrance to the dining room looked vaguely familiar, which probably explained why my name flew from his mouth like a spitball rather than a greeting.

I suspected he knew me.

"Holy crap. You've gotta be kidding me. Emily Andrew? Well, well, well. This explains a lot."

Recognition struck, accompanied by an uncomfortable twinge of guilt. Oh. My. God. He hadn't changed all that much since I'd last seen him. Same chubby chipmunk cheeks. Same bland eyes. Same neat, buttoned-down appearance. He'd traded in his navy-blue blazer and khakis for a pea-green Passages Tours blazer, but if you ignored his expanding waistline and receding hairline, he still looked a lot like the boy next door, in a middle-aged kind of way.

I hazarded a cautious smile. "Wally?"

"Throw the girl a fish. She remembers me."

"Of *course*, I remember you! Golden Swiss Triangle Tours. The Grand Palais Hotel. Lake Lucerne. Mount Pilatus. You were a terrific tour director. How could I forget you?" I pulled a face. "Our local guide was pretty annoying, but you were wonderful. I'm astounded *you* remember *me.*"

"Are you serious? Three days in Switzerland? Three dead bodies? How could I forget you?"

"I had nothing to do with those deaths."

"You found the bodies. Close enough."

"It is not!"

"Besides which, you deliberately ditched me so you could have drinks at the Hotel Chateau Gutsch with that hot police inspector."

Okay, he had me there, "I wouldn't call what I had a drink. It was more like an extravagantly expensive sip."

"You were a jinx!"

"I was n—!" I winced. "You really think so?"

"I know so. The rest of the trip went great after you and your group left, except that the company canned me because they held me responsible for exceeding the allowable number of guests expected to die over a three-day period."

"There's an allowable number?"

"Yah: zero! So I get hired by another company, establish a perfect record, and what happens? My holiday gets canceled so I can replace an otherwise healthy guide who croaks for no reason at all."

"Actually, there was a bicycle involved, so—"

"And who do I find in the middle of it all?"

I forced a smile. "Have I caught you at a bad time?"

"And I'm hearing rumors that not all the guests made it back from an unauthorized excursion to the Red Light District last night. Is that right?"

"Which part?" I asked sheepishly. "That the excursion was unauthorized or that several guests didn't make it back?"

"*Several*? As in, more than one?"

"We were only missing two last night." I lowered my voice to a whisper. "But the number sort of climbed to three this morning."

His eyes seemed to dance in his sockets, aping the kind of reaction you might expect if you stuck a screwdriver into a live electrical outlet.

"I'm right on top of the situation though," I chirped. "I've talked to the police, I have a couple of forms to fill out, and I know exactly what to do if nothing is resolved by early afternoon."

Eye blinking. Panicked silence.

"Come *on*, Wally. No one has been officially in charge since yesterday. I'm just doing my best to help out in the void."

Color drained from his face like dye from a cheap shirt.

"Would you like to sit down?" I asked gently. "You look a little—"

He held up his hand. "I'm changing the itinerary," he choked out in a sandpapery voice. "This morning we'll visit the Rijksmuseum. This afternoon, the Anne Frank house. And in between, I'll be hunkered down in whatever isolated corner I can find, trying to locate our missing guests. Sound like fun?" He glowered at me. "Good thing for you my phone is fully charged. I'll note the changes on the whiteboard."

"I'm sure the missing guests will show up. The policewoman I spoke to sounded really confident that they'd be dragging themselves back any minute now. Her advice was simply to be patient and try not to panic."

"Easy for her to say. She's never traveled with you before." He looked me up and down, as if hoping I'd disappear. "So, you're the official escort for the Iowa contingent, are you?"

I nodded.

"I won't ask you how many guests you've lost in your official capacity."

Which was a good thing, since I'd lost count.

He threw a long look beyond me, as if he were dredging up more unpleasant memories. "Is that irritating woman with the wire-whisk hair and crab walk still part of your group?"

"Bernice? Bernice Zwerg? You remember her, too?"

"You'd better give her a hand. She just walked into the wall."

———

"I'm good," Bernice snuffled when her nose stopped bleeding. "But if my pain and suffering get too overwhelming, I plan to sue."

We'd settled her into a chair in the lobby and plied her with tissues, but had to send Margi running to the restroom for wet paper towels when Osmond keeled over in a dead faint. "Stay calm!" Alice advised as I dug his medical history form out of my shoulder bag. "He's fine with his own blood; it's other people's that gives him the problem."

"That's a stupid place to stick a wall," Bernice complained as we hauled Osmond off the floor.

"Right," said George. "Contractors always make a point of putting load-bearing walls in stupid places, like ... public buildings."

"Don't get smart with me, George," she snapped. "This hotel has got a lot of nerve booby-trapping this place and not bothering to warn us. That wall wasn't there last night, was it?"

This seemed to perk up Osmond, who called for a group vote despite being half-conscious on the sofa. I studied their faces as they cast their yeas and nays, and noticed something astonishing for the very first time.

"Did you know that your eyeglasses are exactly alike? How do nine people as different as you guys end up with the same eye-wear?"

"It's on account of Pills Etcetera," Nana explained. "They was runnin' a special—$39.95 for no-line bifocals."

"And you all selected the same frame?"

"The special only applied to one frame," Tilly chafed. "A detail the pharmacy failed to mention in its weekly flyer."

My brain cells started cranking like the pistons in a steam engine. Identical eyewear? Group vision problems? Hmm. I might be onto something.

"How many of you are accidentally bumping into things this morning?" I questioned.

Nine hands crept slowly into the air.

"How many of you saw fireworks in front of your eyes in the coffeeshop last night?"

Everyone except Nana raised a hand.

"When the symptoms first appeared, how many of you tried on someone else's lenses to see if a different prescription would improve your vision?"

No hands went up.

Nana rolled her eyes. "They was *all* passin' their eyeglasses around the table—the thing is, they was so hopped up on choco-late cake, they can't remember doin' it."

Disbelieving gasps filled the air.

"That's a bunch of hooey," accused Bernice.

"It most certainly is not," said Tilly in her professor's voice. "That's exactly what happened. Now that my brain is operating on all cylinders again, I'm being haunted by colorful memories I'd rather forget."

Nana looked frustrated. "Hold on. If *I* didn't let no one try on my glasses, how come I'm blind as everyone else this mornin'?"

Tilly slid her eyeglasses off her face and offered them to Nana. "See if these help."

"You guys!" I chided. "You *have* to stop doing tha—"

"I can see!" Nana exclaimed. She coaxed the frames up her nose and darted a look around the lobby. "The furniture's not miniaturized no more! Your heads are bigger than mothballs. I can even see the scribblin' on that whiteboard over there."

Tilly shook her head. "When I got up this morning, I must have grabbed your glasses off the bedside table by mistake. Forgive me, Marion." She gestured toward the discarded lenses. "Shall I take those off your hands?"

But once she'd adjusted them on her face, she shook her head. "These aren't mine either. All right." Giving her walking stick an imperious thump on the floor, she steeled her eyes and hardened her jaw. "I have only two things to say. First, we owe Emily a titanic debt of thanks for resolving this imbroglio, and second, one of you is wearing my glasses. I don't know who it is, but I'm giving you notice. I want them back."

Relieved that all nine of them weren't about to suffer kidney failure, I sucked in a calming breath and allowed myself an indulgent sigh.

"Can anyone read the handwritin' on that whiteboard?" Nana asked off-handedly. "I can't figure out where it says we're goin', but the bus better hurry up and get here, 'cause it says we're leavin' at nine-thirty."

I checked my watch. *Jesus, Mary, and Joseph.* I couldn't leave in ten minutes. I hadn't even brushed my teeth yet!

"Get the eyeglasses thing sorted out," I urged as I raced toward the elevator. "I'll see you on the bus."

"What about Dick?" Grace and Helen shouted at me in unison.

"Don't worry about them!" I bypassed the closed elevator door and headed for the stairs. "I'm on top of it!"

———

The Rijksmuseum is a lumbering, red-brick leviathan that sprawls the length of two football fields. Blending the elegance of a French chateau with the ruggedness of a fortified castle, it's an imposing jumble of gothic turrets, decorative gables, grand archways, towering windows, and cold gray stone. Skylights the size of solar panels stud its long expanse of roof, spilling light onto paintings that illustrate the domestic lives of Dutchmen in an age when their galleons ruled the waves, and their burgomeisters ruled the world in periwigs and pumps. The men responsible for creating these portraits are referred to as the Dutch Masters—a group of artistic geniuses whose masterpieces hung in the homes of seventeenth-century patricians before ending up on the lids of twentieth-century cigar boxes.

We were scheduled to meet an art historian on the first floor at eleven o'clock, so we had plenty of time to explore the ground floor exhibits before then. I power-walked through the Dutch history rooms, taking quick notice of the clocks, ships, weapons and armor, then wended my way around to the sculpture and decorative arts rooms, where I found Chip Soucy parked in front of a glass case that housed an exhibit more suited to my taste—a dollhouse.

"Wow." I joined him at the display case. "My Grampa Sippel built a dollhouse for me when I was little, but it didn't look anything like this."

Chip donned his glasses to read the accompanying plaque. "'Dollhouse of Petronella Oortman, 1686–1705.' Cripes, it took nineteen years to complete the thing. I'd like to build one for my granddaughter, but I'd like to finish it before she graduates from college."

The dollhouse was a miniaturized wonder, depicting nine rooms of what were probably high-class digs in Petronella's day. Built inside an open-fronted cabinet of tortoise shell and tin, it boasted Lilliputian-size furnishings, complete with porcelain spittoons, gilt-framed portraits, tapestried walls, China plates, and itty-bitty irons in an array of microscopic sizes.

"All the comforts of home," I quipped. "They even played kids' games." I indicated a wooden game board sitting atop a table in a second-floor salon. "What's your best guess? I'm thinking Parcheesi."

"Backgammon," he said without hesitation.

"How can you tell?"

"I cheated." He nodded at the wall to my left. "You can see it better in the painting."

Petronella had apparently been so proud of her creation, she'd commissioned an artist to reproduce it on canvas. The result was an eight-foot-high painting that replicated the details of the doll-house so perfectly, it looked like something spewed out by the Big Bertha copy machine at Kinko's. But while the painting depicted maids and mistresses in attendance in every room, the dollhouse was strangely unoccupied, or at least, it was now.

"Do you suppose the people in the painting represent dolls that used to be in the dollhouse?" I wondered aloud.

"That'd be my guess," said Chip. "Looks like they all bit the dust."

"They must have been really fragile for not even one of them to survive."

Chip shrugged. "It's been three hundred years. Stuff breaks, gets set aside, goes missing. Speaking of which, I hear a couple of your guys are MIA."

"They're presently unaccounted for, but I'm expecting them back at any moment," I said in an upbeat voice.

"Yeah? Well, good luck with that."

"Please, don't sound so grim. They'll show up. The police *assured* me they would."

He forced an apologetic smile. "Sorry. Guess I'm a little jaded about the prospect of actually finding a missing person. Personal experience and all that."

Was this another reference to Bobby Guerrette? His classmates were talking about him so much, I was beginning to think he was on the trip with us. "Would you do me a favor?" I finally asked. "Would you please get me up to speed with the Bobby Guerrette story? I know he was really smart; he championed Laura LaPierre when she was being ridiculed, and he refused to attend his senior prom with Paula Peavey. I keep hearing everyone bat his name around, but no one has breathed a word about how he disappeared. It's almost as if they're afraid to."

"Sounds like you've been hanging out with the wrong people. No one's afraid to talk about it. It's just that some of these yahoos don't want to waste time talking about Bobby when they could be talking about themselves. So, what do you want to know?"

"How did he disappear?"

"It was on Senior Skip Day, a month before graduation. We decided to spend the day at a park near the Bangor Water Works. It was a great place to hide out from the parents. More like a grotto than a park. A steep hill. Trees. A waterfall. A little manmade sluiceway that funneled water down the hill. A fountain that could have rivaled Vegas at the time. We used to monkey around in the water, acting like dopes. It only reached our ankles, but it was like wading in a brook, without the aggravation of mosquitoes or black flies."

"The whole class went?"

"The whole class never did anything together, except attend assemblies in the auditorium. A bunch of us arrived early, and then kids came and went all day. I don't recall everyone who showed up, but I know Hennessy was there, and Bouchard, Mindy and Sheila, *naturally*, Peewee—"

"—who was much shorter back then than he is now."

"Right. He was a shrimp in high school. He must have overdosed on growth hormone after he graduated. Uh, Bobby was there, of course. Kids got along with him surprisingly well despite the fact that he was so much smarter than the rest of us. Mike McManus showed up—"

"Mike? He told me he was invisible in high school. What was he doing rubbing shoulders with the in-crowd?"

"Bobby really liked Mike, so he asked him to join us. It was probably the first and last time Mike ever found himself in such exalted company."

Pseudo-exalted was more like it.

"Paula was there, even though no one wanted her, but her parents bought her a car for graduation, so she showed up wherever she damn well pleased. I have a mental image of some jocks and cheerleaders whose names escape me, and a few of the more popular smart kids."

"Pete Finnegan?"

"Hell, no. Pete was smart, but that's all he was. He didn't talk to anyone, he didn't participate in anything, he never cracked a smile. He studied. Pete was a dud, even though he was the first kid in our class to get his driver's license, which should have earned him bragging rights, but it didn't. His first big rite of passage, and no one bothered to congratulate him. If I'd been Pete, I would have been so bummed, but he probably never even noticed. He did everything he could to be an outsider, so the rest of us accommodated him. If he'd shown his face at the park, I guarantee he would have been laughed out of the place."

I flinched involuntarily. "And yet he signed up for the reunion."

"A complete one-eighty. Go figure."

"Were Mary Lou and Laura there?"

He scrunched his eyes shut as if trying to picture them in the scene. "I can't visualize them, but that doesn't mean they weren't there." He hesitated. "Well, Mary Lou might have shown up, but not Laura. The popular kids were always merciless with poor Laura. I'm surprised she hasn't suffered permanent emotional damage."

"She apparently rose above it."

Chip pondered this as he massaged the bristly white hairs of his mustache. "Either that, or she's spent a fortune on therapy."

"Whatever the explanation, she's certainly come out the winner. So," I eyed him intently, "at what point did Bobby disappear?"

"Okay, I'm getting to that. We spent the day horsing around— eating junk food, sneaking into the woods to drink the beer we'd smuggled out of our houses, hanging out, making out, getting a buzz on—all the stuff that seems so cool when you're a teenager. When it got later, Bobby said he had to get home before he got locked out, so he decided to hitchhike, and . . . that's the last time we ever saw him."

I stared at him, slightly jarred. "That's it?"

"Pretty much."

"He had the kind of parents who would actually lock him out?"

"He didn't have parents. He lived at the orphanage on the other side of the city. St. Michael's Home. The nuns locked the door at nine o'clock, so if you showed up at 9:01, you were on your own. I guess Bobby had missed curfew a couple of times growing up, and he didn't want to do it again. He wasn't fond of sleeping on the ground."

Bobby Guerrette was an orphan? Huh. Someone had made a reference to an orphan, a misfit, and a girl who was afraid of her own shadow on the dinner cruise last night, but I'd obviously been too distracted by rising tempers to make the connection.

"None of us knew he didn't make it back to the orphanage until he didn't show up for class the next day. What a commotion. The principal called the police. We all got questioned. But hell, we didn't know squat."

"Did anyone see Bobby actually get into a car?"

His eyes flickered with sudden anxiety, as if he were struggling to recall the details. "I didn't see anything, mostly because I was three sheets to the wind, but Hennessy saw a car stop to pick him up. Make and model unknown because it was too dark to tell, but he was reasonably sure it wasn't white, and he didn't think it was a station wagon. Peewee and Mike backed him up, but let's face it, it wasn't much to go on. Little wonder the police never found him."

"That's so sad." I felt an emotional tug, not only for Bobby Guerrette, who never seemed to have gotten a break, but for the bullied kids, like Laura LaPierre, and the square pegs, like Pete Finnegan, who'd never experienced the thrill of having a buddy punch him in the arm in congratulations.

I suffered a twinge of guilt that I might have misjudged Pete. If I'd been a flaming introvert who'd been shunned in high school, I might have become a grouch, too. So maybe he wasn't a villain. Maybe he was just a socially inept guy who was in desperate need of a friend.

"Changing the topic just slightly," I ventured, "were you present for the big blowup last night?"

"In the Red Light District? Sure was. It was the classic battle between good and evil. Paula Peavey versus everyone else."

"Did Pete threaten her?"

"Sure did. Said he'd been wanting to take her out for fifty years, though his choice of words was a bit more, how shall I say, colorful."

"Did you know Paula never made it back to the hotel last night?"

"No kidding? I'd noticed the lack of tension on the bus this morning. Maybe she's hanging out with your two guys. Or better yet, maybe she decided to go home. She got a pretty brutal taste of her own medicine last night. She might be feeling a little chicken-livered about facing her detractors after that. Paula loved to dish it out, but she could never take it."

"You didn't happen to see her after the blowup last night, did you?"

"Who, me?" He leaned back on his heels, as if trying to back away from the question. "Nope. Didn't see her. Uh" —he checked the time— "would you excuse me? I need to make a quick pit stop before we meet up with our art expert."

As a practical matter, it seemed someone should advise Wally of the possibility that Paula could have been too humiliated to continue the tour and might have caught a flight home, and I supposed that person would be me, but I didn't relish the thought of freaking him out any more than I already had.

I cast an uneasy glance around the exhibit room, relieved when I didn't see him.

Okay, at the very least, I felt duty-bound to go through the motions, but if luck was with me, maybe I wouldn't run into him.

Happily, I ran into Mary Lou and Laura instead.

"Am I ever glad to see the two of you," I said in greeting. "Mike was so concerned about you last night. He said one minute you were there, and the next, you were gone. What happened to you?"

Mary Lou offered a hesitant smile. "We got separated in the crowd. It was no big deal. I don't know why Mike made such a fuss."

I laughed. "Duh? He was afraid something might happen to you."

"We're big girls." She linked arms with Laura. "We can take care of ourselves."

Was it just me, or was Mary Lou acting a little testy? "So did you hook up with Mike on the bridge, or did you end up finding your way back to the hotel on your own?"

"We—" It was the only word she got out before freezing up like the proverbial deer in the headlights.

Laura tapped her watch to indicate the hour. "Sorry, Emily, but would you mind if we finished this conversation another time? Mary Lou and I have to powder our noses before the tour begins. See you up there. Okay?"

"Sure," I said, as the two of them headed off in another direction.

Hmm. I seemed to be throwing everyone into a tailspin. They couldn't get away from me fast enough. Maybe I should stop asking people about last night. And yet, if my innocent questions could spark such instantaneous urges to hit the restroom, what did that indicate? Bladder control problems, or something much darker?

A shiver rattled my spine as I searched out the staircase to the first floor.

I was getting a very bad feeling about this.

TEN

"THIS PAINTING IS ONE of Rembrandt's most notable," our art expert informed us. We were gathered in a room with a vaulted ceiling and skylight, mist-colored walls that were embossed with giant fleur-de-lis, a blonde hardwood floor, and a long swath of carpet that mirrored the gray of the walls.

"It's called *The Prophetess Anna*," he continued, "and, as you can see, it depicts a very old woman studying a page in her Bible."

His name was Harold, and he had the clear, well-modulated voice of a natural-born auctioneer. I could imagine him requesting opening bids for diamonds at Sothebys, pearls at Christie's, or hogs at Arnie's Auction Barn.

"According to the Bible story, St. Anna worshiped God day and night in the temple and therefore witnessed the young Jesus when he questioned the holy men about their teachings."

I stood on tiptoe at the back of the group, thinking I'd have to wait until they moved on to the next painting before I could get a good look at this one. It also didn't help that Peewee was hogging the front.

"Please note Rembrandt's use of light and shadow in the portrait. He wants you to focus on both the woman's hand and the Bible page, so he illuminates these details in such a way as to make them appear to be lit by a spotlight. The woman's face, which is oftentimes the most important aspect of a portrait, is entirely in shadow."

Feeling a presence at my back, I looked over my shoulder to find Jackie practically on top of me. "You owe me," she whispered out the corner of her mouth.

"I know," I whispered back.

"Have I mentioned that Tom and I are thinking about starting a family?"

"I am *not* carrying your baby."

"Party pooper."

Harold's voice thrummed with enthusiasm. "The Dutch masters developed a simple technique to draw our eyes to the parts of their paintings they wanted to emphasize. It involves a bit of geometry and..."

"Have you read Beth Ann's recap of last night?" I asked as Harold continued.

"Not every word. Her handwriting is atrocious."

"So, what did you make of it?"

"Rather amateurish, but she has a real gift for metaphors."

I rolled my eyes. "I'm not talking about Beth Ann's writing skills. What did you think about the blowup?"

"Oh, that." She waited a beat to gather her thoughts. "I am *so* ticked off. It would have been the perfect opportunity for a well-dressed life coach to jump in and show these reunion screw-ups the error of their ways. Money in the bank, Emily, and I missed it. I'll tell you one thing. Playing the part of the Good Samaritan is highly overrated."

"Chip Soucy thinks that Paula Peavey suffered so much humiliation at the hands of her classmates last night that she might have left the tour and flown home."

"That's too bad. Now there's one broad who *really* could have used my help. So"—she lowered her voice to a near inaudible whisper—"what's my assignment for today?"

"Keeping your fingers crossed that the Dicks show up."

"Oh, come *on*, Emily. No tailing? No disguises?"

"Not until the Dicks are back." I sighed my frustration as I glanced around the room. "Have you seen Wally anywhere?"

"Men's room. Ground floor. Last stall on the right."

I arched a brow. "How do you know what stall he's in?"

She sucked in her breath as she smoothed her skirt over her hips. "It's like this. I used the old plumbing for so many years, I don't always remember it's been renovated."

"You'll notice this technique being used with absolute perfection in the next painting we're going to discuss," Harold announced. "An exquisite portrait entitled *Maria Trip*, and it's right across the room. But before we move on, are there any questions?"

Bernice's hand shot into the air. "Are you on Facebook?"

Oh, God.

I hung back as Harold herded the group toward the painting and began his spiel. Nana hung back, too, apparently as anxious as I was for a closer look at the masterpiece.

"Can you believe this is a three-hundred-year-old painting?" I asked her. "It looks more like a recent photograph."

"What I can't believe are all them wrinkles on the old girl's hand." Nana tsked. "Didn't they have no hand cream back then? If my hand looked that bad, I wouldn't want it in no spotlight. I'd want it Photoshopped." She held up her own hand for critical analysis. "Mine don't look as wrinkled as hers, does it?"

I regarded her misshapen knuckles, bulging veins, and liver spots and squeezed her hand with affection. "You have beautiful hands." Others might disagree, but to me, they were the most beautiful hands in the world.

"I wish the Dicks was here," she suddenly confided. "I know they can be dicks, but I miss 'em clownin' around and actin' like dopes. Isn't that somethin'? I guess I've gotten used to 'em."

"They'll show up," I asserted with more confidence than I actually felt.

"They better, and soon. I don't know how much longer Grace and Helen can take the pressure. Did you notice Helen today? She don't got no eyebrows. She forgot to draw 'em on. That don't *never* happen."

Uff-da. This was getting serious.

"I'm thinkin' they need a distraction," Nana advised. "Somethin' to take their minds off the boys."

"Good idea." I gave her a hard look. "Were you guys able to get your eyeglasses straightened out back at the hotel?"

"The bus come, so we haven't had no time to do it yet."

"Then why don't you plan to do it soon, and you can put Grace and Helen in charge."

A smile split Nana's face. "I like it." She eyed the group as they streamed into the adjoining exhibit room behind Harold. "But Grace and Helen don't never get elected to be put in charge of nuthin', so I better give Osmond the poop so he can fudge the vote."

"Assure him he won't be prosecuted for voter fraud," I called as she scurried to catch up.

I suddenly found myself the lone occupant of the room, save for Pete Finnegan, who'd lagged behind to study the portrait Harold had just finished discussing.

Hmm. I really needed to track Wally down, but finding Pete so accessible seemed like a sign from Above. Was he truly the bred-in-the-bone miserable cuss everyone accused him of being? The kind of guy who wouldn't think twice about shoving you in front of a bicycle? Or did he have a kinder, gentler nature that was lying dormant just beneath his cranky crust, just waiting to be unleashed?

I bobbed my head in indecision. *Eenie, meenie, mynie ...*

Okay, meenie won. Wally could wait.

I strode quietly across the carpet, stopping at the discreet barrier that fronted the painting of Maria Trip. "Does she look like someone you know?" I asked as I perused her pale face, frizzy hair, and huge man-hands.

Pete observed me out of the corner of his eye before inching sideways to put more space between us. "What's it to you?"

"You look enthralled."

He made a snarky noise in his throat.

"I sympathize with her hair. It looks like mine when the humidity goes off the chart."

"No skin off my teeth."

A declarative sentence! Well, minus the verb. "Unfortunately, I didn't hear Harold's spiel," I lamented. "Did he have any insights to share?"

"No."

"None at all?"

"NO!"

Oh, yah, this was going well. Might as well begin my fishing expedition before he up and left. I softened my voice and forged ahead. "Sad what happened to Charlotte."

He let out a derisive *pish*. "If you say so."

"Poor woman. I bet she never saw what hit her. She probably wasn't bothered by speeding bicycles in rural Kansas."

Silence.

"You must have had a ringside seat when the accident happened."

He turned his head slowly in my direction, eyes slatted, brow puckered. "What?"

"You were already there when I arrived. Remember? I asked you what had happened, and you said you didn't know? Actually, what you said was, 'Dunno.'"

"What of it?"

"Well, my husband—he used to be in law enforcement—says that when we witness accidents, we can be so traumatized by what we've seen that our brains can trick us into thinking we saw nothing at all. It's our body's way of helping us maintain our sanity. Think of it as a computer reverting to safe mode to protect its internal data. But once the initial shock wears off, it's not uncommon to start recalling things we swore we never saw."

His mouth worked itself into a sneer. "You always talk this much?"

"Uh—so here's what I was wondering. Since you were standing so close to the scene of the accident, have you recalled anything today that you didn't realize you saw yesterday?" I was kinda hoping he'd remember pushing Charlotte into the street, but I was probably being too optimistic.

"I'm recalling that I don't like people bothering me when I'm busy."

And his face was turning red. Probably not a good sign. "But this is how people get to know each other," I encouraged. "They talk. Usually to each other. And if they hit it off, they become friends."

"I don't want to be your friend. I don't want to be *anyone's* friend. Now, go away before I have security drag you away."

"You should talk to my grandmother. She's probably seen TV shows that stress the importance of having at least one friend. She likes to surf, so she sees a little bit of everything. How's your cable service in Maine?"

"I've lived my whole live without friends." His voice swelled with anger. "Why the hell do I need one now?"

I countered with a smile. "Is that rhetorical, or do you actually want an answer?"

"Do I look like a complete goober to you? Do you think I don't know what you're doing? You're sniffing around, trying to blame me for that accident because of my run-in with that prissy malcontent. Well, it's not me you should be after. Pester the folks who're the real pros at covering up the truth. Ask 'em about the skeletons they've kept locked in their closets all these years. They knew exactly what they were doing back then, and they know exactly what they're doing now. But don't expect any straight answers. They'll tell you lies and throw buckets of sand in your face. You know why? Because they've done it for so long, that's all they know *how* to do."

Why did I get the feeling we weren't talking about Charlotte anymore?

"Good-for-nothing buggers," he spat. "They don't know I've got secrets of my own. That'd surprise the hell out of them, wouldn't it? I could ruin them all with what I know, and if folks like you don't stop aggravating me, I swear I'll make every last one of you pay." He stabbed a spindly finger at me, forcing me backward. "Stay out of my face, you hear me? I don't like you. I don't trust you. And here's the kicker—that's never going to change. Get it?"

He didn't want to talk to me. He didn't want to be my friend. He absolutely despised me. Okay, I got it. But other than that, I thought the conversation went pretty well!

He stalked across the floor, nearly plowing into Sheila and Gary Bouchard who stood in the middle of the doorway, trying not to look uncomfortable. I didn't know how long they'd been standing there, but if their pinched expressions were any indication, they'd certainly gotten an earful.

"Are you all right?" Gary asked as I joined them.

"I'm fine."

"What's got Pete so riled up?"

"I disturbed him while he was studying the Rembrandt. Apparently, that's a no-no. Hey, you two cleaned up pretty well from the dinner cruise."

Sheila's lips quivered with ill-concealed rage. "Don't ever mention last night again. I've even ripped the page out of my journal to remind myself to forget."

I suppressed a smile. "I hear the situation got pretty ugly in the Red Light District."

"That was jealousy talking," Gary accused. "Pure jealousy."

Sheila elevated her chin to a haughty angle. "Since the outies can't destroy the life Gary and I have built for ourselves, their only recourse is to bring us down by attacking our talent, our intelligence, and our extraordinary good looks. Last night's performance was a classic case of little people mouthing off, and newsflash! Their insults rolled off our backs like water off very expensive nonstick cookware."

"Actually, I was talking about the confrontation between Pete and Paula," I corrected. "Did you happen to see where Paula went after the big to-do? Because I don't know if you're aware or not, but she never made it back to the hotel."

Sheila stared at her husband with wide-eyed innocence. "I'm sure we didn't run into her again. That's right, isn't it, hon?"

"Exactly right. She just took off. Ask anyone."

"Did the two of you walk back to the hotel by yourselves?"

They froze up from knees to eye sockets, giving me the same deer in the headlights look that had paralyzed Mary Lou. Easy to guess what was coming next.

"Do you remember seeing the girls' room anywhere around here?" Sheila blurted, seizing my forearm in a show of urgency. "I'm on a diuretic for my blood pressure and it kicks in at *the* most inconvenient times."

"Ground floor," I said. "By the entrance."

"You're a life saver," she said in a gasp of breath. "Thanks." Locking hands, they charged toward the hallway so fast, they left a trail of dust motes behind them.

"Expect gridlock!" I added for good measure.

Nope. I wasn't buying it. Three people? Three quick getaways to the restroom? One person might be normal. Two could be a coincidence. But three?

Something fishy was definitely going on. The question was what?

Making my way to the adjoining room, I noticed the Hennessys loitering near the doorway, as isolated from the main group as they could be and still be within earshot of Harold. Marching up to them, I cut to the chase.

"For future reference, the restrooms are located on the ground floor."

Ricky blinked his confusion. "What?"

"Did either of you run into Paula on your way back to the hotel last night?"

Mindy stood transfixed, but only for a heartbeat. "Did you say ground floor?" She seized Ricky's arm. "Is that this floor or the one below us? Oh, never mind." She pulled him away from me and hauled him toward the exit. "We'll figure it out ourselves."

That clinched it. There was officially something weird going on, which meant I needed to find Wally so I could do the most responsible thing I could think of.

Dump it all in his lap.

Leaving the group in Harold's hands, I breezed across the floor, stopping short when I noticed Nana and the gang crowded onto the viewing bench at the far end of the next room. Built like an oversized ottoman, the bench provided seating on all four sides—

a design that encouraged patrons to study the room's masterpieces at length, which was exactly what my guys were doing.

Kinda.

"Were the faces in the painting clearer with pair number one, or pair number two?" Grace asked Osmond. She stood in front of him, a pair of eyeglasses clutched in each hand.

"Pair number one," he said definitively.

"I think he means pair number two," corrected Helen, standing beside an exceptionally large painting as if she were Vanna White poised before Wheel of Fortune's letter board. "He mistook the milkmaid for Newt Gingrich with the first pair." She swept her hand toward the milkmaid in question.

Osmond gave his head a scratch. "Can't rightly remember what I saw now. Can I try 'em on again?"

"No retesting!" snapped Bernice. "One chance, that's it, or the rest of us won't get a turn."

"Shouldn't we be sterilizing the equipment after each use?" asked Margi. She yanked a pint bottle out of her handbag and smiled breathlessly. "I have sanitizer."

Oh, good God. They were using a Rembrandt masterpiece as an eye chart.

I regarded the operation with a critical eye and shrugged.

Okay. That could work.

I shot through the remaining exhibit rooms, hit the stairwell, and bounded down the stairs two at a time. To my great relief, I found Wally seated on a bench in the entrance lobby, pocketing his cellphone.

"I'm sorry to bother you," I gasped out, sitting down beside him to catch my breath, "but—"

"Your Dicks haven't shown up yet."

My shoulders sagged with the news. "Oh, no."

"Oh, yes. I just got off the phone with the police."

"But that's partially what I needed to tell you. If Paula Peavey doesn't rejoin us, you have to tell them not to spend a lot of time pounding the pavement for her, because I have it on good authority that she might have caught a flight back to the states."

"Paula Peavey, on the other hand, *has* shown up."

"Oh, my God. Really? See! That'll teach you to be such a pessimist. Is she back at the hotel?"

"No. Her body was dragged out of the Kloveniersburgwal canal about an hour ago."

ELEVEN

I WHEEZED SO FORCEFULLY, I nearly sucked my tonsils up my nose. "Ohmigod." Was this why everyone was running away at the mere mention of Paula's name? Was this why no one would admit how they got back to the hotel last night? They all saw something. Or did something. Or—"Ohmigod." I squeezed Wally's forearm as the puzzle came together. "They killed her."

"What?"

"They. All of them. No wonder they're stonewalling. They've committed murder!"

Wally raised his eyes heavenward. "I had to be put on two different kinds of blood pressure medication after my first run-in with you." He plucked my fingers off his arm. "And I'm not about to fork out the co-pay for a third. Not with my crappy prescription drug benefits. That's why you see me remaining calm and in control."

"You're hypertensive? Have you tried yoga? I've heard it can work wond—"

"Quiet!" He stuck his nose so close to mine, his breath singed my face. "Now, just so we're on the same page, there was *no* murder."

"But—"

"*No* murder. The police aren't even planning to investigate unless the autopsy reveals something suspicious."

"The suspicious stuff is happening right under our noses! The vacant stares. The urgent trips to the restroom. The—"

"They're treating this as an accidental drowning, because as you may have noticed on your city tour—"

"We haven't had the city tour yet."

"As you'll notice when you *take* your city tour, Amsterdam has so many canals, and so few guardrails, that one misstep can spell disaster."

I narrowed my eyes. "Especially if you're pushed."

"She was not pushed."

"How do *you* know? You never met Paula Peavey. She was a mean-spirited, unkind bully whose greatest pleasure in life was humiliating people. No one liked her. Even the people who associated with her hated her."

"That doesn't mean any of them decided to murder her."

"Says you."

"Say the police! I pulled Paula's medical history form earlier. Did you know she suffered from vertigo? Just like in the Alfred Hitchcock movie. It can cause dizziness, loss of equilibrium, and a swimming motion in the head that can result in loss of balance." His eyes gleamed with a "gotcha" look. "Still think she was pushed?"

"Yes." I folded my arms across my chest. "Maybe." I bobbed my head with indecision and tried not to look at him. "All right, how bad was her vertigo?"

"Severe."

"So why would a woman with severe vertigo go anywhere near an open canal?"

"Why would a woman with severe vertigo go anywhere? Because she wasn't living in a box. People travel despite their limitations, Emily. If they didn't, you and I would both be out of a job."

I acknowledged his premise with an ounce of grace and a pound of skepticism. "I don't buy it."

"You don't have to buy it. The police aren't soliciting your opinion."

"They will," I grumbled. "After the autopsy."

He chatted away as if I hadn't spoken. "I'll tell the other guests about the incident once we're gathered back on the bus. I hate to ruin their day with news like this, but they have a right to know what's happened to a fellow member of—"

"No!" I straightened up so fast, I heard my spine crack.

Wally bowed his head, his voice oozing sarcasm. "Now what?"

"Please don't mention Paula, at least not until we get some positive feedback on the Dicks. If my guys learn that Paula went missing because she was floating in a canal, they'll convince themselves that the Dicks are floating in a canal, too, and the emotional upheaval might be too much for them to handle."

"She wasn't exactly floating," he corrected.

"That's not the point. I just want to spare Grace and Helen the needless anxiety of thinking their husbands are dead. Can you meet me halfway on this?"

Indecision flickered in his eyes, followed by a resigned snort. "All right, but I can't wait forever. People have a right to know. I'll give it until after our tour of the Anne Frank house this afternoon, and if we still don't have any word on the Dicks by then, I'll need to inform the group about Paula, whether you think it's advisable or not."

I nodded. "Fair enough. Thanks."

He shrugged it off. "By the way, you might mention to the guests with those 'urgent' needs that they can take pills to treat the condition now, and the side effects are pretty minimal. Death only occurs in rare instances."

My mind wasn't focused on bladder control at the moment though. It was focused on something else he'd said. "If Paula's body wasn't floating, how did they find her so quickly?"

"A bicyclist spied something in the water that looked like a piece of polka-dotted kelp, so he got curious, took a closer look, and discovered it wasn't a new species of kelp, but a woman's polka-dotted scarf. Unfortunately, it still appeared to be attached to its owner. That's when he called the police."

"How did the police know it was Paula?"

"Contents of her fannypack. It was still fastened around her waist, which pretty much rules out robbery as a motive."

Of course, robbery wasn't a motive. Her classmates didn't want to rob her; they wanted to kill her! "What did you say the name of the canal was?"

"Kloveniersburgwal."

"And where is that located?"

"It runs south from Nieuwmarket to the Amstel River, on the edge of the medieval city."

I pinched my lips in exasperation. "I've been here one day. I don't know where any of that is. Can you give me some landmarks I might recognize?"

"Okay, you've been to the Red Light District. If you were walking home from there, you'd have to walk right by it to get back to the hotel."

———

"The bus will pick us up at this exact spot two hours from now," Wally announced over the microphone, "so be sure and orient yourselves to the area so you won't get lost."

This was something of a no-brainer since we'd parked opposite a huge church whose spire reached the stratosphere. You could probably see it from Jupiter.

"The tour of the Anne Frank house takes about an hour," he continued, "and it's unguided, so you can view the rooms at your own pace. Be forewarned, they don't allow large bags, backpacks, luggage, or picture-taking, so stow your cameras. The stairs throughout the house are typical Amsterdam stairs, meaning they're extremely steep, so if you have problems with your knees, hips, or heights, I'd advise you to spend your time reading the display material rather than risk a visit to the secret annex."

"Why can't we take the elevator?" asked Ricky Hennessy.

"There's no elevator," said Wally.

"They should be reported," huffed Bernice in a nasally voice. "It's the law of the land. All public buildings must be handicap accessible."

"We're in Amsterdam," Wally replied with restraint. "There's no elevator." He took a deep breath and continued. "After the tour,

I suggest you pick up a bite to eat in the museum cafeteria. Prices are reasonable, and you can't beat the view overlooking the canal. They serve coffee, tea, lunch, drinks, snacks, and killer apple pie from a local bakery. Any questions?"

"Is there an elevator?" Helen shouted out.

I hung my head. *Oh, God.*

"Where is it you said we're going?" asked Grace.

In their defense, they were so worried about their husbands, they obviously weren't thinking straight, but having them this addled could become dangerous. I leaned close to Nana and lowered my voice to an undertone. "How did Grace and Helen perform on the eyeglasses task?"

Nana gave me a thumbs-up. "They missed their callin', dear. Them two girls are natural-born opticians. They done such a good job, everyone 'ceptin' Bernice and George has got their own glasses back again. When the Dicks show up, we'll do the final swap. And I sure hope it's soon. Bernice is so afraid of walkin' into another wall, have you seen what she done to herself?" Stealing a glance in her direction, she whispered, "She's got so much tissue shootin' out her nose, she looks like a bull walrus."

"We're touring the Anne Frank house," Wally repeated in an even tone, "and for those of you who might need a refresher course, during World War II, thirteen-year-old Anne, her family, and four other people hid from the Gestapo for two years in the back section of this house. They were eventually betrayed, imprisoned, and transported to concentration camps, but Anne's diary survived and remains one of the most seminal documents chronicling life in Amsterdam during Nazi occupation. I think it's been translated into sixty different languages."

"Isn't that somethin'?" marveled Nana. "Who knew there was sixty languages?"

I dropped my voice another decibel. "Do you think Helen and Grace would benefit from having another diversion?"

"What'd you have in mind?"

"Missing person forms. I was going to fill them out, but it might be better if the girls did it. The paperwork is pretty extensive, so it's bound to keep them busy for a while."

"Any word on the Dicks?"

I sighed. "Still missing."

"That's not good. Them drugs musta wore off by now. Could be they're just too stubborn to admit they're lost. Think of the humiliation, dear. How would they ever show their faces in Iowa again if they was forced to break down and ask someone for directions? They'd be broken men."

I prayed it was that innocent, but the longer they were missing, the more frightened I was becoming.

As the doors of the bus *whooshed* open, I scooted into the aisle to catch Helen and Grace before they left. "I have homework for the two of you," I said amiably as I pulled a wad of papers out of my shoulder bag. "We're going to put the police on the trail of the boys, so—"

"You haven't notified the police yet?" cried Grace.

"It's the same protocol as back home," I reassured them. "A person has to be missing for a certain number of hours before the police can get involved."

"Children get Amber alerts," fussed Helen. "You mean to tell me there's nothing like that available to track down old men?"

I shrugged. "Seniors are in a different category. They're sup-posed to be mature enough to take care of themselves."

"I wonder who decided that?" asked Grace.

"Someone who never met our Dicks," said Helen.

"As I was saying"—I passed the forms to both of them—"once you fill out the paperwork, the police can do their part to help find the boys."

As she riffled through the pages, Helen arched what would have been an eyebrow if she'd been wearing any. "How much time have we got to fill them out?"

"It's not a test. You can take as much time as you need. But the sooner you finish, the quicker the police can step in."

"Oh, my goodness," Grace effused as she scanned the first page. "This is wonderful. Absolutely wonderful. Thank you *so* much, Emily." She threw her arms around me in an uncharacteristic hug. "I'm so relieved!"

"No problem." I returned the hug, flattered that she appreci-ated my efforts so much. "I promise you, we'll find the boys if it's the last thing we do."

Helen regarded me, deadpan. "She's not patting you on the back. She's talking about her eyes. This is the first thing she's been able to read since last night."

Wally called out final instructions as we shuffled toward the exits. "Mind the traffic when you cross the street, people. We have reserved tickets, so we need to congregate outside number one-six-seven Prinsengracht and enter the museum as a group. Any more questions?"

He paused. "Okay, take note of the church on the corner as you pass by, because it's where Rembrandt was buried in 1669. It's called the Westerkerk and was built in 1620 as part of the Canal-Ring development. It's famous for its fifty bell carillon, which plays Dutch folksongs for sixty seconds every fifteen minutes, twenty-four hours a day. If any of you have read Anne Frank's diary, you'll recall she mentions the bells of the Westerkerk by name."

I exited through the side door, then corralled my people and herded them toward the traffic light at the corner. "Watch out for the trams," I cautioned as we crossed to the opposite side. "And bicycles!"

Prinsengracht was a picturesque canal street with brick pavers, Victorian street lights, shade trees, park benches, and bicycles cluttered against every rail and railing like discarded erector sets. Watercraft motored up and down the canal, filling the air with sounds reminiscent of buzz saws. Houseboats as long as semitrucks lined the opposite side of the waterway, while glass-topped tour boats glided past them, their engines *putt-putting* along with a muted hum. As we hiked past the church, all fifty bells began ringing in the tower above us, marking the quarter hour with a rousing melody that echoed over the rooftops. The carillon smacked of Old World quaintness and charm, but I wasn't sure how charming the locals found it at two o'clock in the morning. Then again, maybe the peel of bells became such an ordinary part of their lives, they simply stopped noticing it.

The reunion group was ahead of us, clumped in a Greek phalanx kind of formation that walled them off from nosy outsiders, like me, who wanted to pepper them with bothersome questions. Is this how they protected the secrets Pete accused them of hiding? By closing ranks? Were their purported secrets relevant to Paula's drowning? Or were Pete's accusations the rants of an antisocial genius who'd come unhinged and was trying to cover up his own involvement in the deaths of two women?

I was sure of only one thing: My instincts told me that someone in the group was a cold-blooded murderer with a deadly axe to grind, and if we didn't nab him soon, he could very well kill again. But how could I sniff anyone out with all my potential suspects giving me the cold shoulder? If I sent them running in the opposite direction, how would I even get close enough to overhear a conversation or ask a question?

"Emily, will you stop walking so fast?"

I looked over my shoulder, a smile forming on my lips. *Bingo.*

Jackie and Beth Ann jogged toward me, legs pumping and handbags flopping. "You want to hear the latest?" Jackie asked, wheezing to catch her breath. "I just gave Dietger a piece of my mind for stranding us in the Red Light District last night, and you know what he had the nerve to say?" She nodded to Beth Ann. "Go ahead. Tell her."

Beth Ann whipped her notebook out of her coat pocket. "He responded, and I quote—'You want to go to bed with me?'"

I let out a snarky laugh. "I think that must be his standard line with all the girls."

Beth Ann's face fell. "How come he hasn't tried it on me?"

"He will," I assured her. "Give him a little time. So what was your comeback?"

Jackie swept her hand toward Beth Ann in a little ruffles and flourishes gesture. "'Honey,'" Beth Ann recited, "'you wouldn't be able to keep up with me.'"

"Brilliant!" I nodded my approval. "Clever, succinct, with just the right amount of attitude." I wish I'd thought of it first.

Beth Ann regarded her mentor with adoring eyes. "Every off-the-cuff remark from Jackie's mouth is so brilliant, I'm encouraging her to collate them into a book. I've even thought of a title. *Off-the-Cuff.* Don't you think publishers would lap it up? I could record everything she says, and we could edit it together. It could be like a witty compendium of everyday proverbs for Generation Xers."

Jackie patted the top of Beth Ann's head. "Not to toot my own horn, Emily, but my expert coaching has allowed Beth Ann to develop the confidence she needs to open up her mind to great new ideas. Her head is just exploding with them."

It suddenly occurred to me that one of the great ideas exploding in Beth Ann's head might be to co-publish a book riding Jackie's coattails. If she had a hidden agenda to become a writer, this would certainly get her foot in the publishing door. She could skip all the preliminary hardships that newbie writers experience and be granted an instant "in." But this was Jackie's affair, not mine. In the meantime—

I sidled a glance left and right, and seeing that the coast was clear, motioned Jackie and Beth Ann closer. "I need your help."

"Yes!" Jackie tossed her head back and executed a celebratory shimmy that caused all her oversized jewelry to jingle like Christmas bells. "What did I tell you?" she said to Beth Ann. "She always needs help. She just hates to admit it." She patted her metallic bag. "Can I break out the wigs? I just happen to have stashed a couple in my bag."

"I think you can do this without wigs."

"Aw, c'mon." Out went her bottom lip. "But they're so cute." She yanked a mop of luxurious blonde hair out of her bag and gave it a skillful shake, allowing the curls to tumble softly into place.

"Oh, my." If the temperature hadn't been so cool, Beth Ann would have melted all over the sidewalk. "Can I wear that one?"

"You don't need wigs," I repeated.

She touched the fake hair almost reverently. "Okay, but when we *do* need to wear them, can I wear this one?"

"Are you sure you wouldn't rather be a redhead?" asked Jackie as she pulled out a second selection. "With your coloring you could do red quite—"

"Stoppit!" I hissed. "Do you want to help me or not?"

After a long-suffering eye roll, Jackie stuffed the wigs back in her bag. "Okay. Shoot."

"Thank you. Here's the deal. The folks from Maine don't seem willing to talk to me anymore, so—"

"You could try being a little less abrupt," sniped Jackie. "That might help."

"So"—I dismissed her with an ornery look—"I'd like the two of you to mingle as much as you can, chat them up, and eavesdrop on their conversations as much as you can without being too obvious."

"What are we supposed to be listening for?" asked Beth Ann.

"Any mention of last night, especially anything related to something eventful that might have happened on their walk back to the hotel."

"What kind of event are you talking about?" Jackie asked in a coy voice.

I arched my brow. "If I knew that, I probably wouldn't need your help."

"Oh, my God!" she clapped her hand over her mouth. "Some-one whacked Paula Peavey."

My mouth fell open. "How—?"

"Don't deny it. If Paula were alive, she'd be here today, making everyone's life as miserable as possible. I needed about a minute to figure that out about her. She's dead, isn't she?"

"I—"

"So who's our prime suspect?" she urged. "Besides everyone."

Wow. Jack really did boost his brain power when he had his plumbing replaced. "You *can't* tell anyone," I broke down. "Wally wanted to announce it to the whole bus, but he agreed to wait un-til after our tour to give the Dicks a little more time to show up. I'm so afraid Helen and Grace are going to freak out when they hear about Paula. They'll jump to the conclusion that the boys have met the same fate, and that'll be all she wrote. No joke. Stress can be a killer at their age. So you have to give me your word. Not a peep to anyone. Promise?"

"Promise," they said in unison, making the appropriate ges-tures over their hearts and lips.

"EMILY!"

I popped my head up to find Wally making furious beckon-ing motions to us from halfway down the street. He waved sev-eral tickets in the air and stabbed his finger at a house. "ARE YOU COMING?"

"Guess we better go."

"So how did Paula die?" Jackie asked me as we sprinted down the sidewalk.

"She drowned. The police say it was accidental."

"I'd sure question that," said Beth Ann as she kept pace behind us. "If they'd seen her face before she ran away last night, they might not have called it an accident."

"Exactly!" I agreed, realizing that Beth Ann's uterus made her far more perceptive than Wally.

"They might have called it a suicide."

"What?"

I slowed to a stop as Jackie and Beth jogged ahead.

Suicide?

A prickly sensation crawled up my spine.

Shoot. I hadn't thought of that.

TWELVE

By the time I cleared reception and caught up to the rest of the group, they were congregated in a warehouse room with an uneven brick floor—a room, which, according to the posted captions, once served as the spice grinding area for Otto Frank's meat seasonings company. The Mainers were lumped together, watching a video on a TV monitor, while my guys huddled in a corner, whispering back and forth and shushing each other as if they were in a library. Jackie and Beth Ann posted themselves on either side of the Mainers, trying to look as inconspicuous as the barrels stacked along the wall.

Looking for a quiet niche where I could collect my thoughts, I wandered toward the rear of the warehouse and poked my head through a door that led into a narrow shed with a slanted roof made entirely of glass. A blaze of sunshine filled the tiny space and spilled back into the grinding area through windows that looked as if they were part of the building's original outside wall. Without the light from the shed, the grinding room would have been steeped in total blackness, so the skylight made complete sense, despite its being so susceptible to shattering, especially during wartime Holland.

I loved when things made sense and hated when they didn't, which was the impulse driving me to reexamine my thinking about Paula Peavey.

Had she committed suicide? Was it possible her humiliation had been so profound that her only avenue of escape had been to end her own life? And yet, could someone as insensitive as Paula summon the kind of self-reproach it would take to fling herself into a canal? That's what made no sense. People like Paula caused *other* people to jump off bridges, not vice versa.

"You look like you've just lost your best friend," Mike McManus teased as he joined me. "What's up?"

"Hey, Mike." I forced a smile as I wrenched myself back to the present. "Just thinking about how lucky we are not to have lived in Nazi-occupied Europe."

"No argument from me there."

"So, I see that Mary Lou and Laura made it back to the hotel last night. Thank goodness for that, huh?"

He lifted his brows slightly. "Yeah, thank goodness, but I'm pretty ticked off about the whole thing."

"Did you figure out how you got separated?"

"Nope, and neither Mary Lou nor Laura want to discuss it. All they're saying is that they got turned around in the crowd and couldn't find me anywhere. Guess they never bothered to look on the damn bridge where I stood for three frickin' hours, looking for them. Would you believe they made it back to the hotel before I did last night? So I blew up in a fit of temper, and now Mary

Lou's not speaking to me. What a great vacation, huh? I'm so glad I came."

"Excuse me, Emily." Grace approached us on tiptoe, questionnaire in hand. "If I could bother you for just a moment."

"Problems with the form?" I inquired.

"And how. I'm having an ethical crisis with question number two."

I angled my head to read the line she indicated. "'What is subject's hair color?'"

"That's the one. What am I supposed to say?"

"Uh—steel gray? Salt and pepper? Plain old gray?"

She gnawed her bottom lip like a squirrel gnawing a nut. "Here's the thing. If I'm going to be absolutely honest, I'd have to list his actual hair color as 'bald,' and his fake hair color as gray, but Dick would be mortified if I told the police he's wearing a toupee. You know how sensitive he is about his hair loss. So should I keep his secret and tell the police he has a thick head of natural hair, or should I spill my guts and admit he's bald, which will crush his ego if he finds out?"

"Well…" How did I not see this coming? I could hardly wait until she got to the hard questions. "Having a visual description of Dick will help the police find him. So you need to ask yourself, what's more likely—that Dick is still wearing his toupee, or that he discarded it?"

"He better not have discarded it!" Her eyes spat fire. "I could have remodeled my kitchen for what it cost him to buy that thing. It's real hair! Harvested from virgins living on a mountaintop in some remote part of India and FedExed to Iowa overnight."

Well, duh? I didn't want to point out the obvious, but it wasn't the hair that was so flipping expensive. It was the shipping.

"How is his hair attached?" I asked her.

"To his head."

I smiled indulgently. "Do you happen to know how he prevents it from falling *off* his head?"

"Glue. Industrial strength. It does for toupees what mortar does for bricks. It's formulated with some kind of super-duper bonding agent that makes it impervious to blizzards, tornadoes, and hurricane force winds, so once he plasters it on his skull, he knows his hair ain't going anywhere."

"Well, there you go. You've answered your own question. If the glue is that strong, his hair is probably still in place, so the answer to question number two would be steel gray."

"Right." Her mouth inched into a relieved smile. "I wonder why I couldn't figure that out? Thanks, Emily."

"You bet."

Mike grinned when she'd left. "That was very considerate of you. As a man who boasts an undue vanity about his own hair, I thank you for urging her to keep her husband's secret. People don't respect the right of other people to have secrets anymore. They think everyone's life should be broadcast on YouTube for public viewing."

"Dick's rug really isn't a secret," I confessed. "We all know he wears one. We just pretend like we don't."

"So what kind of questionnaire is your friend filling out?"

After I explained what it was and how it would be used, he grew pensive. "Paula's missing, too, isn't she? Did you elect someone to fill one out for her?"

I blurted the first thing that popped into my head. "Wally's taking care of that." But I saw an opening that I couldn't ignore. "Why? Did you want to volunteer?"

"Who me? No way. I wouldn't be able to describe her without having the entire text censored for use of obscenities, not so much for the way she treated me, but for the way she treated everyone else. Most notably my wife."

"Seems unimaginable that Paula doesn't possess even one redeeming quality."

He laughed derisively. "Maybe she does. She's just doing a damned fine job of keeping it a secret."

"Secrets seem to be the topic of the day," I reflected. "When I broached the subject of Charlotte's accident with Pete Finnegan back at the museum, he suggested I should direct my questions at the people who are the real professionals at covering up the truth."

"What's that supposed to mean?"

"I suspect he's referring to all the reunion people, but I was hoping you might be able to provide a little more insight."

"Sounds like he's calling everyone a liar."

"That was my take. But the real question is, what's he accusing everyone of lying about?"

He quirked his mouth and shook his head. "Hell if I know."

"He hinted that his classmates have been hiding skeletons in their closets for a lot of years. Do you know anything about that?"

"Sounds like Pete has finally hit the paranoid-schizophrenia button."

"I don't know." I paused in thought. "I got the impression that whatever he was talking about related back to the incident with Bobby Guerrette. Chip Soucy filled me in on Senior Skip Day and its aftermath, but Pete's harangue made me think there still might be unresolved issues about Bobby's disappearance. Are there?"

His expression morphed from puzzled to wary. "He disappeared without a trace. That was pretty much the end of it."

"Chip told me Bobby invited you to hang out with the innies that day, so you were right there in the middle of everything."

His eyes grew pained. "My one big event with the in crowd. What a disaster. Look, Emily, I'd really prefer not dredging all that up again. It was bad enough going through it the first time."

"But you saw something, didn't you?"

Alarm registered on his sun-bronzed face. "What?"

"Chip said you saw the car that picked Bobby up."

"Oh, right. The one that wasn't white and wasn't a station wagon. Hennessy got the best look at it. I just kind of caught a glimpse."

"And the police never found the car or the driver."

He swallowed with such difficulty, his Adam's apple bobbed in slow motion. "Yeah. No happy ending."

"Did the police ever question Pete about the incident?"

"Not that I recall. He wasn't there that day, so they had no reason to question him."

"But Chip said Pete was the first person in your class to get his driver's license, so theoretically, he could have driven by the park without your ever seeing him, right?"

His gaze hardened. "Can I ask what you're getting at?"

"I'm trying to figure out how Pete might know things that no one realizes he knows, because he claims he's chock full of secrets that could ruin everyone."

"Really?" He sounded more amused than skeptical.

"Really."

"He's full of it."

"I have no idea if he is or not, but he sure sounded convinced."

He looked over his shoulder to find the video on the monitor still playing and the Mainers nowhere in sight. "Where'd everyone go?"

"Next room." I nodded toward the front of the warehouse, taking note that my guys were still huddled in the corner.

"Gotta abandon you, Emily. Sorry. But I want to catch up with the group before they get too far ahead. I'm not about to let Mary Lou get separated from me again, whether we're speaking to each other or not."

"No problem." As he headed off in the opposite direction, I added a parting shot. "If you run across any skeletons in your closet, let me know, okay?"

"You got it." But I knew he wouldn't. He'd looked so uneasy when we were discussing Pete that I found it a bit unsettling. Maybe I shouldn't have revealed so much to him, but Mike was so nice, he couldn't be hiding a ragbag of dark secrets, could he?

"Are we ready to move on to the next room?" I asked the gang as I paused by the huddle.

"Emily will know," asserted Helen.

"Don't count on it," said Bernice.

"Emily will know what?" I inquired.

Helen let out a frustrated sigh. "We've been going over and over this and we can't agree. What was Dick wearing last night?"

"It's question number four on the form," Grace added helpfully.

I gave them a blank look. "Uhh—"

"What'd I tell you," droned Bernice.

"That's a toughie," I admitted, unable to recall even seeing Dick Teig last night. "Did any of you take a picture of him?"

"I tried," said Tilly. "When we were in the coffeeshop. With my phone. But I ended up calling a shaman in New Guinea instead."

"Anyone else take a picture?"

"I wanted to," said George, "but the buttons on my keypad kept moving around."

"Nana?" I eyed her expectantly. She was such a photo hound, she had to have taken pictures last night.

She shook her head. "I couldn't snap the shutter, dear. It was too embarrassin'."

"Okay, no pictures, but you know for sure he was wearing a shirt, slacks, and jacket. Can you remember the color of the jacket?"

"Gray," said Alice.

"Green," said George.

"Aha!" I regarded Helen hopefully. "Does Dick own a sage colored jacket?"

Her eyes crinkled at the corners as she pondered the question. "The grandkids bought him a jacket for Christmas a few years back, but I don't think it was sage. It was more like the color of baby asparagus when you overcook it in the microwave."

"Black?" asked Margi.

"Morons!" snapped Bernice. "His jacket is denim with a fleece collar that makes him look like he has a flock of sheep living under his chins. What's wrong with you people? Are you all blind?"

They obviously were last night. "I tell you what," I intervened, "why don't you skip this question for now and go back to it later?"

"Am I allowed to do that?" asked Helen.

"You bet. In fact, answering all the other questions might help jog your memory with these earlier ones."

"I doubt it," she fretted.

"Unh-unh-unh." I wagged my finger. "Don't you dare sell yourself short. Once you put your mind to it, I suspect you'll be able to remember every last detail of what Dick was wearing last night."

"I can't honestly say as I remember the last time I really looked at Dick." She let out a wistful sigh. "Is his head still big as an inflatable pumpkin?"

"More like an inflatable planet," said Bernice.

She set a placating hand on my arm. "Maybe no one's explained this to you, Emily, but when you've been married as long as Dick and I have, you notice certain changes in your relationship. Like, you don't actually see each other anymore. You already know what each other looks like, so what's the point? Dick could hang around the house in a ruffled tutu, and I could run errands in a sausage casing, and the truth is, neither one of us would probably notice."

"Oh." I stared dumbly, a little taken aback. Is this how Etienne and I would end up in a few years? So bored with each other's company that we'd be blind to each other's fatal clothing choices?

"Emily and her young man don't gotta worry about that for another fifty years," Nana spoke up, "which is about how long it's gonna take us to fill out these forms if we keep dillydallyin."

Nods. Grunts of agreement.

"Before you get back to work," I broke in as Helen smoothed the folds out of her papers, "please don't spend all your time filling out forms. We only have two hours, so if you want to see the whole house, you have to get moving. Okay?"

More nods.

157

"I'm going to continue the tour, so I'll be on the first floor if you need me."

"I thought we were *on* the first floor," said Margi.

"We're on the ground floor," explained Tilly. "The first floor is one level up. Europeans number their floors differently."

"But…" Margi regarded the ceiling in confusion. "I thought we were *on* the first floor."

"Question number five," Helen read in a rush of words. "'Does the subject in question have any distinguishing features that would make him stand out in a crowd?'"

"'Bout time we got an easy one," said George.

"His head," Helen scribbled with authority.

I proceeded through the room at the front of the building and entered a vestibule that housed a staircase as steep as a cliff, with treads no wider than my hand. *Uff-da.* These must be the notorious Dutch stairs that Wally had warned us about. I wondered if Ricky and Mindy had made it to the top, hampered, as they were, by their excessive weight and possible balance problems. But they must have managed somehow, because they were nowhere in sight.

The first floor was a rabbit warren of rooms off a long hallway. I followed the prescribed route through private offices and supply rooms, learning that Otto Frank operated a second business while he was in hiding—one that distributed pectin used for making jam. I browsed the exhibits, taking note of identity cards, accounting books, and Anne's favorite movie magazine, *Cinema & Theater*, then climbed a circular staircase to the next floor, where the memorabilia on display told tales of both extraordinary heroism and unimaginable horror.

The Mainers must have breezed through this level, because I didn't see a one of them until I entered a narrow hallway that funneled traffic to the rear of the building. At the far end of this passageway, where a hinged bookcase swung away from the wall to reveal the once secret entrance to the annex, Mike and Peewee stood toe to toe, locked in an intense exchange.

Hmm. I wondered what that was about. But before I could get close enough to hear what they were saying, Mike saw me coming, broke off his discussion with Peewee, and tossed me a furtive wave before disappearing into a doorway beneath an awkwardly placed map on the wall. Peewee followed close behind, doubling over at his waist to clear the space without bumping his head.

I quickened my steps. Nuts. Where were Jackie and Beth Ann when I needed them?

The door to the secret annex was wedged open and held in place by a steel brace that blocked access to an ascending stairway. Patrons were apparently expected to reach the next story by climbing what looked like a bookshelf, but only after touring the Frank's apartment and passing through a door on the opposite side of the barrier. I peered up the nearly vertical staircase to the opening cut in the floor above and felt the bottoms of my feet tingle in alarm. *Holy crap!* My guys couldn't climb these things. I wasn't sure *I* could climb them!

I pulled out my cellphone, hoping they were still on the ground floor, dithering over the questionnaires. I checked the screen.

No service.

Shoot! I looked back down the hallway to find a crowd of tourists streaming toward me. Swimming against the tide would take too long. I had to go forward. If I didn't stop to look at anything, I could probably reach the ground floor in a few minutes.

Mike suddenly appeared on the other side of the barrier, aiming to head up the stairs.

"That was quick," I said nonchalantly.

He gave me a palms-up. "Not much to linger over."

I hurried through a short hallway to arrive in the Frank's family room—a modest space with pinkish wallpaper and woodwork painted institutionalized green. I blew past several people into an even narrower room, where the photos of long-dead movie stars graced the walls, then hurried into a connecting room that housed a sink and toilet. Following the tour route out the bathroom door, I stepped into the hallway to find myself back at the entrance to the annex, on the opposite side of the barrier, at the foot of the staircase I really didn't want to climb.

I inhaled a deep breath to bolster my courage. It was a good thing Paula Peavey wasn't here. Given her struggles with vertigo, there was no way she—

The thought went unfinished as a body came crashing down the stairs and fell in a mangled heap at my feet.

THIRTEEN

Our visit ended up lasting a lot longer than two hours.

"Question number one hundred-eighteen," said Helen, trying unsuccessfully to stifle a yawn. She blinked away tears as she stared bleary-eyed at the questionnaire. "'What is the subject's favorite television program?'"

George's head fell onto his chest, startling him awake. "Make something up," he grumbled.

We were gathered in the museum cafeteria, battling spotty cellphone service while seated at tables with sweeping views of bicyclists, pedestrians, and canal traffic. The police were still questioning patrons about the tragic mishap that had forced the museum to close its doors for the remainder of the day. Interviewees were being held in the administrative offices in another part of the complex and were being released one at a time in a very orderly process. I complimented the police on their efficiency and thoroughness. But the downside was, it was taking forever.

I guess it was no easy task determining what had caused Pete Finnegan to plunge to his death.

"How much longer have we gotta sit here?" Bernice griped as Gary Bouchard sauntered into the room.

"We almost got everyone back," said Nana, recording Gary's arrival with a hash mark on her napkin. She tallied the count. "Only three to go."

Being on the ground floor when the mishap occurred had proven to be fortuitous for my group. No interrogation for them. But the reunion people had fared less well. The police wanted to interview all patrons who'd been touring the third floor rooms when Pete took his header down the stairs. And, wouldn't you know? Every single Mainer had apparently been crowded into the apartment when Pete fell. Little wonder the interrogation was taking so long. I couldn't imagine how underwhelmed the police must be with the feedback.

I rubbed my hands together, trying to warm my icy fingertips. I'd finally stopped shaking after downing six pots of hot tea, but I still felt brittle and a little wobbly. Every time I closed my eyes, all I could see was Pete, frantically windmilling his arms as he plummeted toward me. All I could hear was the bone-jarring *thunk* as he landed at my feet. I found solace in only one detail: Had I been standing a hairsbreadth closer, I'd be lying in the morgue with him.

I shuddered at the thought.

Grace flipped through the remaining pages of her questionnaire. "We're making progress, everyone," she announced proudly. "Only eight pages left."

A collective groan.

"Look at the woman across the street!" Margi leaped from her chair and pressed her nose to the window glass, her voice trembling with anguish. "She's talking on a cellphone. She's probably even able to text."

"Where?" cried Osmond and Alice, racing to the window to join her.

"You want I should fetch you another pot a tea, dear?" Nana spoke softly, as if a louder tone might cause me to shatter. "Your great-gramma Maccoull used to say there wasn't no misery in this world what couldn't be made better by a hot cup a tea."

I squeezed her hand and smiled. "I'm good, Nana." Which wasn't exactly true, because if Pete died the way I suspected he died, I'd never be able to live with myself again. "But, I do think I'm about to float away, so if you'll excuse me." I pushed away from the table.

"Going back to the television question," Helen fussed, "what do you think they want to know? Dick's favorite show of all-time, or his pick in the new fall lineup?"

Since the museum had been cleared of all patrons except us, I didn't have to wait in line to use the ladies' room. In fact, I had the room all to myself ... until Jackie charged through the door, fisting her hands on her hips when she saw me.

"Why is it that every time *you* find a dead body, *I* end up getting grilled by the police?" she asked in a tight voice.

"Finally!" I sloughed water from my hands as I spun around to face her. "I've been going nuts not knowing what's going on. Why is it taking so long? What did they ask you? What did you tell them? Did you actually see anything?"

She made a beeline toward the closest mirror and plopped her metallic bag on the countertop. "You don't mind if I multi-task while I answer, do you? My lip gloss is in desperate need of freshening up."

"Your lips are fine, Jack. Talk to me!"

"What did I see?" she repeated as she removed a lip brush from her cosmetic bag. "A sink and wall spigot. World War II vintage. Not in the best of shape. An alcove where a stove used to sit. A closed off fireplace. Beamed ceiling. A menu for an anniversary dinner. An adjoining room I never got to see because of Pete Finnegan's swan dive down the staircase."

"Were you near him when it happened?"

"Everyone was near him, Emily. We were packed in like sardines. I bumped into, stepped on, or smacked elbows with every person in the stupid room. But that's what makes eavesdropping such a specialized skill. You can't stand in one place. You have to keep moving around."

"And?"

"And my boots have scuff marks all over them because of it." She pivoted her foot, toe out, to show me. "You don't happen to have a suede cleaner bar on you, do you?"

"Jack!"

"What! I was on the other side of the room when all the commotion started, along with a whole host of other people, who, by the way, were blowing off the rules and taking photos."

"Was Mike McManus on your side of the room? Tall, good-looking guy with a golf tan and Wolf Blitzer's hair?"

"Mmmm…" She unscrewed the cap on her lip gloss. "Not that I recall. I was surrounded by a clique of plushy women who were rehashing their dislike of some nun named Sister Hippolytus when the wheels fell off."

"So Mike could have been standing near the staircase when Pete fell?"

She leaned close to the mirror as she brushed a dab of gloss over her lips. "I don't know who was standing nearest the staircase, but you might want to ask Beth Ann, because she was working that side of the room for me. I had this ingenious idea to divide the room into two hal—" She gasped suddenly, wheeling around to face me. "Oh, my God. Do you think this Mike McManus pushed Pete?"

"I don't *know*." I inhaled a breath and let it out, but it did nothing to lessen the taste of guilt lingering in my mouth. "I … I'm terrified *I* might have killed him."

"WHAT?"

"I feel so horrible, Jack. Pete ranted at me earlier today that he could ruin all his classmates by blabbing some secrets no one realized he knew, and I made the mistake of telling Mike, and a few flights of stairs later, Pete ends up dead. See?" My voice rose to a breathless squeal. "I killed him!"

Jackie rolled her eyes. "Can I give you some friendly advice, Emily? Stop making everything about yourself. You were nowhere near Pete when he took his dive, so cool your jets. You didn't do it."

"I know I didn't do it directly. What I did was worse. I drove someone else to do it!"

"The guy tripped and fell. Have you seen the stairs in this place? They're enough to scare the climbers who scaled Everest. One misstep, and *splat*!"

I winced. "But what about—"

"When Pete dive-bombed at you, was he wearing the kind of look that screamed, 'Holy shit! Someone just pushed me?'"

I regarded her blandly. "I don't know how he looked. I mean, I didn't see his face. It all happened too quickly."

"My point exactly. These stairs are killers." She recapped her lip gloss and brush and stuffed them back in her bag. "Look, Em, if it'll make you feel any better, the police seem to be treating Pete's death as an accident. These guys are very thorough interrogators, so trust me, if Mike McManus had entertained even a fleeting thought about shoving Pete down the stairs, they would know. Their interrogation techniques are brilliant. You wouldn't believe what they were able to get out of me."

"Like what?"

She gave her eyelashes a demure flutter. "Like, I had written a novel that can still be purchased on Amazon from select sellers."

Oh, right. Who knew what sordid threats they'd had to make to get that out of her?

The restroom door swung open.

"Thank God," Jackie gushed as Beth Ann crossed the threshold. "Could you *please* do me a colossal favor and convince Emily she didn't kill Pete Finnegan?"

Beth Ann did a double-take. "Pardon me?"

"Go ahead." She made a scooting motion with her hand. "Tell her what you saw just before Pete fell down the stairs."

"Uh—he was hanging out by the stairs, waiting for the queue to Peter Van Pels' room to shorten, and the next thing I knew, I heard a series of thumps, a scream, and *poof*. He wasn't there anymore."

My heart did a little stutter step. "Was he doing anything unusual while he was waiting? Talking to anyone? Looking at anything?"

"The last time I saw him, he was checking out the ceiling beams. Did you notice them, Jackie? The dark wood added so much warmth and character to the room. I wish they could have displayed some of the original furniture. My dad's house was full of antique fixtures and furniture, so I have a real appreciation for period pieces."

"So, Pete was … looking up when he probably should have been looking down?" I persisted.

Beth Ann nodded. "He seemed mesmerized by those beams. Kind of like a bricklayer would be mesmerized by the craftsmanship of a really intricate chimney."

Was this what Pete's mishap boiled down to? One inattentive step in the wrong direction? "Did the police find it likely that Pete's accident might have been caused by nothing more than a misstep?"

She shrugged. "They didn't comment one way or the other. They just took down my account and told me I could leave."

"See?" Jackie gave my shoulder an "I told you so" poke. "No one pushed him. He fell."

Beth Ann's cheeks flushed with exuberance. "This whole experience has been so exciting. I've never been questioned by the authorities before." She flashed Jackie a breathless smile. "Have you ever thought of writing a police procedural novel?"

My pulse slowed to a more natural rhythm. Calm leavened my guilt. Reason replaced paranoia. *Why* did I do this to myself? Why did I always leap to conclusions, rush to judgment, see everyone as a suspect? I needed to get a grip. But more than that, I needed to stop thinking that I, Emily Andrew Miceli, knew more than the police.

I propped my hip against the edge of the vanity, feeling my adrenalin high start to fade. "So I guess neither one of you got to see Peter Van Pels room," I said in a less frenzied voice.

"The queue was ridiculous," said Beth Ann. "And the people who were waiting to jump in line were all clustered around me, which was great for eavesdropping, but bad for touring."

"I hope you heard more than I did." Jackie primped in the mirror. "I was surrounded by duds."

Beth Ann referred to her notebook, which suddenly seemed affixed to her hand like a tattoo. "Ricky Hennessy was complaining to Chip Soucy about his bad knees and the prospect of total knee replacements in the near future. Mindy was staring at the floor, looking bored. Gary and Sheila Bouchard were standing close to the wall, saying nothing, but looking very uncomfortable. Laura LaPierre and Mary Lou McManus had their heads together, talking, but they were speaking so softly, I couldn't hear what they were saying. Sorry."

Jackie cocked her head like the Victrola dog peering into the phonograph speaker. "How do you know everyone's name already?"

"Uhh—nametags?" Beth Ann regarded her wide-eyed. "Everyone's wearing one. Haven't you noticed?"

Jackie twitched her freshly glossed lips. "Good point. Anything else?"

"Mike McManus and Peewee were latecomers, so they were only there a couple of minutes, but I did overhear Mike ask Peewee if he'd been in school the day a few members of the football team let the air out of someone named Mr. Albert's tires."

"Wait a sec." I held up my hand to slow her down. If she was saying what I think she was saying, then—"All the people you've just mentioned were a stone's throw away from you, right?"

"Right."

"And you were a stone's throw away from Pete Finnegan?"

"Yeah."

"So *everyone* was within a stone's throw of Pete?"

Beth Ann looked a little cowed. "Ye*aaa*h." She dragged the word out as if it were caught in a slide flute.

My heart raced. My mouth went dry. I pressed my palms to my forehead and squeezed my eyelids shut. "They were all there," I choked. "Mike. Peewee. Ricky. Watching him like hawks. How could the police think it was an accident?"

Beth Ann raised her eyebrows. "Do you suppose they never got the memo that Pete is the third person we've lost in two days? What if they don't have police scanners over here? What if the officers who interrogated us didn't know about Paula and Charlotte?"

I glanced from one to the other. "Neither of you mentioned Paula to the police?"

Jackie shot me *the look*. "Duh? You made us promise not to say a word to anyone. What do we look like? Stool pigeons?" But her expression registered slow enlightenment as she put two and two together. "OH, MY GOD! Pete didn't fall. Someone pushed him!"

"Hel-l*ooo*?" I cried.

"Hello to you, too, dear," said Nana, peeking over her shoulder as she scooted into the room. She pressed her back against the wall just inside the door and stood motionless for a moment, like a cat burglar waiting for the coast to clear. She offered us a placid smile as we stared across the room at her. "You girls go on with what you was talkin' about. Just pretend like I'm not here."

What in the world? "Let me guess," I said impassively. "You're trying to avoid someone."

"Dang." She pumped her fist. "What gave it away?"

169

"Who are you hiding from?"

Her eyes flickered with guilt. "Grace and Helen. I can't take no more of them questions, so I'm goin' rogue."

"In the restroom?" I regarded the cold tile and harsh lighting. "You can't find someplace more relaxing?"

"This'll do. Especially since I don't gotta haul water to flush the commode."

I looked at Jackie, Jackie looked at Beth, Beth looked at me—our glances posing a silent question. *What now?*

I made an executive decision. "Nana, if I share something with you, will you promise to keep it under your hat until it's officially made public later today?"

"You don't even gotta ask, dear." She locked her lips with an imaginary key and dropped it down her bosom. "Good enough?"

The door burst open. Tilly and Alice scuttled inside, pulling up short when they spied Nana. "Found you!" Tilly said breathlessly. "They're stuck on question one-thirty-two. 'If the subject could come back to earth as a vegetable, what would it be?'"

"Back to earth from where?" asked Nana.

"It doesn't matter," said Alice. "The Dicks don't like vegetables."

I hung my head. *Oh, God.*

"This is real bad timin', girls," Nana said apologetically. "Emily was about to tell me somethin' I gotta keep under my hat."

Tilly regarded me with doe eyes. "I'm so sorry, Emily. Alice and I would be happy to leave."

Alice nodded agreement. "If we go now, we might even catch the tail end of the debate."

"Debate?" I asked.

Tilly's voice crackled with self-restraint. "Helen said she could picture Dick coming back as a tomato, but Bernice decreed that he'd have to come back as something else, because a tomato isn't a vegetable. It's a fruit."

"So Osmond is compiling a list of every fruit and vegetable known to man so the girls can see what their options are." Alice sighed. "And naturally, there's been some disagreement. Breadfruit was particularly contentious."

"Well, don't go back without armin' yourselves first," instructed Nana as she mined the contents of her pocketbook. "Where'd I put them things? They'll help you to end things real quick."

"Nana!" I started to hyperventilate as I imagined my grandmother being hauled off to jail on weapons charges. "Oh, my God. What are you packing?"

She opened her palm. "Earplugs."

Hearing a sudden chorus of voices in the hall, I fired a glance at the door just as Margi came barreling through. "Told you so," she called back into the hall. "They're all holed up in the potty."

Helen and Grace rushed into the room as if their hair were on fire.

"Wally wants everyone back in the cafeteria," snapped Helen in her drill sergeant's voice. "And you're already late, so move it."

"He has a big announcement," said Grace.

Unh-oh. Sounded as if he was going to break the news about Paula.

Beads of sweat started popping up at my hairline. I needed to stay close to Helen and Grace. Lord, this was going to be brutal on them.

"I wonder what all the intrigue is about?" tittered Margi. "Do you think he's going to change the itinerary again?"

Nana gave a little suck on her dentures. "If you was to ask me, I'd say he probably wants to tell us about that poor Peavey woman. I suspect them folks from Maine are gonna be real devastated when they find out."

What? I blinked dumbly. "You know? But—you can't know. No one knows! How do you know?"

"About the Peavey woman?" asked Nana.

"*Yes*, about the Peavey woman."

"Bernice told us," said Margi.

My jaw dropped like an anvil. "How does Bernice know? No one knows. She can't possibly know!"

"She knows," said Nana.

"But—" I felt my throat constrict as I studied Helen and Grace. I hurried over to them, blubbering words of encouragement and consolation. "Please don't jump to the conclusion that the boys are going to suffer the same fate as Paula. I promise you, they're not dead. They'll show up. I guarantee it. They're alive, and well, and probably just made a wrong turn somewhere. In fact, I bet they're back at the hotel even as we speak."

"I hope not," said Helen. "If they stay lost just a little longer, we'll have a shot at finishing these stupid questionnaires."

I frowned as she scooted everyone out the door.

What?

Nana crept back into the restroom and shuffled over to me. "Sorry about the interruption, dear. I thought they was never gonna leave. Now, what was it you wanted to tell me?"

FOURTEEN

"Emily don't know nuthin' about text messagin', so we're gonna have to vote by secret ballot."

Groans. Whines. Eye rolling.

I regarded the gang in exasperation. "Hey, I admit it. I'm electronically challenged, but in fifty years, when everyone else's thumbs are paralyzed with arthritis, I'll be seen as a visionary. You'll see. The proof will be in the pudding."

Margi raised her hand, her face alit with anticipation. "Are we having dessert?"

The day had been so emotionally draining, we'd decided to hang up our walking shoes and eat dinner in the hotel dining room rather than hoof around Amsterdam, trying to find a fancy restaurant. I requested a group meeting in my room afterward, so we were all present, except for Jackie and Beth Ann, who'd stopped for an after-dinner drink in the lounge. I'd invited Wally, too, but having just returned from the police station, where he'd delivered the completed questionnaires and had the Dicks declared officially missing, he said he needed to spend the evening with his laptop.

"I'll get right to the point," I began. "I need your help."

They came to attention like eager pups, eyes forward, ears perked, tongues practically hanging out of their mouths.

"I'm hoping if I tell you what I've learned in the last two days, you might be able to see something I'm missing. I know accidents happen all the time, but if you ask me, three fatal accidents in two days smash the law of averages."

"Three?" argued Bernice. "How about five? Have you forgotten the Dicks? You're all just too lily-livered to talk about them."

Silence ensued, followed by a collective intake of breath that sucked all the air from the room. Grace snatched up Tilly's walking stick and brandished the rubber end cap at Bernice's chest. "One more comment like that, Bernice Zwerg, and you'll be looking at a major time-out in the potty, *minus* your hearing aid batteries. And we won't need to vote on it."

"Grace's edict carries by unanimous consent," declared Osmond. "Put a lid on it, Bernice."

I leveled a piercing look at her. "And while we're on the subject of hearing aids, would you like to tell me how you heard about Paula's death before Wally announced it to everyone in the cafeteria?"

She folded her arms across her chest and tucked in her lips. "No can do. I plead the fifth."

"Don't pay Bernice no nevermind," Nana urged. "Go on with what you was gonna tell us, dear."

After providing them with a brief primer on who was who in the Maine contingent, I told them everything I'd learned over the last two days, starting with Paula Peavey's fondness for humiliating people and Pete Finnegan's offer to neutralize her. I recounted my dinner on the canal cruise, where Gary Bouchard had accused Ricky Hennessy of ruining his prospects for a basketball scholarship, where it became obvious that both Gary and Pete had benefited from the death of a fellow classmate, and where I'd learned just how mercilessly the people at my table had mocked Laura LaPierre. I pointed out how both Charlotte and Paula had crossed Pete and ended up dead, and how Pete had threatened to ruin all his classmates by revealing secrets he'd known about them for years. "But before he can make good on his threat, he ends up dead himself."

"Did anyone from Maine know Pete was a ticking time bomb?" asked Tilly.

"Mike McManus," I said, then recalling the scene outside the secret annex, "and Peewee, I think."

"Pushing Pete down the stairs would have been a pretty convenient way to shut him up," said George. "You think one of those fellas did it?"

"I know they were standing practically on top of him when he fell, so they certainly had the opportunity."

"What do you s'pose Pete knew that them two fellas wanted kept secret?" asked Nana.

"That's the sixty-four-thousand-dollar question. I don't have a clue, but every time I talk to a reunion person, the conversation always finds its way around to a classmate named Bobby Guerrette, who disappeared on their Senior Skip Day and was never seen again. If they're hiding skeletons in their closets, my gut tells me, the skeletons are wearing Bobby Guerrette's face."

"Sounds like we're flirtin' with a cold case file," said Nana.

175

"But it's spilling over into the present day," fretted Helen. "How do we know my Dick's disappearance isn't connected with one or more of them trying to keep their skeletons hidden?"

I had no answer to that.

"Did anyone notice how composed all the Mainers were when Wally announced that Paula Peavey was dead?" asked Tilly. "It was almost as if the news didn't come as a surprise. I didn't notice a single tear being shed."

"There wasn't no tears for Pete neither," said Nana.

"Good thing Wally didn't threaten to cancel the tour," said George. "I think the Mainers would have staged a rebellion."

"Isn't it nice how the tour company is going to handle all the arrangements for flying the bodies back to the states?" Alice chimed in. "It must give folks great peace of mind to know that if they get knocked off in Amsterdam, their bodies won't be left to molder away in a forgotten corner somewhere, while their cheap relatives bicker over who's going to get stuck with the air freight bill."

Helen looked intrigued. "Do you suppose there are other perks in our travel packages that we don't know about yet?"

Before they could take off on another unrelated tangent, I let out an attention-getting whistle. "Do you want me to tell you what I know about Bobby Guerrette and Senior Skip Day?"

Nods. Mumbles of assent.

"It's pretty depressing, just so you know."

Margi grabbed a box off my bedside table and waved it in the air. "I've got tissues."

I recounted every detail I could remember about Bobby Guerrette, focusing on the qualities that seemed to define him—his intelligence, his popularity, his strong self-image—qualities he'd developed

176

despite having no family other than the nuns at the orphanage. I told them how he'd appointed himself as Laura LaPierre's protector, and how he'd befriended Mike McManus in the days when Mike had been a super geek. I related how he'd stayed home from his senior prom rather than attend with Paula Peavey ,and how he'd been in line to be valedictorian of his class. "When he disappeared, Pete got bumped up to valedictorian, Laura became salutatorian, and Gary Bouchard got elevated to fifth in his graduating class, which was apparently a big status thing for Gary's father."

I talked briefly about Senior Skip Day, how the in crowd had dropped in and out of the gathering that was going on at a local park, how most of the kids spent the day getting hammered, how Bobby was forced to hitchhike back to the orphanage later that night, how Ricky Hennessy saw Bobby get into the car that apparently drove him into oblivion, and how Mike and Peewee backed up Ricky's eyewitness account.

"Was Paula Peavey considered a member of the in crowd?" asked Tilly.

"I got the impression that she ran with the in crowd because she was so vicious, they were afraid what she might say about them if they ignored her. Chip Soucy told me that she wasn't specifically invited to hang out with them on Senior Skip Day, but her parents had given her a car for graduation, so she showed up anyway." I threw them a pleading look. "Can you see why my head is about to explode?"

Tilly removed a pen and notepad from her pocketbook and began taking notes. "Pete Finnegan, Laura LaPierre, and Gary Bouchard benefited most from young Bobby's disappearance. Is that correct?"

I nodded. "All three reaped the academic rewards of Bobby's not graduating."

"You s'pose one a them coulda done that young man in?" asked Nana.

I sighed. "Laura idolized him, so I'd take her name off the board. I don't know about Pete and Gary. Do you think they would have had the stomach to kill a fellow student to improve their academic ranking?" I shivered. "It's just so brutal."

"Were Pete and Gary at the park when Bobby got into that car?" asked George.

"Pete wasn't. No one invited him to participate. But Gary was there, which pretty much gives him an airtight alibi."

"Who said he was still there?" asked Bernice. "His buddies? If you believe that, I've got some land in Florida I'd like to sell you."

I stared at Bernice, her accusation zapping me like a shot of stray voltage. *Uff-da*! This whole time I'd been operating on the assumption that everyone was telling me the truth. But what if that wasn't the case? What if everyone was lying to cover up what had really happened? Duh?

"Why was Pete left out?" Alice asked me.

"He wasn't socially adept, he didn't try to fit in, and no one enjoyed his company."

Eight sets of eyes riveted on Bernice.

"What?" she balked.

Helen bristled with indignation. "If folks snubbed me like that, I wouldn't take kindly to it at all. I might even find a way to make them regret it."

Nana raised her hand. "If Pete Finnegan wasn't at the park, where was he?"

I regarded her dumbly. "I don't know. But I do know that he was the first person in the class to get his driver's license, even though no one bothered to acknowledge it. So if he had access to a car, he could have easily cruised by to see what was going on with his classmates."

"And seen something he shouldn't have?" asked George.

A stillness fell over the room. Yes, he could have gotten an eyeful that day. But what in God's name had he seen?

Tilly thumped her walking stick on the floor. "Have you considered the possibility that the person who picked Bobby up might not have been a random stranger? What if the person driving the car had been Pete Finnegan?"

Collective gasps, the loudest of which was my own.

"Pete could easily have offered Bobby a ride back to the orphanage," she continued, "then made sure he never got there. What better way to wield power over the ruling elite than by eliminating the one student who stood in the way of your receiving the highest honor in your graduating class?"

"I think you're all ignoring the obvious," Grace spoke up. "Bobby Guerrette refused to attend the senior prom with Paula Peavey. Can you imagine how angry that must have made her? Don't you think she would have wanted to get even? You said yourself she was vicious, Emily. And she had her own car. Maybe *she* was the one who picked up Bobby that night."

"And made him pay the ultimate price," said Helen.

"Hell hath no fury," offered Osmond.

Was it Paula who'd picked Bobby up? Had Pete witnessed it? Could he have carried that secret around with him for five decades? But why wouldn't he have spoken up at the time? "*Arrrrhh!*" I scrubbed my face with my hands. "I can't think."

"You people are so delusional," Bernice grumbled. "What are you trying to prove? You think there was a murder fifty years ago? There wasn't. That kid ran away. It happens all the time. They're called runaways."

"Oh, yeah?" countered Margi. "So if there was no murder to cover up back then, how come so many people are dying now?"

Bernice stared at her. "Is that supposed to make sense?"

Margi stared back. "It does to me."

"It doesn't make sense to Bernice because she doesn't know how to connect the dots," said Grace.

"Here's some dots for you," huffed Bernice. "Pete fell down a staircase because he wasn't looking where he was going. Paula fell into a canal because she wasn't looking where *she* was going. Not to mention, she had vertigo."

My mouth fell open. "You knew about that, too?"

"Charlotte plowed into a speeding bicycle because ... *she wasn't looking where she was going.* Do you see any dots?"

George shooed something away from his line of vision. "I see 'em, but are you sure they're not floaters?"

"Emily is getting us all hopped up over nothing," accused Bernice. "If we listen to her, we're all gonna end up having another lousy vacation, because she'll convince us to waste all our time trying to prove her stupid conspiracy theories."

"I thought that was the reason we come on these trips," said Nana.

Eight sets of eyes pingponged from Bernice, to me, to Bernice again. "Show of hands," announced Osmond. "How many people are in favor of ousting Bernice from our caucus?"

While he counted the eight hands that shot into the air, I excused myself to answer a sudden knock on my door.

"Don't ask," Jackie fumed as she stormed into the room. Beth Ann followed close behind her, like a beagle chasing a squirrel.

"Whatever you say," I agreed as I closed the door.

Jackie paused in the center of the room, feet apart, hands on hips, eyes snapping. "Men!"

Silence. Gaping. Uncertainty.

"What's wrong with 'em?" asked Nana.

She flashed a grateful smile. "You're so sweet to ask, Mrs. S. I'll tell you what's wrong with them." She snapped her fingers at Beth Ann.

"'Our drinks arrived,'" Beth Ann read from her notebook. "'My strawberry daiquiri was as pink as liquid antacid and twice as frothy. Jackie's selection was more cosmopolitan—James Bond's favorite, a vodka martini, shaken not stirred.'"

"I thought it was stirred, not shaken," said Helen.

"What's the difference?" asked Margi.

George scratched his head. "Are we talking about martinis or cosmopolitans?"

"Do cosmopolitans have olives?" asked Grace. "I love olives."

"I love them little baby onions," said Nana. "But they don't taste real good in a Shirley Temple."

I shot a pathetic look heavenward.

Knockknockknock.

"Hold that thought," I said as I answered the door.

Wally stood in the doorway, out of breath and frazzled. He nodded toward Jackie. "Good. I was hoping she'd be here. Can I come in?"

I swept my hand toward the inner sanctum. "Be my guest."

He gave a little wave of acknowledgment to everyone before confronting Jackie. "I want you to know I'm really sorry about what happened downstairs, and you have my word that it'll never happen again."

"Words are cheap," she fired back. "What are you planning to do if it does?"

"Dietger will be looking at immediate dismissal, not only from this tour, but from the company. We have a zero tolerance policy against any type of fraternization between guests and drivers. I'll file a report. If it happens again, he's outta here."

Jackie twitched her lips, unwilling to give an inch. "His people skills are abhorrent."

"I know," Wally said contritely.

"I hope you realize that the fiasco last night was all his fault. How does he get off leading a bunch of old geezers into the Red Light District and then just dumping them?"

"I'll include that in my report," he promised.

She flexed her shoulders, thawing slightly. "All right then. I'm not a total troglodyte."

"What's a troglodyte?" whispered Nana

"Neanderthal," Tilly whispered back.

Nana waited a beat. "That don't help none."

"Is there any way I can make it up to you?" Wally glanced from Jackie to Beth Ann.

"Well, you did act the gallant when you came to our rescue." Jackie batted her lashes and brushed an imaginary fleck off his shoulder. "I didn't know you had it in you."

"Me either," said Beth Ann a little breathlessly.

"Just doing my job." But if his chest puffed out any more, his buttons would be history. "I—uh, I guess I should be getting back to my computer before the bartender forgets he's supposed to be keeping an eye on it for me. I just wanted to make sure we were squared away."

Bernice raised her hand. "Are you on Facebook?"

"Company requirement. Look for me under Peppers. Wally Peppers. I'm the only one listed."

Halfway to the door he paused, then turned around to offer Beth Ann a come-hither smile. "You mentioned you were pretty good with computers. Could I steal you away for a few minutes to help me with mine? I keep getting a message that tells me I have a runtime error 28, but I don't know what that means."

"It means you're out of stack space."

"Do you know how to fix it?"

She shoved her notebook into her purse and returned his smile, looking delirious to be singled out for special duty. "Piece of cake."

I closed the door behind them and tossed Jackie an inquiring look. "What's up with that?"

"Long story short. Dietger was making a pest of himself wanting to join us for drinks. I told him it was a private party. He interpreted that to mean we'd like to sleep with him. I told him to bugger off. He sat down at the next table, leering at us. Wally saw what was going on and read Dietger the riot act, which is when Beth

Ann and I split. Not a good scene. Dietger was *sooo* angry that he was being dressed down. No good is going to come of this. Mark my words. Our little Belgian coach driver is trouble."

I shook my head. "What I meant was, what's up with Wally? Do I detect a little sexual chemistry going on between him and your favorite client?"

"There better not be any sexual chemistry going on." Jackie trained an arch look at the door. "How can I teach Beth Ann anything about the fine art of decision-making if she decides to hang out with him instead of me? Do you realize how devastating that would be to my career? I can't have clients making their own decisions. I'd be rendered obsolete!"

She worried her bottom lip, unconsciously gnawing the gloss clear off. "You know, I should have suspected he was up to something. Before he burrowed himself into a corner with his computer, Wally stopped by our table all friendly and chatty and polite. I figured he was hitting on me." She let out a long-suffering sigh. "It happens a lot, you know."

"Maybe not this time," I suggested.

"But … but … h\ow could he prefer Beth over me?" Her face crumpled in slow, agonizing waves, her voice became a plaintive wail. "Oh, my God, Emily. I've lost my touch. I'm all washed up. I've become invisible!"

"I wish to heck you'd become invisible," cracked Bernice. "Will you park it someplace? You're blocking my view."

"Oh. Sorry." She sat down on the edge of the bed and offered smiles all around. "So, what were you doing before yours truly barged in on you?"

Pursed lips. Puckered brows. Blank looks.

"Isn't that somethin'?" Nana said, chiding herself. "I can't rightly recall what we was doin'."

"I think we were discussing snack foods," said Helen.

"Seems like we were fixing to vote on something," said Osmond. "But doggone if I can remember what."

I beamed. Failing memory wasn't such a bad thing, especially when you were trying to keep the troops focused. "We were discussing our murder investigation and what we should do next."

"That's right," said Margi. "Someone suggested we should all pitch in to help Emily prove her theory."

"I think it was Bernice," Alice marveled.

"First time that's ever happened," muttered George.

"*Eww.*" Jackie did a little pattycake clap. "The noose tightens. So, whose neck is in the noose?"

It took me less than a millisecond to pare down our tsunami of hunches into a single coherent thought. "I think that someone is killing reunion guests... to avenge something that happened at a high school outing fifty years ago." I nodded approval at myself. That's what I'd been wanting to say all along, wasn't it?

"Who?" pressed Jackie.

I frowned. "That's the part I haven't figured out yet."

"But Pete Finnegan and Paula Peavey are at the top of the leader board," said Helen.

"Pete and Paula?" Jackie let out a hoot. "Hel-looo? Your main suspects are *dead*. I can hardly wait to hear the confessions you drag out of them."

"Laura LaPierre and Gary Bouchard might be suspect," said Tilly, reading the names she'd written on her notepad.

"I think there's somethin' shady about that Hennessy fella's wife," said Nana. "She don't look like no cheerleader I ever seen."

"You think there's something shady about her?" Bernice snorted. "Get a gander of Peewee's graduation picture on his nametag. He didn't even look like the same species back then."

"People in glass houses shouldn't throw stones," Margi said in a small, tight voice.

"Should we take a vote?" asked Osmond.

"No." I waved off the idea with both hands. "Research first, then voting."

"What kinda research?" asked Nana.

"You're the ones with the smartphones and Web access, so would each of you be responsible for a single name and dig up whatever information you can on that one person? Anything you can find. Public records. Newspaper articles. Obituaries. Service organization rosters. Genealogical records. Anything that looks in the least bit relevant. When we get together again, we'll pool our findings to see if we can establish any new leads."

I could feel the energy level rise like the mercury in a Fahrenheit thermometer. "We only need to investigate about twelve people, so that should be doable. Maybe we should call them the dirty dozen."

"Can we choose the name we want to research?" asked Alice.

"Sure," I agreed. "Out of a hat."

But since I didn't have a hat, I put the names into my ice bucket instead.

"I don't like this name," whined Bernice. "Anyone want to trade?"

There were no apparent takers as everyone held fast to the slips of paper they'd selected.

"Twits."

"How am I going to do this?" asked Jackie. "I don't have a smartphone."

"The hotel has a business center. Maybe you can access a computer there. I'll have to do that, too." Either that, or call Mom, which could leave me with a bad case of hives. "Any other questions?"

They looked a little twitchy, as if they'd overdosed on caffeine. Snatching up their belongings, they put a bead on the door and began shuffling their feet.

"Okay, then." I stepped out of the way. "Meeting adjourned."

They raced across the room in a tangle of hips, legs, and elbows.

"Get to bed early," I reminded them as they shouldered their way out the door. "We have a long day ahead of us tomorrow."

Jackie stared after them. "Why do they always have to run?"

I gave her a palms-up. "Because they can?"

"What*evvv*er. Say, you got stuck with two names. You want me to give one to Beth Ann?"

"I think Wally might have plans to keep Beth Ann a little preoccupied in the days to come, so I'd better handle them myself. I don't want anyone accusing me of standing in the way of true love."

"It's so unfair," she pouted as I ushered her to the door. "She's supposed to be furthering *my* career, not *his* lovelife. What'll I do if they decide to get married?"

I snapped my fingers. "The perfect career change for you, Jack. Wedding planner!"

She cocked her head and flashed a broad smile. "Ooh. That could work."

Having orchestrated Jack's next career move, I flopped onto my bed and unfolded the slips of paper I'd pulled from the ice bucket. "Sheila Bouchard" read the first one. "Gary Bouchard" read the second.

It was only then that I recalled my brief encounter with them in the Rijksmuseum—the one where they'd been standing within earshot of Pete Finnegan as he'd ranted about divulging secrets powerful enough to ruin all his classmates.

Damn. I'd forgotten about that.

FIFTEEN

"In the fourteenth century, the medieval city of Bruges was hailed as the premier center for trade and commerce in all of northern Europe," Wally announced over the mike the next morning. "A hundred and fifty years later, a majority of its residents were living in poverty. Can you guess why?"

"Black Death!" called someone from the front of the bus.

"Nope."

"Extension of the Bush tax cuts!" blurted Margi.

"Nope."

I lunged for the seat in front of me as Dietger swerved into the passing lane, causing the whole bus to shimmy.

"Total economic collapse brung on by competition from foreign wool markets," spouted Nana. "And then one of their big rivers silted up, so they couldn't ship nuthin' to no seaports."

Wally paused. "That's right," he said, sounding a bit shocked.

She leaned toward me. "Globalization screwed 'em, but they didn't call it that back then on account of in them days, the world wasn't shaped like no globe. It was flat."

I regarded her indulgently. "National Geographic Channel?"

"*Reader's Digest.* I been a little irregular lately."

"Bruges remained economically crippled for three hundred years," Wally continued, "until British tourists rediscovered it in the mid-nineteenth century, prompting new cottage industries to spring up around chocolates, beer, and lace. It's nicknamed the 'Venice of the North' for its many canals and waterways, but you'll note that unlike Venice, it's not sinking. Its guildhalls, warehouses, cathedrals, and merchants' houses are some of the finest examples of Medieval Gothic architecture on the Continent, and lucky for us, perfectly preserved. Hitler's armies left it untouched in the war, so the city you're going to see today is the same city you would have seen six hundred years ago, with some minor updating to accommodate modern-day traffic and sanitation."

The bus swerved back into the traveling lane, causing the contents of my stomach to slosh like a rogue wave.

"Geez!" Wally barked, making me think his stomach was sloshing, too. "If you can't keep this rig on the road, how's about I find someone who can?"

Dietger had been swerving a lot since our early morning departure from Amsterdam, jolting us awake from our catnaps with his dramatic over-corrections, accelerations, and staggering lurches to left and right. Our seat belts prevented us from slamming face first into the seat in front of us, but there was nothing we could do about the sleep deprivation, which meant, we'd be touring Bruges looking like an army of zombies.

I interpreted Dietger's little temper tantrum to mean he hadn't been pleased about Wally's rebuke in the bar. Jackie had predicted there'd be consequences. Boy, she'd sure called that right.

"I'm sorry I don't got no research to report to you this mornin'," Nana apologized as she fussed with her seat belt. "Me and Tilly was full a good intentions last night, but listenin' to the financial news put us both to sleep."

"Pretty boring stuff, huh?"

"Don't know. It was in Dutch."

I'd had good intentions, too. I'd trekked down to the business center a couple of times, but on each occasion, someone was using the computer, so around midnight, I'd thrown in the towel and gone to bed, without finding out any more about Sheila and Gary Bouchard than I'd known the day before.

"You want we should call you the minute we dig up anything promisin' on our suspects?" asked Nana.

I frowned. "That could get awkward, especially if I'm standing beside the person you're ratting on."

"We could text you."

I perked up, suddenly enamored with the new advances in phone technology. "That could actually work."

"You bet it could. And all's you'd have to do is read the message. You wouldn't have to send nuthin' back."

"Okay. Show me what I need to know."

So while Wally continued to entertain us with a brief history of Bruges, Nana instructed me on the dos and don'ts of text messaging. By the time we entered the city limits, I figured I knew as much about sending text messages as a fifth grader, so I could hardly wait to strut my stuff.

"When the little alert goes off, all's you gotta do is read what's on the screen. It's real easy, dear. And if you got questions about the message, type in a reply just like I showed you."

I regarded my cellphone with newfound affection. "Okay. I can do this." I slid it back into the side pocket of my shoulder bag. "By the way, whose name did you draw last night?"

She pulled the paper out of the handwarming pouch of her Vikings sweatshirt. "Ricky Hennessy," she said, after rechecking the name.

We catapulted forward as Dietger jumped the curb and jammed on the brakes, executing a tooth-rattling stop in front of a row of two-story mercantile shops.

Gasps. Grunts. Groans.

"Did we stop like that on purpose, or was our tires shot out?" asked Nana.

Wally made a robotic move into the center aisle, his stiff body language signaling that his temper was simmering on low burn. "The streets in the old town can't accommodate coaches, so we need to travel the rest of the way on foot. Does everyone have their map?"

We waved them above our heads in response.

"I've starred the spot where we're parked because it's where Dietger will pick us up again in four hours"—his voice bristled with sarcasm—"if he's able to navigate the road without putting the bus in a ditch someplace. And as I look out the window, I see that our local guide is waiting for us, so why don't we step off the bus and join her?"

We gathered around our guide like drones around the queen bee. She was middle-aged, wore sturdy shoes, and kinda had a

French/Dutch/German thing going on with her accent that forced us to have to listen really closely to what she was saying. Her name was Gheertrude.

"I welcome you to Flanders," she said cheerily.

Stunned silence.

"Wait just a darned minute," balked Bernice. "We're supposed to be in Bruges."

Gheertrude laughed. "You *are* in Bruges. But Bruges is in Flanders."

"I thought Bruges was in Belgium," said Helen.

"It is," Gheertrude allowed.

"So we're not in Flanders?" asked Grace.

"No, no. You're still in Flanders."

"You just said we're in Belgium," corrected Bernice.

"We *are* in Belgium. Bruges is the capital of the province of West Flanders in the Flemish region of Belgium."

Thoughtful silence.

Margi raised her hand. "I'm sorry. Where are we?"

"Why don't we straighten that out later?" suggested Wally. "Moving right along, we're giving you a host of options today. Option one: you can remain with Gheertrude and me for the walking tour and canal ride, and we'll escort you back here to the pickup point. Option two: you can take the walking tour as far as the market square, then part company with us to get a bite to eat, shop, or take a carriage ride. You'll be on your own to find your way back. Option three: head into Old Town on your own, eat, shop, then meet up with us for the canal ride, which I've marked on your maps. Option four: none of the above. Just make sure you get back to the pickup point on time."

My guys looked stricken. For people afflicted with lateness anxiety, being presented with options that could make them late was no option at all. Even if they could read a map better than the Rand McNally atlas guys, they needed to be reassured that someone in charge would guide them through the city streets and back to this spot before the bus took off. And there was really only one person in charge.

"We'll take option one," I told Wally, making an executive decision for the group.

"Me, too," said Jackie.

"And me," said Beth Ann, causing Wally's eyes to brighten and a hint of a smile to soften his lips.

In the final tally, everyone took option one, though a few reunion people reserved the right to change their minds once they had a looksee at the central market. I wasn't sure how the gang would be able to handle their individual investigations with the Mainers breathing down their necks, but I figured they were all pretty clever, so they'd find a way.

"Our first stop this morning is only a few steps away," announced Gheertrude as she gestured toward a side street. "The Begijnhof, a serene cluster of white-washed houses, where, for six hundred years, girls and widows dedicated their lives to charitable work without taking religious vows, and Minnewater, also called 'the Lake of Love', a thirteenth-century, man-made reservoir, famous for its beautiful white swans and utter tranquility. Please to follow after me."

The side street was called Wijngaardstraat, and was possibly as wide as a New York City alley, but a lot more high class. Tidy brick buildings lined both sides of the tidy brick pavement, their decorative doors inviting passersby into tea rooms, chocolate shops, and art galleries. As we strolled past an unassuming hotel hidden among the bricks, I glanced through the lobby window, noticing something that caused me to hesitate, then stop dead in my tracks.

"*Psssst!* Jack."

She turned her head in my direction.

"I'm ducking in here for a minute. I'll catch up."

She gave me a thumbs-up before stutter-stepping over the pavers in her stiletto boots. I guess she hadn't been daunted by the fact that the streets in Bruges were cobbled.

I entered the hotel and made a beeline for a table that sat in front of the lobby window. On the table sat two computers—powered up and sitting idle.

Yes! This was my chance.

I approached the front desk and smiled at the clerk, a handsome young man with a buff body and bedroom eyes. "Would it be possible for me to use one of your lobby computers?"

"Of course, madam. The computers are set up for the convenience of our guests."

"I'm not a guest. I'm staying at another hotel. In Amsterdam."

"Ahh. That presents something of a problem."

"Could I pay you to use it for a short time?"

"We're not set up to accept off-the-books fees, madam."

"Even if it's a matter of life or death?"

He lifted his brows. "You're American?"

"Guilty."

He motioned me closer. "Do you watch the Fox Network show *American Idol*?"

"Wouldn't miss it," I lied.

"Me, too! I watch it at my cousin's. He has a satellite dish. I even follow it on Facebook."

"Me, too!" I lied again.

Curving his mouth into a slow smile, he scribbled something on a piece of paper and handed it to me. "The code to access the computer."

"Really?"

He winked. "Let it be our secret."

With the small front lobby all to myself, I typed in the access code and in a few keystrokes was staring at the Google homepage. Now, where to begin? I typed "Gary Bouchard," hit the return key, and in less than a nanosecond pulled up more than four million bits of information on the Gary Bouchards of the world. Four million. *You gotta be kidding me.*

I decided to narrow my search. My fingers flew over the keyboard. "Gary Bouchard Bangor Maine." I hit the return.

Twelve thousand hits.

Okay. Twelve thousand I could handle.

I spent the next fifteen minutes unearthing pieces of Gary Bouchard's life on a website called, *Who's Who in Bangor.* His car dealership was apparently the largest in southern Maine, with satellite dealerships as far north as Presque Isle, which practically sat on the Canadian border. He'd received several Businessman of the Year awards from local service organizations, was an officer in the Knights of Columbus, and sponsored a basketball camp every summer for underprivileged youth. Gee, that was nice of him. He was a longtime member of the Bangor city council, president of the fine arts commission, and served on the board of trustees for

St. Francis Xavier High School. My eyes slowly glazed over. The guy sounded like a saint. An elitist saint, but a saint nonetheless. I obviously needed to dig deeper into his background to find the real dirt.

I accessed the local paper and plunged into the archives, hitting the mother lode under "weddings." Gary's name led me to a bridal photo of Sheila in her "*peau de soie* gown, sewn with seed pearls and aurora borealis crystals." Wow. The article described every single detail of the wedding, from the bride's and attendants' gowns, to the altar flowers and mother-of-the-bride outfits. It listed out-of-town guests, the country club where the reception was held, and where the newlyweds would be traveling on their honeymoon.

I studied the photo of Sheila (Eaton) Bouchard, thinking how incredibly young she'd been when she married. Babies having babies. But she and Gary were still together, so they'd obviously found a way to make it work. The article mentioned that she'd graduated third in her class from St. Francis Xavier and would be "at home" after the honeymoon, setting up housekeeping in their new house, which had been a wedding gift from her parents.

I read that twice to make sure I wasn't seeing things. A house as a wedding gift? Who could afford it? My parents had given us a blender, but it had twenty-four speeds and a self-cleaning button, so it was a really good one.

The article wrapped up with the scoop on the groom. He'd been the highest scoring basketball player in Xavier's history, graduated fifth in his class, and planned to attend Husson College in the fall to pursue a degree in business, while at the same time joining his father at Bouchard Motors as part owner.

Gary's life had apparently been all mapped out for him, but I wondered if Gary had done any of the planning. He might have pursued a basketball career if Ricky Hennessy hadn't monkeyed with the toilet paper in the boys' bathroom. He might have attended one of the big Ivy League schools if Sheila hadn't been pushing marriage. He might have tested his wings in another part of the country if his in-laws hadn't anchored him in place with a new house. At some point in his life had he rebelled against the status quo and exacted revenge on the people who'd stolen his options? But what could he have done that Pete Finnegan might have found out about? And how did Paula fit in?

I accessed birth announcements, obituaries, and entries in Bangor's social calendar. I found a birth announcement for Gary Allen Bouchard III a few months after the wedding and an obituary for Gary Bouchard Senior two years later. Gee. He'd only been forty-five years old. Died in a hunting accident. I clicked on a link to find that Gary Senior had been fatally wounded when his gun accidentally discharged while he was deer hunting with Gary Junior.

I stared at the words until the letters ran into each other. Holy crap. Was this my smoking gun? Literally?

I scanned the rest of the article, learning that Gary Junior would be taking over the family car dealership, insuring that loyal customers would suffer no disruption in sales or service. Armed with his two-year business degree, twenty-one-year-old Gary professed readiness to step into his father's shoes, although his mother would remain the titular head of the business. Accessing a second link, I found another obituary—that of Gary's mother, who died in a car accident eight months later. "A defect in the braking system of her Chrysler Saratoga," a subsequent article reported, explaining how Mrs. Bouchard had careened down Newbury Street hill and crashed headlong into a tree. I didn't know if Gary's dealership had been responsible for maintaining her brakes, but I did know that with both his parents dead, Gary was free to run the whole show without interference from anyone. Barely in his twenties, he becomes one of the wealthiest men in the city, which probably did a lot to make up for a few of his earlier disappointments.

Coincidence, or deliberate plan?

I expanded my search to include Sheila Bouchard and in a few clicks discovered entries in the social calendar announcing her induction onto the boards of the Maine State Historical Society, the Daughters of the American Revolution, and the Junior League of Bangor. She even established her own social club, the Minerva Society, where local women came together on a weekly basis to discuss literature and the arts. I found pictures of an ever-evolving Sheila with the conductor of the Bangor Symphony orchestra at a Christmas extravaganza, and with St. Xavier's Sister Hippolytus at the parish's annual Coffee Party. I studied the photo of the nun, remembering this was the teacher none of the girls had liked. Sister Hippo. I wondered if she was still alive. She'd be pretty old now, but when nuns retired to the Mother House, they oftentimes seemed to live forever. Kinda like Osmond.

Sheila graced the pages of the *Bangor Daily News* throughout the decades, and almost exclusively on the front page—at the opening of the State Fair, at the ribbon cutting for a new wing of the medical center, at the Bowdoin College graduation ceremony when Gary III received his degree, at the county courthouse where she gazed sourly at a jubilant Paula Peavey.

Courthouse?

I scanned the accompanying article. Oh, my God. Paula had won a discrimination suit against Sheila and the Minerva Society. Paula's application for membership had been rejected on the basis that since she hadn't graduated in the top tenth of her class, she wasn't actually smart enough to discuss *Lolita* or *Green Eggs and Ham*. Paula had called foul, and the judgment had been decided in her favor, along with a significant cash payment for damages. A week later, another article announced the dissolution of the Minerva Society, which "in its two years of existence, had become the premier ladies group in Bangor, surpassing even the Junior League in popularity among the well-heeled."

I leaned back in my chair, thinking. Had Sheila eventually forgiven Paula for the lawsuit, or had she bided her time until she could even the score? Paula had definitely knocked her down a few pegs. Sheila wouldn't have liked that. But how far would Sheila have gone to get even? Could she have been bitter and angry enough to commit murder? The idea seemed pretty far-fetched, and yet one thing I'd learned in my travel experience was that, what seemed far-fetched to me might seem perfectly normal to a homicidal maniac.

I stared out the lobby window in a daze. Was this the kind of information that would be useful to the police? Or would they tell me to come back when I'd found a direct link between my suspects and their victims? I'd already found a link between Paula and Sheila, but I needed something concrete to connect Pete to Gary. Something that I could point to and say, "See this? I think Pete is dead because he threatened to reveal this about Gary." But what could Pete possibly know?

I heard a loud rapping on the window. Jackie grimaced at me with every muscle in her face before mouthing something I couldn't hear.

"What?" I mouthed back.

Rolling her eyes in disgust, she charged through the front door and into the lobby. "I said—What are you doing in here? Gheertrude isn't waiting for you. But I know which way she's headed, so if we leave now, we might be able to catch up."

I typed a flurry of words, my eyes riveted on the monitor. "Gimme a minute. I need to find out what Pete Finnegan did for a living."

She hovered over me, her foot tapping out an impatient rhythm on the floor. "Are you coming?"

"Just ... just ... I'm almost there."

"Are you supposed to be using this computer?"

"The front desk clerk gave me the access code. Free of charge."

"Get out of here." She stilled her foot and settled into the chair beside me. "What is it?"

I gave her the code.

"*Ooh*. Google access." She paused. "I can't just Google the word Peewee. What's the guy's real name?"

I continued clicking on links. "Check the guest roster in your tour packet."

She rummaged through her designer bag. Shuffling. Sorting. Swearing. "Let's see. Here it is. 'Peewee' Crowley. Phoenix, Arizona. This can't be right. Are they telling us his real name *is* Peewee?"

"Try the Francis Xavier yearbook. Maybe they've archived copies online." I combined Pete's name with various businesses in Bangor and got no hits. Guess he wasn't a local merchant.

"Okay, his real name is Norman Crowley," said Jackie, fingers flying and screen changing as fast as the beams in a laser light show.

I tried banking, the bar association, the medical field. Nothing.

"Ta-da!" She veed her arms over her head. "Norman Crowley was drafted right out of high school. Here's a picture of him and some of his buddies packing up and heading off to boot camp. 'Local Boys Put College on Hold to Serve Country First,' is the title of the newspaper article. Man, he really was a squirt back then."

I sat straight up in my chair. The draft? That's right! Up until the early seventies, all men had been inducted into the military, even my dad. Was it possible that Pete and Gary had served together? Maybe even been in the same platoon or regiment?

I Googled the United States Military.

"I know people change," Jackie quipped, "but this kid in the picture looks *nothing* like the guy who's on the tour with us."

"You don't look anything like your high school graduation picture either," I reminded her. I stared at the required fields I needed to fill in to access any information on Peter Finnegan's military history. Damn. I didn't know any of this stuff.

"At least I have the same nose," Jackie argued. "And cheekbones. That's more than I can say for Norman Crowley."

Impasse. I'd have to forget the military for now. What next? Could Pete have been an undertaker? A teacher?

"Maybe Peewee underwent a growth spurt when he was in the service." Jackie's fingers danced over the keyboard, nails clicking. "I wonder if the newspaper shot a picture when he came home?"

I leaned back in my chair. Flummoxed.

"Aha! Private Norman Crowley . . . blah, blah, blah . . . discharged after two years . . . blah, blah, blah . . . There's an article, but no picture. I guess we'll just have to assume he grew, and had a nose job."

I checked the time. "We better go. Let's hope Gheertrude is walking slowly."

"Did you see this photo of Pete Finnegan? It's on the same page."

"What photo?"

"The one where he's posing with the carcass of a deer he shot on the first day of hunting season. 'Local Man Shoots Twenty-Four Point Buck.' Ick."

Pete had been a deer hunter?

Bingo.

SIXTEEN

"So, does this blow the hell out of your senior class outing theory?"

"I don't know what it does, but I'll feel less anxious if I can convince Wally to pass the information along to the Amsterdam police, for whatever it's worth."

We were taking a breather on an ancient stone bridge that offered a panoramic view of the city with its towering church spires, witch-capped turrets, winding lanes, iconic gables, hidden alleyways, moss-covered walls, and ivy-clad dwellings. Beneath us, in a narrow canal flanked by houses that looked centuries old, fairytale swans glided in silence, their passage barely ruffling the water.

We hadn't spied the rest of the group yet, but given that Jackie had developed a killer limp that was slowing us down to a crawl, I wasn't surprised. In a footrace between seniors in flats and transsexuals in stilettos, seniors win hands down, especially if there's food involved.

"Both Gary and Pete were hunters," I rattled on as I snapped a photo of a step-gabled house across the street. "What if Pete had been hunting the day Gary Senior suffered his mishap? What if he saw the whole thing?"

Jackie winced as she tested her weight on her right foot. "You don't think the Bouchards would have noticed Pete Finnegan standing around, gawking at them?"

"Not if Pete had built a blind for himself. He could have been so well camouflaged, he might have been invisible to the human eye."

"So you're speculating that Pete saw something he wasn't meant to see?"

I panned to the left and pressed my shutter, capturing a horse and open carriage as they clattered over the cobblestones. "Think about it, Jack. What if the accident didn't happen exactly like Gary Junior said? What if Pete could implicate Gary in his father's death?"

"Then Gary would have good reason to push Pete down a flight of stairs and hope for the worst. But if Pete saw something, why didn't he speak up at the time of the accident? I mean, wouldn't that be the normal thing to do? And if Gary *knew* that Pete knew, why did he wait over forty years to deal with him?"

"Okay, I still have a few holes in my theory, but I'm getting closer."

Ting!

"Text message alert," Jackie deadpanned. She nodded at my shoulder bag. "It's yours."

"How do you know?" I quickly dug out my phone.

"My ring tones are a lot more annoying."

I felt a sudden rush of excitement. "It's from Nana. My first!" I read the message on the screen. "'Where r u?' Aw, isn't that cute?"

205

I held the phone up so she could read the message for herself. "It's like reading a little vanity license plate."

"Really, Emily," Jackie said in an undertone. "Please don't tell me you've never seen texting shorthand. What planet have you been living on?"

"The same one you've been living on, only in the technologically challenged section. Do you want to send the reply?" I handed her the phone. "Go ahead, smartie. Wow me."

She flexed her thumbs in the same way a gunslinger might flex his trigger finger. "If you insist."

I spread my map out on the low wall of the bridge and traced several squiggly lines before stabbing an unremarkable speck. "Tell her we're standing right here."

Jackie looked over my shoulder. "Oh, yeah. That's really helpful."

With a theatrical sigh, she labored over my phone for the next two minutes before handing it back. "Would you do me a favor and buy yourself a phone with a dedicated keypad?"

"Sure. Right after I buy the Lear jet I've been eying. So what did you tell her?"

"Sightseeing. Will catch up."

I eyed my screen as the alert chimed again. "Text message from Margi Swanson." I punched the view key. "Bless her heart. She's really been doing her research. Listen to this. 'Paula Peavey sued Penobscot Auto Repair forty years ago. Claimed faulty brake repair work caused accident.'" I exchanged a look with Jackie. "Do you suppose Paula did anything with her life besides sue people?"

"Maybe she was a serial suer," said Jackie. "Winning frivolous lawsuits can be a lucrative profession for people who prefer not to work for a living."

Ting!

In the next few minutes I was bombarded with a flurry of messages that pointed to one conclusion: If you need to dig up information on the Internet, have an eighty-year-old do the searching for you.

From Alice: "Mike McManus attended U of Maine, served in military, married Mary Lou O'Leary, relocated to DC. Spent none of adult life in Bangor. Worked in insurance industry as safety inspector. Retired after thirty years of service."

From Helen: "Chip Soucy sued by Paula Peavey after she slipped on wet floor in his grocery market. Damages bankrupted him. Lost store. Unresolved tax issues up the wazoo."

From Bernice: "We're in stupid lace store watching demonstration. BORING. No poop on Bobby Guerrette. What a waste of time."

From Nana: "Ricky Hennessy opened Penobscot Auto Repair after high school. Went bankrupt after being sued by Paula Peavey ten years later. Spotty work record until landing job as gas station attendant and repairman at Pine Tree State Tires and Auto Repair. Lots of tax troubles."

From Osmond: "Mary Lou McManus (born O'Leary) earned nursing degree from Eastern Maine General Hospital. Moved to DC area after marrying Mike McManus. Worked at Walter Reed Hospital in surgical unit. Two children, Mike Junior and Laura."

From Grace: "Mindy Hennessy's wedding took up five columns in newspaper. Name appears eight times in birth announcement section. Worked part-time at Freese's Department Store, J. J. Newberry's Five and Dime Store, and Standard Shoes. Trouble with IRS."

From Bernice: "No one wears lace. Why do I have to watch this? I notice YOU'RE not here."

From George: "Laura LaPierre attended Colby College and did graduate work at Stanford. Remained in CA. Headed admissions office at Berkeley. Married decorated army vet. One daughter."

From Margi again: "Paula Peavey lived in family home on Maple Street entire life. Can't find work record. Showed dogs. Many awards. Constant trouble with IRS."

From Tilly: "Pete Finnegan attended Bowdoin College. Worked for local IRS as tax examiner and later tax compliance officer. Never married. Avid hunter and woodworker. Photo of him and 24-point buck in paper."

"Oh, my God, Jack. Look at this."

She frowned as she read. "Tilly must have found the same picture I did, but I don't get it. What's so special about a twenty-four point buck? How many points are they supposed to have?"

"The buck isn't the important part. Pete was the tax police. An IRS agent. A G-man! Do you know what that means?"

"Of course I know what it means. Federal retirement. The government offers much better benefits than Social Security."

"No! It means he was in a position to make his classmates' lives a living hell, and I suspect that's exactly what he did." I scrolled back through my messages. "A slew of them had a history of tax troubles—Chip Soucy, Ricky and Mindy, Paula Peavey. I bet if I were a better searcher, I'd probably discover that the Bouchards have been battling the IRS most of their married lives, too."

Jackie's eyes glazed over with horror. "My Tom was audited once. He said it was the most terrifying experience of his life. Even more terrifying than his first Brazilian wax."

My brain was clicking at a thousand miles an hour. "Paula drove them into bankruptcy and Pete rode roughshod over whatever money they had left. What a duo. They must have been the two most hated people in Bangor."

"Which makes you wonder why they ever came on this trip. They sign up to spend eight days with the enemy, and they think nothing's going to happen? Duh?"

My thought process executed a sudden detour. Would anyone have had the opportunity to settle old scores with Pete and Paula if the reunion had been held in Bangor? Would the hometown setting have been too safe to create any kind of chaos? Was the reunion held abroad for the sole purpose of inserting Pete and Paula into unfamiliar surroundings so they'd be more vulnerable? Oh, my God. Were Pete and Paula's deaths premeditated? Could the reunion be nothing more than a convenient ruse to commit murder?

"Whose idea was it to have a class reunion in Holland anyway?" asked Jackie.

I felt a wrenching in my gut as I supplied the answer.

"Mary Lou McManus."

———

"You been able to figure out who done it yet, dear?"

After a fifteen-minute hike over meandering canals, through parks with umbrellaed tables, around whimsical sculptures, and past stone houses rippling with ivy, we arrived at the Market Square, to find Nana and the gang exactly where her latest text message said they'd be—in front of an official-looking building with a soaring octagonal tower.

"I'm coming up with a new suspect every five minutes," I confessed. "I'm making myself crazy."

"You want we should hold off sendin' you any more messages?"

"No! Keep them coming. They're helping me piece together a narrative of the Mainers' lives. I just don't know how many pieces are involved."

Market Square reminded me of some of the grand squares of Italy. The center was filled with canopied booths as plentiful as carnival tents, where vendors hawked flowers and food, clothing and jewelry. Flagpoles ringed the far side, their heraldic banners floating overhead like United Nations flags. Horse-drawn carriages clattered by in the street, chased by bicycles pedaled by men in three-piece suits, and women in skirts and high heels. A row of guild houses flanked the opposite side of the square, their brick facades boasting vibrant shades of red and brown, their stepped gables as picturesque as the cafes that spilled onto the sidewalks beneath them. I doubted many Americans had ever heard of Bruges, but it was their loss, because walking through Bruges was like strolling through the pages of a storybook, where all the ugly ducklings had turned into swans, and every house was a fairytale castle.

Ting!

I retrieved a message from Osmond, who was leaning against a bicycle rack about six feet away, his eyes glued to his phone. "Maid of Honor at Mary Lou's wedding was Laura LaPierre. After the wedding, little contact between them. Checked old phone logs. No record of long-distance calls between DC and CA until about a year ago."

A year ago? Had Mary Lou and Laura planned the reunion to-gether?

But wait a minute, Osmond had checked old phone logs? Logs from four or five decades ago? I tossed him a curious look. How in the world had he done that?

"Would you excuse me for a minute, Nana?"

I held my phone in front of Osmond's face. "Good work on Mary Lou McManus," I complimented him. "But how were you able to check old phone logs? Who are you? The CIA?"

"Your grandmother showed me a website where I could access all sorts of archived classified files. Phone records. Buying habits. Financial records. Medical records. Did you know the government keeps records on all that stuff?"

I guess I did now. I narrowed my eyes suspiciously. "When you say Nana 'showed' you, do you mean she gave you the web address, or she helped you hack into the site?"

"Oh, she helped me hack into the site, all right. I wouldn't have known how to do it otherwise. But it was pretty easy once she showed me, so maybe I can do it on my own next time."

Oh, God. "No! No more hacking. Ever. Here's the thing: It's against the law! Do you want to become the world's oldest person to serve time in the Big House?"

He mulled that over. "Would I get my name printed in the *Guinness Book of World Records?* I've always wanted to see my name in print for something other than an obituary."

"This is serious, Osmond. You can search legitimate sites on the Web without having to resort to the cloak-and-dagger stuff. Okay?"

He sighed. "Does that mean you don't want to hear about the e-mails Mary Lou and Laura have been sending to each other?"

I froze in place. "E-mails?"

"Yeah. E-mail accounts are really easy to break into. Mary Lou and Laura reconnected on Facebook right after Laura's husband passed away, and they began to correspond by e-mail—the usual chitchat about kids and grandkids and a lot of talk about plans for the reunion. They did a lot of reminiscing, too. Mostly about how mean Paula Peavey had been in high school and wondering if she'd dare show up at the reunion."

But Paula *had* shown up and, from what I'd seen, had been acting as mean as the teenager she'd once been. Had I missed an angry exchange between the three women? In the Red Light District? After the group had split up? Is that why Mike hadn't been able to find Mary Lou and Laura that night? Had the two women run into Paula on the way back to the hotel and dealt with her once and for all?

No. I didn't want to point the finger at Mary Lou and Laura. I liked them too much.

"Excuse me, Emily." Alice flashed her phone in front of me. "I know I'm supposed to be researching Mike McManus, but I ran across this and thought you might want to see it anyway." She pressed a button that activated a murky, reddish-yellow image of a sidewalk.

"What am I looking at?" I squinted at the screen.

"Video from our hotel's surveillance camera on the night Paula Peavey died."

I stared at her, wide-eyed, my voice dropping to a whisper. "You accessed a surveillance camera? A private surveillance camera that's probably protected by all kinds of Dutch laws?"

"Oh, sure. It's a high-tech system, but the software program was really easy to hack into. Your grandmother—"

I slapped my hands over my ears. "I'm not listening. Just play the video. Then erase it!"

I continued looking at the same image on the screen. Sidewalk. Sidewalk. Heavyset man and woman coming into the frame. Walking quickly. Looking over their shoulders as if afraid they were being followed. Pausing. Looking both ways.

I studied the screen more closely. Who was that? The Hennessys? Mindy thrust her arm in the direction from which they'd come. Ricky getting in her face, his body language implying that he was yelling. What was she pointing at? Why was he yelling? Who did they think was following them?

Mindy crying. Ricky yelling some more. Mindy storming out of frame. Ricky pulling something that looked like a scarf out of the pocket of his letter jacket. Ricky rubbing the material against his cheek before crumpling it into a ball. Ricky disappearing from the frame in the direction of the canal. Ricky walking back into frame without the scarf in his hand. Hmm. What had he done? Thrown it into the canal? Whose scarf was it? And why did he have to get rid of it? Black screen.

"Do you still want me to erase it?" asked Alice.

Did I? I hedged. "*Nnn*not quite yet." Damn. If the police caught up to us, we'd all be sharing a cell in the Big House.

Ting!

"Text message alert!" Alice and Osmond tittered in unison.

I opened my message. From Jackie: "Mrs. S. just helped me hack into the AZ Dept. of Motor Vehicles. Here's the most recent driver's license photo for Norman Peewee Crowley. Notice anything?"

I switched screens to access the photo.

Nuts. The guy in Norman Crowley's license photo wasn't the same guy who was on the trip with us.

I sucked in my breath. *Holy Crap*! So if our Peewee wasn't the real Peewee, who the heck was he?

Ting!

From Jackie: "Told you so."

I swung around to find her kibitzing with Nana beneath a streetlight that looked to have been imported from Victorian England. She acknowledged my reaction with a self-satisfied smile before tossing her head toward Mike McManus, who was chatting with the fake Peewee. She typed a quick message that arrived almost instantly.

"What now?"

A hand clapped down on my shoulder. I turned around to find Wally standing grim-faced behind me. "Could I speak to you privately, Emily?"

A mantra kept playing in my head as I followed him through the crowd to a spot that was beyond earshot of the tour group. *Please don't tell me the Dicks are dead. Please don't tell me the Dicks are dead.*

"I owe you an apology," he said without preamble.

"For what?"

"You were right. I was wrong."

"Well, good for me." I had no idea what he was referring to. "So, what was I right about?"

"You said the police would want to investigate Paula's death more closely after the autopsy, and you were spot-on."

I kinda remembered saying that, but I'd said so much over the last twenty-four hours that I was having a hard time keeping it all straight. But one thing seemed clear. "Are you saying the police are back on the case?"

He nodded. "It was because of the bruising that showed up post-mortem. The medical examiner determined Paula's death couldn't have been an accident. You were right about that, too. She didn't fall. She was pushed."

SEVENTEEN

THE CANAL RIDE HAD been a blur.

I vaguely remember ducking as we'd motored beneath bridges low enough to knock our heads off, oohing as we'd passed a quiet commune of whitewashed almshouses, and aahing as we'd sped along the Canal of Ghent with its buzzing boat traffic. But mostly what I remember was wishing I hadn't been right about Paula Peavey.

Things had gotten entirely too complicated.

Had Mary Lou and Laura teamed up to push Paula into the canal? Or had Mindy and Ricky Hennessy beaten them to it? Chip Soucy had sidestepped the question about whether he'd seen Paula after the blowup in the Red Light District. Was that because he'd taken a long look at her before he'd pushed her into the water? Were my suspicions about the Bouchards legitimate? Or was I doing nothing more than grasping at straws?

And what about Pete? Could Mary Lou and Laura have ganged up on him, too? But why would they want to? They'd had little to do with him in high school and even less to do with him afterward. Chip and the Hennessys might have wanted the IRS out of their financial hair, but would they have murdered Pete to resolve the problem? Why did the Hennessys look so guilty on the surveillance video? What was with the scarf that Ricky had gotten rid of? And if Peewee wasn't Norman Crowley, who was he, and why was he here?

Most puzzling of all, was any of this connected to Charlotte's death?

I grabbed the handrail on the seat in front of me as the bus exited the off-ramp on three wheels, sending packages flying and our stomachs into our throats.

"I have motion sickness pills!" announced Margi as she waved a carton over her head. "A sampler pack. In six delicious flavors."

I placed a steadying hand on Nana, who sat calm as a clock beside me, flipping through the most recent photos she'd shot with her camera phone.

"Jesus, Mary, and Joseph," I sputtered when the tires stopping screeching.

"Don't pay him no mind, dear," she advised without looking up. "I spent fifty years ridin' with your Grampa Sippel. Compared to him, this fella's a regular Mario Andretti." She angled her phone toward me. "Isn't this a nice shot of Wally and Beth Ann?"

It was a head shot of the two of them, eyes twinkling and smiles stretching from ear to ear. "You must have taken this before Wally found out about Paula's autop—" I froze mid-word, the final syllable sliding back down my throat. Wally had asked me to keep mum about the autopsy results until we got back to Amsterdam and received further instructions from the police. *Good going, Emily. Way to keep mum.*

I sidled a look at Nana. On a brighter note, if her attention had wandered, maybe she hadn't heard me.

"When you was talkin' to Wally, dear, he didn't have no bad news to share about the Dicks, did he? Since we run outta stuff for Grace and Helen to do, they're gettin' awful worried."

I settled back in my seat, relieved she'd missed my *faux pas*. "As a matter of fact, Wally talked to the police earlier, and they told him they haven't received any leads on the Dicks, but they've assigned an officer to the case. That's encouraging, isn't it?"

"I s'pose. Maybe I should tell the girls that no news is good news."

"That's the spirit."

She fidgeted with her camera photos once again. "So when's Wally gonna tell us that Paula was pushed?"

My eyelids flapped upward so fast, they nearly drove my eyelashes into my skull. Leaning in her direction, I said in a manic rush of breath, "Howdoyouknowthat? Nooneknowsthat." I wheezed in sudden horror. "Didyouhackintotheautopsyreport?"

"I'm not that brave, dear. Holland don't like foreigners hackin' into their government files, so if they was to convict me, I'd have to serve more years in the pokey than I got left on the earth."

"Here's a thought. You can be thrown into jail back home, too."

"But if I was back home, I'd get more visitors."

"Howdidyoufindout? OhmyGod. DidBernicetellyou?"

"It's on account of the course they was offerin' at the senior center, dear. A young fella from the clinic showed us ways to deal with hearin' loss, and I turned out to be pretty good at one a them."

I eyed her narrowly. "Which one? Eavesdropping?"

"Lip readin'. He said he never seen no one take to it quicker than me. Isn't that somethin'?"

I stared at her, dumbfounded. "You can read lips? Really?"

"You bet. At least, I can read 'em as long as I can see someone's mouth, but it's kinda hard when folks walk in front of you. If it hadn't been for Peewee, I mighta caught Wally's whole conversation."

"How many people have you told about Paula?"

"I been keepin' it to myself, dear. No tellin' what the killer might do if word leaks out that the police are on to 'im. Folks like that will do crazy things when they're backed into a corner."

Yeah, just like a rat.

"Emily, I been thinkin'. You don't s'pose the Dicks have ended up like Paula, do you?"

"No!" I lied. "They're lost. I'm sure they're lost, or, or something. Remember, they're still wearing the wrong glasses, so they probably can't read street signs worth beans."

"I just hope they wasn't nowhere around Paula when she got pushed. I worry that if the killer seen 'em..." She paused, her voice faltering.

"I know," I finished for her in a hushed tone. I clasped her hand in mine. "I'm worried about that, too."

———

After a brief stop at Flanders Fields to visit a cemetery dedicated to the soldiers who died in the Great War, we headed toward the coast, to another town I'd never heard of.

"Oostende is a resort town on the North Sea," Wally informed us as we rattled down roads that cut through land as wide and flat as an Indiana corn field. "The city center is a concrete jungle of high rises, shops, and grand promenades, but the real attraction in Oostende is its uninterrupted stretch of white sand beach, which played a prominent role in World War II. Hitler was so fearful that the coastal beaches of Europe would be invaded by allied armies, that as a deterrent, he ordered an intricate system of trenches, bunkers, and pillboxes to be built from Norway to the Spanish border. It was called the Atlantic Wall, and we're going to see a well-preserved section of it today."

"I thought we were scheduled to stop for Belgian waffles," shouted Ricky.

"We are," said Wally. "After our visit."

"But I'm hungry now."

A tightlipped pause. "There's a cafeteria in the museum if you'd prefer to eat rather than tour the site."

"Do they serve Belgian waffles?" asked Mindy.

"I don't know what the cafeteria serves," admitted Wally. "But the tour takes ninety minutes, so pick your poison. Food or history? It's your choice. But you'll need a ticket no matter what you decide to do, so you need to pick that up first."

Dietger gunned the engine as we passed through the entrance gates, laying rubber across the parking lot like a hood on a joyride. Screeching into an empty space, he jammed on the brakes and snickered into the rearview mirror as the bus shimmied to a full stop. Wally was first out the door, and from what I could tell by his body language, he wasn't a happy camper.

We followed a well-marked path through a field of tall coastal grasses toward a sprawling complex of buildings that were all painted the same color yellow. I hung out behind my group like an old mother hen, wanting them to enjoy the open-air museum, but hesitant to let them out of my sight. I was battling an unnerving feeling that something bad was about to happen, but my psychic wires were so crossed right now, my reception was probably a little dodgy. I mean, maybe what I was feeling was nothing more than an acute case of hunger pangs.

"Emily! Slow down, will you?"

I turned to find Jackie leaning on Beth Ann's shoulder as she hobbled toward me, her mouth rounded into an O of pain. "Maintaining status as a fashion icon can be such a bitch." She braced her free arm on my shoulder and hung her head, studying her spike-heeled size fourteens. "Tell me honestly, Emily, do these boots make my feet look big?"

Everything made her feet look big. Shoes. Boots. Sidewalks. But the great thing about a true friend is, she'd rather dodge the truth than hurt your feelings. "What a dumb question. I'm not even going to dignify it with an answer. But you don't look as if you're up for a ninety-minute walking tour."

"My feet and I are going to sit this one out in the cafeteria. But I'm sending in Beth Ann to do reconnaissance."

"On what?"

She broke out in a smile. "I have a plan."

As we shuffled our way to the ticket office, she laid out the elaborate plan she'd concocted to discover Peewee's true identity. "I figure his real name is on his driver's license, so if we relieve him of his wallet, we just might find out who the heck he is."

"We'll handle it like a tag team," said Beth Ann. "If he heads for the cafeteria, the ball will be in Jackie's court, but if he decides to tour the wall, he'll be all mine."

I regarded them skeptically. "Do either of you have experience lifting wallets?"

"I accidentally shoplifted a ballpoint pen once," said Beth Ann, her eyes clouding with guilt. "I had it in my hand and walked right out of the store without paying for it."

"See?" said Jackie. "Accidental shoplifting. That counts, doesn't it?"

I rolled my eyes.

"It's a great plan," Jackie defended. "Peewee might have gotten away with giving the tour company a fake name, but to board an international flight, he had to have made airline reservations under the name that's on his passport and/or driver's license."

I puffed up my cheeks and blew out a slow breath. "How about I speak to Wally about requesting some type of trumped-up passport check back at the hotel? It's bound to be less dangerous than petty thievery."

Jackie pondered my suggestion as we watched the group file into the ticket office building. "You can ask him, but if we see a bulge in Peewee's back pocket, we're going in."

By the time we got inside, people were hitting the restrooms, checking out the photos and war artifacts that were on display throughout the room, testing the electronic audio guides that were being handed out as part of the self-guided tour, and picking up their tickets from Wally, who was finding a way to smile despite the angry set of his jaw. Peewee was notably absent, so assuming he was in the men's room, Jackie and Beth Ann posted themselves outside the door to await his reappearance. I picked up my ticket from Wally, mentioning that I needed to speak to him when he was done, then hit the restroom myself, to find Nana and the other girls queuing up at the sink so Margi could wipe their audio guides down with hand sanitizer.

"This thing smells like doggie breath," whined Bernice as she sniffed her freshly decontaminated device. "Where's the lemon scented stuff?"

"Gone!" snapped Margi in a wild-eyed frenzy. "All I have left is peony-pumpkin. You see? *This* is what happens when you're restricted to forty-five pounds of luggage. I can't fight the norovirus with only thirty pounds of hand sanitizer. It's impossible!"

"Stick together out there, okay?" I advised, reverting to the old safety in numbers philosophy. "I'm serious about this. Do not wander away from the group."

A groan from Helen. "But what if some people are slowpokes?"

Six sets of eyes riveted on Bernice.

"What?" she complained. "Why are you looking at me?"

"If people are slow, be polite and wait for them," I instructed. "It won't kill you. I'll catch up to you as soon as I can."

"Where are you going?" accused Bernice. "The cafeteria?"

"Nope. I have to see a man about a horse."

They finished up their sanitizing and were out the door before I left my stall. When I stepped back into the main lobby area, I was surprised to find it deserted, save for Wally, who was in a far corner talking on his cellphone, and Jackie and Beth Ann, who continued to linger by the men's room entrance in anticipation of ambushing Peewee.

"He's still in there?" I marveled.

"With our luck he'll have prostate problems, and it'll take him all day to whiz," griped Jackie. Running her hands over her skirt, she smoothed out imaginary wrinkles. "Thank God I don't have to anticipate *that* happening anymore."

I picked up my audio guide from the bin on the front desk, and when Wally pocketed his cellphone, I hurried over to him. "I need your help. Would it be terribly inconvenient for you to request everyone's passport when we get back to the hotel so we can check if everyone is who they say they are?"

He threw up his hands. "Why not? Glad to oblige. Maybe the police will give me a pat on the back for thinking ahead and doing part of their job for them. Isn't that what tour guides are supposed to do? Smile in spite of all the crap that people throw at us?"

I quietly tucked in my lips. Somebody was still angry.

"Why am I still in this business?" he ranted. He drilled me with a hard look. "Why are *you* still in this business?"

"Well, I was out of the business for a little while."

"Got fed up with the loonies, did you?"

I shook my head. "Bank collapse."

"Ahh, that's right. You were part of some bank-sponsored travel club. Damn recession. Did your bank go belly up?"

"It collapsed. Literally." I compressed air between my hands until my palms were flattened together. "F-4 category tornado."

"And you came back?" He looked bewildered. "Why?"

Why? "Because … I love what I'm doing," I said without hesitation. "I love the whole nine yards. The people. The places. The cuisine. The—"

"The coach drivers?"

"Aha. The truth comes out. So what are you going to do about Dietger's showboating?"

"I already took care of it. I just called the company to request a substitute driver."

"Oh, my God. You sacked Dietger?"

"Hell, yes. I'm not about to jeopardize the lives of forty-four people by tolerating any more of his antics."

"You have the authority to do that?"

"I'm claiming the authority." He marked the time. "The new driver should be here within the hour. His name is Jens."

"Wow. That's pretty gutsy of you. How did Dietger take the news?"

He squared his shoulders and jaw as Dietger swaggered through the front door. "I'll let you know after I tell him."

Unh-oh. No way did I want to be any part of this. In the next moment Peewee swooped out of the men's room and blew past Jackie and Beth Ann, his jacket slung over his shoulder and his shoes squeaking across the floor. He picked up his audio guide at the front desk and without even giving it a trial run, charged out the door. Caught off guard, the girls sprinted after him, wrestling through the doorway at the same time like a couple of Iowans vying to be first in the buffet line.

I hurried out the door after them, intent on being out of earshot when Wally brought the hammer down. Dietger might be nothing more than an immature blowhard, but something about him made me nervous, so I was more than happy to have him traded in for a more functional model.

"He's heading for the site," said Jackie as we watched Peewee stride down the path signposted, Atlantikwall. She gave Beth Ann a thumbs-up. "He's all yours, so as your coach and confidante, I have only one bit of advice: If he notices your hand on his butt, tell him there's a string hanging out of his pocket that you're pulling out. Guys always buy that line."

Yup. This had disaster written all over it. "You know, ladies, Wally has agreed to collect passports when we get back to the hotel, so maybe you should forget about—"

"No," objected Beth Ann. "I made my decision, and now I'm going to follow through. I want to show Jackie how far I've come. I want to prove to her that I could be the poster girl for *Jackie's Life Improvements, Inc.*"

"Isn't she adorable?" asked Jackie, preening like a proud parent.

"And maybe if we crack the case, we could write a story about it," Beth Ann continued breathlessly. "A novel. Or a screenplay. We could have our names on the big screen! Or on a six-ninety-nine paperback. Really, I wouldn't be fussy."

I bet she wouldn't, I thought, as a light bulb suddenly went on over my head.

"We could," Jackie agreed, then warming to the idea, "We could! We could be writing partners. Co-authors. Two brains, one pseudonym. *EEEEEEEE!*"

They hopped up and down with their arms wrapped around each other. I threw a long look down the path.

"Peewee's gone," I said dryly.

"Get going," Jackie urged, sending us both on our way. "Meet you back at the cafeteria."

"I hope we haven't lost sight of him permanently," Beth Ann fretted as we followed the arrows around a series of embankments to the first venue.

"So how long have you wanted to be a writer?" I asked as I kept pace beside her.

She immediately slowed her steps, my question seeming to cut her off at the knees. "Everyone wants to be a writer, don't they?"

"Apparently some more than others."

"Come on, Emily. Haven't you ever wanted to pen the great American novel?"

"Nope. I have a hard enough time writing notes in birthday cards."

"They say everyone has at least one book in them."

"And Jackie's already written hers. It wasn't a bestseller, but that's not the point. She's still a published author." I went in for the kill. "Does she have any idea that the only reason you signed up for her life coaching instruction was because of her connections to publishing?"

She slowed to a standstill, her face reflecting the throes of self-conscious guilt. She threw her hands up as if surrendering to the police. "Busted. I was trying to be so subtle, but subtlety isn't Jackie's strong suit. I was having to drag out the neon arrows and baseball bats. I love Jackie, but at times, she can be really dense."

I led the way up a short flight of stairs that opened onto a battery emplaced with a World War II anti-aircraft gun.

"Why didn't you just tell her the truth?" I asked. "I bet she would have been thrilled to give you pointers on novel writing. She loves handing out advice."

"Tom told me she had such a bad publishing experience that she swore she'd never have anything to do with writing again, so I figured I had to break down her defenses by taking the back door approach."

"You couldn't have just joined a critique group? Isn't that what aspiring writers do?"

"That's what I *should* have done, but what do they say about hindsight being 20/20? A critique group sure would have been cheaper. Jackie charges a bloody fortune for her life coaching services."

We wandered over to the far embankment and peered across the noisy highway to the wide strip of sand beach that Hitler had been so fanatical about protecting.

"How can you afford to pay her? She said you'd lost your job."

"My job, my husband, my dad. Dad had a life insurance policy, so that's kept me flush for awhile. But to be honest, after he was gone, I lapped up the one-on-one attention from Jackie. It was like a spa treatment for my emotional health. I was so depressed after he died that I turned to journal writing as a kind of catharsis. And then I thought, why not a book? Something that could generate income. But I got impatient."

"Which is when you decided to take advantage of Jackie's ad?"

"Yeah. Everyone in the salon knows she wrote a book, so I thought if I could establish a good rapport with her, I could coax her back to novel writing, and maybe convince her that I could be a worthy partner. I have some great plots in my head. I just need her to show me the ropes. Really, Emily, with her *chutzpah* and my determination, we could be the next big brand name in publishing."

"You and Jackie would be to books what Huntley and Brinkley were to TV?"

"Yeah! Kind of. Please don't think I'm a charlatan. I'm not proud of what I've done. And now that you've found me out, I'm even less proud." She had the decency to look embarrassed and a little humble. "Life is funny isn't it? I came on this trip hoping to find a writing partner, and I may have found a soulmate instead. And I didn't even have sign up with Match.com."

From the depths of a nearby concrete pillbox, we heard a loud sneeze, followed by another, and another, and—

Adrenalin pumped through me as Peewee emerged from the stairwell.

"Don't go down there if you've got allergies!" He waggled his audio phone in our direction before tromping back down the stairs to the path.

"His jacket is too long," fretted Beth Ann, reverting back to detective mode. "It falls clear over his tush. How am I supposed to check out his pockets?"

"Forget his pockets! Would you just tell Jackie the truth?"

"I'll tell her the truth. I promise. But I really need to follow this guy. If I can't snatch his wallet, the least I can do is tail him. He's not who he says he is, Emily. And he's carrying a weapon. This is serious. Wish me luck."

She charged across the battery and hit the stairs, leaving me to puzzle over her words. *A weapon?* What weapon?

Only then did I consider what I was carrying in my hand—a fifteen-inch-long hard plastic shaft, equipped with a ten-digit keypad, a readout window, and a speaker tucked inside the molded earpiece. It might look like an audiophone, intended to provide visitors with taped information about each venue, but Beth Ann had been right to call it a weapon. It could easily double as a truncheon or billy club ... and everybody had one.

Holy crap. I pounded down the stairs and hiked down the path, through flat, sandy terrain blanketed with dune grass and around embankments reminiscent of Indian burial mounds. At the end of the path, a brick staircase descended into a gully surrounded by towering dunes. I pelted down the staircase and crossed a short footbridge that opened onto a supply platform and guardhouse, then worked my way back to an enclosed field, where anti-tank and anti-landing craft obstacles dotted the landscape like gigantic weapons of torture. *Euw*. But the good news was that Nana and company were captivated by the display, because they were all here, listening dutifully to their audio phones.

Peewee and Beth Ann, on the other hand, were nowhere in sight.

"Isn't this somethin'?" Nana marveled when I joined her. "The Germans planted all them contraptions on the beach so's the allies couldn't land their boats. I bet they couldn't get away with it today. They'd probably get fined for litterin'."

It was quite a display. Long metal bars angled into concrete blocks. Iron bars bolted into the shape of supersized isosceles triangles. Deadly looking metal configurations that resembled giant jacks. And farther afield searchlights, field cannons, and machine guns that would have made Al Capone salivate.

"Did you see Beth Ann go by?" I asked her.

"Yup. And just about everyone else, too. For all the talkin' that Ricky Hennessy done about bein' hungry, him and his missus never set foot in the cafeteria. They're up ahead, doin' their best to ignore that Bouchard fella and his wife."

"Mike McManus and his wife are ahead of us, too," said Alice.

"And Laura LaPierre," added George.

"And Peewee and Chip," said Helen. "They shot past like streakers, only with their clothes on."

Gee, if none of my prime suspects went to the cafeteria, that meant they were all wandering around the site. Great. But at least if my guys stuck together, they'd be out of harm's way, and I aimed to keep it that way.

"How's the narrative?" I asked Nana as I punched the site number into my audiophone.

"Good, dear."

"Lousy!" sniped Bernice. "It's not even in English."

Nana gave me the eye. "She reached in the wrong bin. Hers is in Italian."

Ten minutes later, as I was mustering everyone along the path toward the next exhibit, I felt a tap on my shoulder.

"Mission accomplished," Wally whispered as he drew alongside me. He rattled a set of keys in his pants pocket, looking extremely satisfied with himself.

"Bus keys?" I asked.

He nodded.

"You fired him?"

"One of the greatest pleasures of my life."

"How'd he take it?"

"Not well. He's probably still back at the ticket office spewing epithets in five languages."

"You are the *man.*"

"I gave him cab fare to his apartment and told him I wanted him gone by the time I got back."

"Thank you from all of us. We may yet live to tour another day."

He winked impishly. "You bet."

I eyed his audio guide. "What are you doing now? Taking the self-guided tour? Haven't you been here before?"

"Years ago, but I want to blow off some steam, so I'm visiting it again. Maybe by the time I reach the end of the tour, I'll feel more like myself again."

The path morphed into a brick-lined trench that cut deeply through the terrain. Tunnels radiated in every direction, ushering us into life-like dioramas of the officers' quarters, communications bunkers, storage bunkers, men's sleeping quarters, munitions bunkers, and lookout bunkers that sported panoramic views of the sea, with cheat sheets identifying enemy aircraft still attached to the wall. We climbed up stairs and down stairs, inside and outside, observing gun pits, machine gun nests, field guns, anti-tank grenades, and swiveling flak guns. We found ourselves encased by bricks, concrete blocks, and sandbags, with camouflage netting above and darkness below, in bunkers that burrowed deep into the bowels of the earth. That fortifications like this had once stretched for five thousand miles boggled the mind.

Forty minutes into the tour, slowed by Bernice's having to borrow someone's audio guide at each venue, my natives started to get restless.

"If you hadn't been so all fired up to get your device before everyone else, you might have reached into the right bin," scolded Helen. "The bin that said 'English'!"

Bernice ripped her wire rims off her face and brandished them in the air. "I'm wearing your husband's freaking glasses! I thought it *did* say English!"

Alice worried her lip as she checked the time. "We only have forty-five minutes left. We'll never make it through this whole thing."

"We'll be left behind," fretted Margi.

"Alice has a point," said George. "We're lagging so far back, all the folks who were straggling behind us are ahead of us now."

"Even the bus driver's ahead of us," lamented Nana, "and he started out way behind."

I drilled a look at her. "Which bus driver?"

"Our bus driver."

"Which one?"

She looked confused. "We got more than one?"

"We do now." My heart slammed into my ribcage. Acid bubbled up my windpipe. "Look everyone, I need to run ahead. Stay together. *Do not* wander off alone. And here—" I handed Bernice my audio guide. "Try to pick up the pace."

I could be overreacting. I hoped I was overreacting. But why was Dietger on the Atlantic Wall when he should be in a cab on his way to banishment right now?

Anxiety quickened my step. I raced through narrow trenches and low-ceilinged tunnels, poked my head into bunkers, and checked out exterior gun emplacements. The other guests must have breezed through the site, because save for the uniformed mannequins on display behind protective glass, the place was deserted. No Peewee. No Bouchards. No Hennessys. No—

I ducked inside a darkened pillbox, pausing a millesecond for my eyes to adjust to the lack of light. The stairs were made of brick and descended deep into the earth, but it wasn't their steepness that forced a sudden scream out of me.

It was the body lying at their base.

EIGHTEEN

WITH DREAD KNOTTING MY stomach, I watched the ambulance tear out of the parking lot, lights flashing and siren wailing.

"He'll be okay," Jackie assured me. "He's probably had a spill at every historical site in Europe. Five-hundred-year-old staircases weren't constructed with safety features in mind."

"The stairs back there aren't five hundred years old. They're not even a hundred years old." The blaring *weeooo!* of the siren faded as the yellow medical van headed south.

I'd called the emergency services number on my cellphone when I'd found Wally at the bottom of the stairs, but to my horror, the operator spoke no English. "Atlantic Wall!" I kept repeating. "Ambulance!" Unsure of my success, I hung up, called Nana's cell, gave her the scoop, then asked her to send someone to the ticket office to request an ambulance. "Your fastest runner. And don't you dare waste time voting. Just do it. Pronto!"

The ambulance arrived sooner than I expected, which was a relief, because although Wally was maintaining a strong pulse, he hadn't regained consciousness, and that worried me. I'd dealt with head traumas before and knew they could have devastating consequences. I'd asked Beth Ann to ride in the ambulance and remain in the hospital with him, and she'd agreed, so I felt good that we were covering that base. Jackie had even lent her cellphone to Beth Ann so she could report back to us on Wally's progress. I suspected he might be happy to see a familiar face when he woke up.

If he woke up.

I banished the thought as the ambulance disappeared from sight.

The police car, however, was still here.

"Do you think Wally tripped?" Jackie asked as we headed back to the ticket office.

"I think he had unwelcome help down the stairs," I told her. And I knew exactly whose hand had done the helping.

————

"You accuse me?" Dietger railed, florid-faced and indignant. "I was one who found him! I was one who ran back here for help!"

"What was wrong with your cellphone?" I challenged. "Why didn't you call for help from the site?"

He whipped his phone out of its holster and shoved it in my face. "I have no bars! Is it crime to forget to charge your mobile phone?"

The police officer who'd responded to the emergency call stepped between us. "You realize the charge you're making is a serious one, madam?"

"You bet I do. Wally fired him from his job just over an hour ago, and he was supposed to be gone by now. But he didn't leave. He decided to stalk Wally instead."

The officer's expression remained neutral. "Is this true?" he asked Dietger. "Mr. Peppers discharged you?"

"So he fired me. What of it? Is there law preventing me from visiting my country's number-one tourist attraction?"

"There's a law preventing you from pushing someone down a flight of stairs!" I cried.

"You crazy woman! I tell you already. *I* find him! *I* run back here to phone ambulance!" He stabbed his finger at the ticket clerk. "Ask him. He has landline. He make the call."

"I did," the clerk agreed. "I dialed the emergency number to request an ambulance for the gentleman."

"See?" Dietger crowed.

"And then I called a taxi to pick this man up as quickly as possible."

The officer's eyebrow slanted upward.

"This looks maybe not so good," offered Dietger, his voice losing its bluster. "But I can explain."

"I'm sure you can," said the officer, manacling his hand around Dietger's arm. "At the station."

"I did nothing," Dietger fumed as the officer escorted him out the door. "I was mad, but try to kill him? No! I wanted we should talk. But he was at the bottom of the stairs, unable to talk. So what was I supposed to do? Wait until he woke up?"

A second officer took over as mayhem erupted within the room.

"He's our bus driver!" yelled Gary Bouchard. "How are we supposed to get back to Amsterdam without him?"

"How can we take a tour without a tour director?" griped Ricky.

"This trip has been cursed from day one," carped Sheila in a damning voice. "I've had it. I'm leaving."

"Me, too," said Mindy, "*after* the Belgian waffles we were promised."

"Does anyone have an address for Wally so we can send him a get-well card?" asked Margi.

Anger. Anxiety. Agitation. With the police officer looking a little overwhelmed, I curled my lips over my teeth and let fly my signature whistle, shocking the room into immediate silence.

"There," I announced. "That's more like it. How can you hear anything the police officer says if you're all talking at the same time?"

"Are you in charge?" the officer asked me.

I surrendered to the inevitable. "I guess I am now."

We conducted a quick question and answer session between us, going over a litany of loose ends. Wally would be taken to one of the many hospitals in Oostende. Our substitute bus driver would ferry us back to Amsterdam. The officer would call me if they decided to press charges against Dietger. Could he have my name and mobile phone number? And by the way, I told him in parting, we'd lost our first tour director and two other guests on this trip already, so he might want to phone the Amsterdam police for information because at least one of the deaths was being investigated as a murder.

"Is it possible your bus driver is responsible for this other death?" he asked me.

"Now there's a thought," I remarked. "Why don't you ask him?" Dietger was about the only person on the tour whose name I *hadn't* connected with the other deaths.

The ride back to Amsterdam, hindered by road construction and lane-clogging traffic jams, was interminable. Halfway back, I received a call from an exuberant Beth Ann. "He's conscious! He has a mean headache, but the doctors are going to do some kind of scan, and if there's no indication of brain swelling, they're going to keep him under observation for a few hours and then release him. Isn't that great?"

A flood of relief washed over me. "Thank God."

"And I have even better news. He remembers exactly what happened, which his doctor says is an excellent sign. He slipped on some loose mortar halfway down the staircase and went flying. He's pretty embarrassed about the whole thing, and he apologizes for leaving you in the lurch, but his doctor told him that considering the stairs were made of brick, he's lucky to be alive."

"He fell?"

"Arse over teacup."

"He wasn't pushed?"

"Excuse me?"

"Nothing. Tell him we're all thinking about him, and—and let me know how the scan turns out."

I blew a long breath of air upward and reflected upon my recent gut instincts, analysis, and accusations. Could I have been any more wrong about Dietger?

Damn.

I slouched down in my seat, mortified.

I wondered who else I was wrong about?

NINETEEN

I DIDN'T HAVE TO wait long for an answer.

The police greeted us at the hotel and led us to a ground floor conference room set up with several rows of folding chairs arranged in a semicircle. A podium stood in the front of the room. "Sit anywhere," the officer in charge instructed us.

"Are you going to be serving snacks?" asked Mindy, as she pondered her seating choices. "Because we never stopped for the Belgian waffles we were promised and *already paid for*. Don't think you can fool us with these bait and switch methods. I'm firing off a letter to corporate."

"Would you prefer to send an e-mail?" Margi chirped helpfully. "I can access the Passages website from my phone."

"What she'd prefer to do is make a scene and draw attention to herself," sniped Sheila Bouchard. "She's still operating under the misperception that she's sixteen and a size 2."

Mindy cackled with laughter. "And Sheila's still operating under the misperception that she's *not* a dried-up old stick!"

If we'd had access to snacks, this would be the point when someone would jump up and yell, "Food fight!"

"Would you two knock it off?" Mary Lou chided with a sharpness that cut through the chatter. "Wasn't it enough that the world revolved around your bleeping dramas back in high school? It was more than enough for us. Didn't it sink in the other night? We're sick to death of your bleeping shallowness, and your bleeping self-absorption, and your bleeping *towering* conceit."

"I'm sick of Ricky thinking he was such a good bleeping quarterback," shouted a man at the back of the room. "He bleeping sucked!"

"I'm sick of Sheila acting so bleeping uppity when everyone knows she's in debt up to her bleeping eyebrows," blasted a voice I didn't recognize.

"Grow up!" Mary Lou screamed at the two women, her face splotchy with angry patches of red. "The rest of us have! Get over your bleeping selves. And if you can't do that, do us all a favor and shut the *bleep* up!"

Whoa! Beth Ann had warned me these Mainers knew how to cuss when they got provoked. But who knew she'd been talking about Mary Lou? I mean, it just seemed so out of character.

Her outburst, however, was not unappreciated. As Mike wrapped a comforting arm around her shoulders, a solitary clap echoed through the room, followed by another, and another, until the entire room was thundering with applause. Mindy and Sheila slinked off to opposite ends of the room, bristling with indignation, their displeasure palpable as they took their seats. Ricky and Gary walked shamefaced behind them, looking as if they might have spent better days spread-eagled on a proctologist's examine table.

When the noise died down, the officer looked out over the room, his expression unreadable. "If you have acted dis way since your tour began, I'm surprised you have any guests left. Such delight in savaging each other. Are you politicians?"

"I apologize, Officer," Mary Lou said in a small voice, minus the expletives. "I don't usually allow my temper to get the better of me."

He raised his eyebrows noncommittally. "My name is Officer Vanden Boogard." He had a long face, a narrow nose, and piercing blue eyes that looked more predatory than a hawk's.

"Are you on Facebook?" Margi called out.

"Hey," Bernice piped up. "You can't ask him that. That's *my* line."

"Wasn't that a quiz show?" asked Osmond. "I think I used to watch it."

"Maybe it has a Facebook page," enthused Alice as she whipped out her smartphone. "We could become fans!"

Nana raised her hand politely. "Will we be takin' a potty break any time soon, young man? Us old folks has got needs, 'specially the fellas."

Ignoring the room at large, Officer Vanden Boogard removed a clipboard from the podium and leafed through several sheets of paper before looking up again. "Charlotte Gooch," he said in an even tone. "Her death must seem like ancient history to you now. Do you recall Charlotte?"

"She was completely unsuited to deal with adults," said Laura LaPierre. "She treated us as if we were kindergarteners."

"She was a pain in the butt," Ricky wisecracked.

"She yelled at us," Gary spoke up. "If I wanted to be yelled at, I could have stayed home and let Sheila do it."

Officer Vanden Boogard referenced his papers once again. "She died as a result of injuries suffered in a collision in Volendam. She stepped off a curb into der path of a bicyclist and died immediately." He gave us a hard look. "Visitors to our country are always at risk to be struck by bicyclists. They never remember to look both ways before crossing a street or stepping onto a sidewalk. You Americans are der worst offenders, followed closely by der Canadians. Always listening to your iPods, or MP3 players, or text messaging on your cellphones. You come here to see der sights, but you're so preoccupied with your electronic gadgetry, you see nothing."

In the chairs around me, hands stilled on cellphones, fingers paused on keypads, backsides shifted uncomfortably on seat cushions. Hey, I liked this guy! But I wasn't sure he had the most up-to-date information.

I raised my hand. "In light of the fact that two more people died after Charlotte, is there any evidence that the accident happened differently than it was first reported?"

"That she didn't step in front of der bicyclist?" he asked.

"No, that she might have been pushed off the curb."

Whispers from the Mainers. Gasps. Rubbernecking.

"Do you have any evidence that contradicts der original report?" he inquired.

"She always thinks she does," mocked Bernice.

I shot her an exasperated look. "I don't have any hard evidence," I confessed, "but Charlotte had created such a poisonous atmosphere, and her accident seemed such a convenient coincidence, that—"

"You suspected one of der guests had taken matters into his own hands?"

242

I nodded. "Pete Finnegan. He'd had a terrible run-in with her on our first stop."

Officer Vanden Boogard eyed his clipboard. "Mr. Finnegan is also dead."

"I know, but he was alive when we were in Volendam."

He flipped through his sheaf of papers and cleared his throat when he found what he was looking for. "Ms. Gooch stepped off der curb into der path of a speeding bicycle. This account is corroborated by videotape presented at der Volendam police station yesterday by a Mrs. Dafne Herold, whose camcorder was accidentally left on der record position while she and her daughter were dining in der restaurant across der street. She was seated at a window table, purported to be der best seat in der house, and unknowingly videotaped dee entire event. The camcorder is apparently new, so she admits confusion about its operation. She was unaware of der recording until she played back der footage yesterday, at which point she contacted der local police."

Mindy thwacked Ricky's chest. "We ate at that restaurant! Remember? There was only one table in the window and we got it after those two women left. Do you hear that, Sheila?" She megaphoned her hands around her mouth. "It was the best seat in the house and Ricky and me got it!"

"Pete didn't push her?" I asked Officer Vanden Boogard, my voice a mere decibel above a squeak.

"Ms. Gooch stepped off der curb of her own accord. She received no unwanted assistance."

I slid down in my chair, wanting to crawl into the nearest sinkhole, which, with my luck, was probably in Florida.

"Ms. Paula Peavey, however, *was* pushed into der Kloveniers-burgwal canal, and with such force, she exhibited significant bruising on her back."

Nana nudged me with her elbow. "You hear that, dear? You're right about this one."

"So." Officer Vanden Boogard scrutinized us with cool detachment. "Would any of Ms. Peavey's former classmates care to paint a portrait of who she was, and why anyone would want to kill her?"

I scanned the room, anticipating a Tower of Babel type moment when everyone would leap into a pitched battle to have his voice heard above everyone else's in denunciation of their nemesis, but what greeted me instead was silence. Prolonged silence. Uncomfortable silence. Self-conscience silence.

I spotted Mary Lou, who'd cried a river of tears at Paula's hands, and Laura LaPierre, who'd been cruelly bullied by her. Both of them sitting quietly with their lips buttoned. I glanced at the classmates who'd suffered financial disaster because of her—Chip Soucy, Ricky and Mindy, looking satisfied to keep their mouths shut. I eyed Sheila Bouchard, whose social status had taken a hit because of Paula, stiff-lipped and wooden in the corner. What was wrong with them? This was their chance. Why weren't they saying anything?

The answer to that seemed painfully obvious. No one was speaking up, because in the matter of Paula Peavey, everyone had something to hide.

Officer Vanden Boogard lifted his brows. "You may tear der lady apart if you like. She's not here. What are you waiting for?"

More silence.

"Surely one of you must have something hateful to say about her."

Nana stood up. "I got somethin' to say, Officer. When I go out this door here, is the potty on the left or the right?"

After giving Nana directions and allowing Tilly and Margi to accompany her, Officer Vanden Boogard tried a different tact. He smiled. Albeit grimly.

"Perhaps I should approach dis in another way. We know Ms. Peavey was killed on her way back from der Red Light District two nights ago. How many of you were part of der group who went down there?"

Nearly everyone raised their hand.

"Good, good. How did you all get back?"

"Most of us walked," Chip spoke up.

"Together?"

"The group broke up pretty early on," said Mike McManus. "Around nine. So we all found our way back on our own."

Vanden Boogard tipped his head. "Thank you. Dis is what der surveillance cameras indicate."

Low grumbles of unease.

"What surveillance cameras?" asked Ricky.

"Der ones throughout der city—on your hotel, at large intersections, on university property, on buildings in dee Old City center. Wherever you go, you're being watched. Oddly, some of our foreign visitors don't find dis a comforting thought. I tell them, our streets are not as well monitored as those in London, but we're getting there."

I boosted myself back up to vertical. This guy knew something. He might not be Sherlock Holmes or Hercule Poirot, but as he presented his case, I could sense that he was methodically tightening the noose around the killer's neck.

"Mr. and Mrs. Hennessy." He fixed his gaze on Mindy and Ricky. "Der hotel surveillance camera shows you returning from your outing just after midnight two nights ago. You appear to be arguing over a scarf dat Mr. Hennessy disposes of after Mrs. Hennessy walks out of der frame. "

"How do you know it's us?" Ricky challenged.

Vanden Boogard stared. "Seriously?"

Ricky snorted. "It's those damn bows you stick in your hair," he sniped at Mindy. "What'd I tell you? Didn't I warn you that people could use them to identify us? It's a dead giveaway. Who wears bows in their hair anymore? If you'd listened to me, this wouldn't be happening. They could have looked at their flippin' tapes all day and had nothin'!"

Except a refrigerator-sized bald guy stuffed into a varsity letter jacket with the words "St. Francis Xavier" plastered across the back. Yup. No way Ricky could have been identified by that description.

"Don't you get snippy with me, Ricky Hennessy! I told you it was a bad idea from the start, but *no-ooo*. You had to have your way." Mindy thwacked his arm.

"Mr. and Mrs. Hennessy," Vanden Boogard persisted, "did you run into Ms. Peavey after you departed der Red Light District?"

"No," they responded in unison.

"If your group broke up at nine, what took you so long to return to your hotel? And let me remind you once again, there are surveillance tapes."

"Even in the Red Light District?" asked Ricky.

"Especially in der Red Light District," said Vanden Boogard.

Ricky and Mindy rocked back and forth in their seats, har-rumphing and hissing and glaring at each other, until Mindy spat, "You might as well tell him. He's bound to find out anyway."

Ricky ran his palm over his bald pate as if polishing a cue ball. "Okay," he said flatly. "We took so long getting back because ... well ... we stopped to take in a show."

"A show?" asked Vanden Boogard.

"You know. A *show*." Ricky lowered his voice. "At the Live Sex Theater."

Gasps of shock and ridicule. Hisses of condemnation.

"Did it have English subtitles?" questioned Osmond. "I can't see paying good money to watch a show over here if there's no subtitles."

"Ah, yes," said Vanden Boogard. "Der Sex Theater is in some-what of a lower rent district."

"I caught a souvenir," Ricky confessed, hardening his tone when he turned to his wife, "but Mindy made me get rid of it. The gal on the stage had this scarf that she rubbed over every luscious curve of her nak—"

"Shut up, Ricky." Mindy gave her hair a pouf. "I never witnessed anything so disgusting in all my life. The perversion. The wicked-ness. The immorality of all those sweaty, over-endowed nymphos with their gyrating bodies. And the men with their rock hard mus-cles, performing such obscene acts right before our naked eyes. It was appalling."

A hush fell over the room.

"Do you remember the address for this place?" asked George.

"Leave it to Hennessy to take his wife to a low-brow strip joint," taunted Gary. "You should have gone a little higher class,

Rick. Like, the place with the neon pink elephant. I bet what we saw was a helluva lot more obscene than what you witnessed. Hey, you get what you pay for."

"It was an eye-opening experience," agreed Sheila. "Should anything so vile come to Bangor, I'll be the first person in line to file an objection with the zoning commission."

"Did you guys see men *and* women?" asked Chip. "How come the place I went only had women?"

"Der Bananenbar features women only," Vanden Boogard informed him.

"I was at a banana bar," Peewee told Chip. "Was it the same one you went to? How come I didn't see you there?"

"I got absorbed into a bachelor party in a private salon, so I wasn't in the main room. You wouldn't have believed the raunchiness. Lap dances. Pole dances. I wanted to leave, but hell, I didn't want to appear rude."

My gaze bounced from one to the other as they compared the depravity levels of the shows they'd seen. And since they all professed abject horror at what the Dutch offered up as entertainment, they agreed not to tell anyone back in Bangor about their adventure. "People would only criticize," said Mindy. "Can you imagine the gossip? People might suggest that devout Catholics like us might actually have enjoyed watching that filth."

"Father Harvey would recommend we go to confession," said Sheila.

"What people don't know won't hurt them," said Gary. "It'll be our little secret. Agreed?"

I stared at them, thunderstruck. Is that why everyone had run away from me when I'd questioned them about Paula Peavey and the Red Light District? Not because they were trying to cover up their complicity in Paula's death, but because they didn't want anyone to know that they'd sneaked into a bunch of seamy sex shows?

The atmosphere all of a sudden seemed more cordial, kind of like a room gets when its occupants discover they support the same cause, denounce the same enemy, or are trying the same diet. They laughed. They exchanged quips. They made a pact to keep their dip in the naughty pool to themselves. And as quickly as that, sworn enemies became friends, fused by their bond of secrecy.

But the fact still remained, someone had killed Paula.

I popped out of my chair. "Did your surveillance tapes show Pete Finnegan buying a ticket to any of the erotic theaters?"

"There are many tapes," Officer Vanden Boogard admitted, "not all of which we have analyzed."

"Pete Finnegan threatened Paula on the night she died, and just about everyone in this room heard him."

Helen looked surprised. "We didn't hear him. Where were we?"

"Playing croquet with George's leg in lala land," Jackie said under her breath.

"If Pete didn't spend the evening in a sex club like everyone else," I hurried on, "he would have had ample time to stalk ... and maybe even kill Paula."

Vanden Boogard made a quick notation on his papers. "Mr. Finnegan kills Ms. Peavey, and der following day, ends up dead himself? Are you suggesting der possibility that he may have committed suicide in remorse for his actions?"

"No. Actually, I think Pete was killed, too."

He stood statue-still, regarding me oddly, while the Mainers whispered behind their hands and gasped some more. "Could I have your name, please?"

"Emily Andrew, but my married name is Miceli."

The door to the conference room creaked open and Nana appeared, her face lit up like Lars Bakke's grain elevator at Christmas time. "Would you look at what the cat drug in?" she announced, stepping aside to allow Dick Teig and Dick Stolee to precede her into the room.

"Oh, my God!" I cried. "You're back!" We left our seats en masse and descended upon them like a swarm of locusts, group hugging, smiling, sobbing, laughing.

"Where have you been?" demanded Helen after squeezing sufficient air out of her Dick to shrink him by an inch.

"Forget that," griped Bernice. "Gimme back my glasses."

"Why didn't you call?" spat Grace, her voice escalating into a Palin screech. "Do you know how worried we were? Do you know how long it took us to fill out your stupid missing person questionnaires? And by the way, what's your favorite color? Black or white?"

"I dropped my phone," Dick Stolee explained in a contrite voice, "and not only did it fall apart when it hit the ground, it got run over by a girl on a bike."

"I suppose you're going to tell me *your* phone ended up on the pavement, too?" Helen taunted her husband.

He shook his head. "Mine ended up in the canal."

"Of course, it did," she said skeptically. "Which one?"

"The one that had the pretty flying saucers hovering over it."

Osmond scratched his jaw. "Now that you mention it, I think I mighta seen them, too."

"I never should have tried taking a picture," Dick lamented, "but I wanted to show my little lovebug that I wasn't hallucinating."

I didn't know what I found more disturbing—that Dick Teig had been high enough on weed to see flying saucers, or that his pet name for Helen was lovebug.

"Why didn't you just walk back to the hotel?" asked Grace.

"Couldn't remember the name," said one Dick.

"Didn't know where it was," said the other.

"You weren't carrying your itineraries with you?" I scolded.

They shrugged in unison. "We don't carry that stuff with us," explained Dick Teig. "That's *your* job."

Helen sniffed the air around her husband. "Dick Teig! Is that cheap perfume I smell on your jacket?"

He took a whiff of his sleeve. "It doesn't smell that bad, Helen. You have stuff that smells worse."

"If I may," said Dick Stolee, raising his palms for calm. "The girl on the bicycle felt so bad about running over my smartphone that she offered to take us under her wing until we got our bearings back. She was a real Samaritan, Grace. She took us to her apartment, let us sleep on her sofa, plied us with coffee and some very nice Dutch apple pastry. She's a student at the university, studying to be a doctor. I don't know how we would have survived without her. And today, she drove us up and down every street in the downtown area until we spotted our hotel. So, here we are."

Helen twitched her nose. "She has terrible taste in perfume."

"Did you offer her any money for her trouble?" asked Grace. "If she's a student, she could probably use a few extra dollars."

"She works a part-time job at a grocery store," said Dick Teig, "and she says the pay is great, so she refused our money. It had a funny name. Sounded like some kind of fruit market. You remember the name, Dick?"

"The Bananenbar." He pulled several small rectangular boxes out of his pocket and held them up. "They give away souvenir matchboxes with real wooden matches inside, so I stocked up. Chantal had a whole bowlful, so she told us to help ourselves."

"Her name is *Chantal*?" questioned Helen. "A doctor named Chantal? Hildegard I could believe, but Chantal?"

Helen eyed Grace. Grace eyed Helen. Without exchanging a single syllable, they grabbed their husbands by their prospective ears and marched them to the nearest seats.

"Ow!" wailed Dick Stolee.

"What?" howled Dick Teig.

"Der missing Dicks have returned?" asked Officer Vanden Boogard, his gaze fixed on Grace and Helen.

"Call off your search," demanded Helen. "Your department wasted enough man hours looking for these two bozos while they were holed up with *Chantal*."

Stepping away from the podium, he released his mobile phone, and leaving us with an, "Excuse me for a moment, please," disappeared into the hallway. As Nana, Tilly, and the rest of the gang jockeyed around each other to arrive back at their seats first, I regarded the two Dicks, relieved beyond words that nothing calamitous had happened to them. That they were safe. That no one had harmed them because of some heinous act they might have witnessed.

My brain suddenly hit "rewind" as that last thought sunk in, causing my synapses to light up like the bulbs in an old-fashioned switchboard.

The Dicks hadn't seen Paula being pushed into the canal that night. But what if someone else had? Oh, my God. Could I have ascribed the wrong motive to Pete's death? Was all the information I'd learned about him irrelevant? Did his classmates actually give a hoot that he'd dragged them into IRS hell? Could he have been targeted not because of something he'd done, but because of something he'd seen? Was it Pete who'd witnessed Paula's death and been killed because of it?

I ranged a look around the room, my gaze lingering on my list of prime suspects.

"We were so offended by the entertainment, we sat through the show a second time just to make sure it was as bad as we thought," Gary Bouchard told Chip.

"We did the same thing," crowed the Hennessys.

"The shock wore off for me by the third go around," confessed Peewee.

How could they have killed Paula when they'd been nowhere near her? How could they have pushed her into a canal at the same time they were clamoring to catch scarves and pasties with their bare teeth? They couldn't have been in two places at once, could they?

But I soon realized that not everyone was joining in the banter. Mike, Mary Lou, and Laura, while seated together, were having little to say to each other or anyone else. Mike was clasping Mary Lou's hand, but she was wearing a pinched expression that indicated he might be squeezing too tightly. Laura stared at the ceiling, looking as if she could hardly wait for the convocation to end. Had the three of them resolved their differences over the miscommunication problems they'd had the other night? Or were the ladies' ears still ringing from the lecture Mike had probably served up about losing him in the crowd and making him wait on the bridge so many hours?

It was that thought that caused a puzzle piece to quietly shift into place.

That's right. Mike hadn't explored the erotica scene because he'd been on the bridge with the JESUS SAVES people, frantically scouring the crowd for Mary Lou and Laura. Mary Lou and Laura—who'd both been victimized and verbally abused by Paula in high school, and now seemed connected at the hip, acting like proverbial best friends forever. And then there was Mike, smothering Mary Lou's hand as if it were a lifeline. Hadn't he confessed as much on the bridge? Hadn't he questioned what he would do without Mary Lou because she was, in essence, his whole life?

A shiver feathered down my spine as I studied the three of them, sitting a few seats away from me in the front row, their name badges flaunting their once youthful faces. Mary Lou O'Leary, currently Mary Lou McManus, and Laura LaPierre, currently—

I zoomed in on the name that appeared in larger print beneath her high school graduation picture, my eyes suddenly widening with recognition. Why hadn't I noticed it before? Was that her real name, or had she made this particular change as a cruel ironic twist?

Oh, my God. There wasn't one killer.

There were three.

TWENTY

"It was you," I accused, leaping up to stand before them. "The three of you! You killed Pete and Paula."

"I beg your pardon?" said Mary Lou.

"Are you crazy?" said Mike.

"Look," I said, pointing to Laura's name badge. "Her last name is Battles. *Battles!*" I made an appeal to the room. "Don't any of you get it?"

"Show of hands," announced Osmond. "How many of you get it?"

"Battles is the English translation of Guerrette!" I choked out. "*Guerre.* The French word for war, or battle, or—"

Feeling a presence behind me, I turned to find Officer Vanden Boogard observing with keen interest. "You've solved der crime, have you, Ms. Andrew?"

I thrust my finger at the guilty trio. "They did it! Mary Lou and Laura stalked Paula through the Red Light District and pushed her into the canal on their way back to the hotel. But Pete Finnegan saw the whole thing, and Mary Lou and Laura knew it, so the next day at the Anne Frank house, Mike pushed Pete down the stairs to keep him quiet. It was like a *Gift of the Magi* kind of thing, only more warped. The women killed Paula to avenge her cruelty, and Mike killed Pete to protect his wife."

"That's kind of romantic," said Margi.

"No it's not romantic!" I cried. "They've committed a double murder!"

Laura regarded me in bemusement. "Exactly what does my name have to do with your version of the facts?"

"Bobby Guerrette was your protector. You idolized him. So not only were you bent on getting even with Paula for her mistreatment of *you*, you wanted to stick it to her for the role she might have played in Bobby's disappearance on Senior Skip Day." I shot an accusatory look at the abashed faces of the reunion crowd. "Something unlawful took place that day, and a lot of you know what it is, but you've kept it secret for five decades. Pete told me you were good at keeping secrets, and he was right. Haven't you already agreed to keep your sex theater adventures a secret for the *next* five decades?"

Whispers of shock from the Iowa contingent. "S'cuse me, dear," interrupted Nana, "but if them folks are gonna be around for the next fifty years, you might wanna suggest they speak to their financial planners about bulkin' up their investment portfolios, on account a Social Security probably won't be around no more."

Laura smiled, her eyes flinty. "I killed Paula to avenge Bobby Guerrette? Why would I do that? I didn't need to kill anyone to avenge Bobby Guerrette. I *married* Bobby Guerrette."

What?

The room exploded with a single, ear-popping gasp.

"Come again?" barked Mike, coming straight out of his chair.

"I married him," she repeated. "He applied to Berkeley after completing his military service, and that's where we ran into each other again. He didn't look exactly like the Bobby I'd known in high school." She raised her hand to her face, touching her forehead and cheek. "He was involved in a pretty serious vehicle accident during his tour of duty, but I would have known him anywhere, even with his new name."

"You married him?" Mike's voice echoed off the ceiling lights. "He's been alive all these years, and he never bothered to contact anyone back home to let us know?"

"He didn't *want* anyone to know," Laura fired back. "Why do you think he left in the first place? He wanted to start over again, away from Bangor, away from the small town social elite, away from the idea that he'd never make anything of himself because he was an orphan."

Mike sank back into his chair. "But how? I don't understand. How did he pull it off? Hennessy said—"

"The SOB is alive?" snarled Ricky. "That dirty jeezer. All these years thinking I'd killed him, and he turns up alive?"

"What do you mean you thought you killed him?" Mindy's face turned ashen. "You said he got into a car. Remember? A car that was something other than white and a station wagon?"

"So I lied. Big deal. Everyone lied after he went missing."

"You *intimidated* us into lying," accused Mike. "You told us your lame story, and you swore it was the truth. And you threatened to rat us out to the police about our drinking if we didn't regurgitate the story back to them. All to save your guilty butt."

"Hey, Guerrette got on my case about Laura, so I called him out," defended Ricky. "That's what guys in high school do. They get bombed, and they call each other out. If you'd walked down to the river with us, you might have saved me fifty years of nightmares, but *nooo*, the rest of you were either hurling or passed out, so you missed the big showdown. Bunch of wusses."

"Would you get to the part about where you thought you killed him?" asked Peewee.

"Yeah, dumbass," yelled Gary. "We'd all like to hear that part."

Ricky boosted himself to his feet. "When we got beyond the railroad tracks, Bobby said he was gonna teach me the lesson of my life. But the idiot just stood there, smiling at me, so I slugged him but good. I hit him so hard I spun around and landed on the ground. And that's the last thing I remember until I woke up and found him gone."

"Why did you think you'd killed him if his body was gone when you regained consciousness?" I asked.

Ricky looked suddenly hangdog. "After I hit him, I thought I heard something fall into the water. Something big. So I figured I'd probably knocked him unconscious into the river...and he drowned."

"You freaking coward," bellowed Mike. "Threatening me. Threatening Peewee!"

"Don't drag me into this," squawked Peewee. "I don't know anything about it."

Mike shot him a look. "What do you mean you don't know anything about it?"

"I'm not Peewee."

"What did I tell you!" hooted Jackie.

Mike's voice exploded like a sonic boom. "You're not Peewee? Then who the hell are you?"

Peewee shrugged. "Melvin Crowley. Peewee's cousin. He didn't want to participate in the reunion, but the discounted tour price was so good, I couldn't pass it up, so he told me I could come in his place. Sorry I got you so hot under the collar yesterday, man, but when you were reliving all those high school memories, I didn't know who the hell you were talking about." He elevated his hand, waving to the room like an English monarch. "Thanks for being so nice to me, everyone. You're all right, despite what Peewee had to say about you."

"I *told* you morons that that Bobby kid ran away," crowed Bernice. "But no one ever listens to me."

I stared at Laura. "How did he do it? How did he just disappear?"

"Ricky's punch never landed, but he was so drunk, he didn't realize it. He pretty much knocked himself silly when he tried to slug Bobby, and while he was groaning on the riverbank, Bobby chucked an old railroad tie into the river, kind of imitating the same sound a body might make if it fell into the Penobscot."

"He did it on purpose?" Ricky sputtered. "He wanted me to think I'd caused him to drown *on purpose*? Miserable bastard!"

Yup. I guess Bobby Guerrette had sure taught Ricky Hennessy the lesson of his life.

"So did Bobby get into a car with someone or not?" Chip threw out. "All my life I believed what Hennessy—"

"Oh, shut up about me," yelled Ricky.

259

"Bobby hiked along the railroad tracks until he reached another town," said Laura, "and then he hitched a ride with a truck driver headed for Boston."

"He walked the railroad tracks?" said Gary. "Why didn't he just hitch a ride from the park? We were so wasted, none of us would have noticed."

"Because he spied Pete Finnegan's car parked at the side of the road by the Water Works, so if he'd shown his face again, Pete would have seen him."

"Isn't that just like Finnegan to spy on us," sneered Ricky.

"Maybe if you'd treated him differently, he wouldn't have had to spy," snapped Laura. "But he got an eyeful that night. He saw Bobby and Ricky disappear across the railroad tracks. And he most probably saw Ricky return to the park alone, and knew that everyone was lying about Bobby catching a ride in a mysterious car."

"So why didn't Pete ever say anything to the cops?" asked Mike.

Laura shrugged. "Only Pete knows the answer to that, and it's too late to ask him now."

"What happened after Bobby got to Boston?" asked Chip.

"He found a room at the YMCA, got a job busing tables, enlisted in the military, spent time recuperating from his injuries at Walter Reed, headed to California to attend college, married yours truly, and became one of the most respected psychiatrists in the Bay area. He led a good life, right up until the day he died."

"He was at Walter Reed?" asked Mike, leveling a look at Mary Lou. "Did you know about that?"

Mary Lou nodded self-consciously. "I was in the operating room for one of his facial reconstructive surgeries."

"You knew?" blasted Mike. "You knew he was alive and you never told me?"

"He swore me to secrecy! What was I supposed to do, Mike? Be disloyal? Betray his trust? Reveal the secret he'd struggled so hard to keep?"

Mike thumped his chest with an angry fist. "*I'm* your husband! Your first loyalty was to me! Jeesuz-Mighty, Mary Lou, didn't you think I'd want to know he was still alive?"

"You think it was easy for me?" she yelled, tears starring her eyes. "You think I didn't stay awake at night wondering if I should throw professional ethics and confidentiality out the window and tell you? Well, it *wasn't* easy. It was the hardest decision I've ever had to make!"

"Don't be so hard on her, Mike," chided Laura as she banded her arm around Mary Lou's shoulders. "If not for Mary Lou, I never would have become Mrs. Battles. She's the one who told him where I was. She's the one who got the ball rolling. And if you ask me, she did good." She clasped Mary Lou's hand and smiled. "She did real good."

Officer Vanden Boogard retrieved his clipboard from the podium and tapped his pen on the metal clip, his gaze focused on Mary Lou and Laura. "You have no alibi, ladies. Dat was an intriguing human interest story, but if you weren't pushing Ms. Peavey into der canal, what were you doing?"

Looking both chagrined and embarrassed, Laura slid her hand into her purse and extracted a matchbox that she tossed to Vanden Boogard.

"Der Dungeon Bar?"

Mary Lou cleared her throat. "It's an all-male revue. Kind of like the Chippendales, only the dancers are dressed up as macho historical figures like Attila the Hun and Genghis Khan before they, uhh—strip down to the good parts."

"Do them folks knock money off the cover charge for seniors?" asked Nana.

"You were whooping it up at a strip club while I waited half the night for you on that damn bridge?" railed Mike.

"Give it a rest, hon," soothed Mary Lou. "After spending all those years at Walter Reed, I was dying to see a few body parts that weren't screaming out to be stapled, drained, or sutured back together again. And it wasn't as exciting as I thought it would be. Think busman's holiday."

Officer Vanden Boogard rolled his eyes. Glaring at the bunch of us, he let fly a stream of exasperated Dutch that I had no trouble translating into English: *So if Mike didn't kill Pete, and Mary Lou and Laura didn't kill Paula, who did?*

TWENTY-ONE

We dined fashionably late in the hotel restaurant again that night.

After subjecting us to two more hours of questioning with no relevant information to show for it, Officer Vanden Boogard had thrown in the towel and released us, with the caveat that he wasn't satisfied with our timeline, so we weren't off the hook yet. The reunion crowd had dispersed in every direction afterward, some forming into little cliques in the lobby, some exiting through the revolving door, others crowding into the elevator for the upper floors. My gang swore to be suffering such stomach-gnawing hunger that they didn't have the energy to dodge bicyclists while searching for a nice restaurant, so I'd ushered them into the hotel dining room, where the staff had been kind enough to set us up at a table that could accommodate all of us.

"Wasn't it somethin' how that Bobby Guerrette fella invented a whole new life for hisself," commented Nana as she dug into her cinnamon ice cream.

"Probably wasn't too hard to do back then," said George.

Tilly nodded agreement. "There were so few forms of identification in those days. No national credit cards. No local charge cards. No photos on drivers' licenses. And the communication highway had yet to be constructed. Most households didn't even have a telephone."

They bobbed their heads in silence, looking as if they were wondering how they'd ever endured the horror of such privation.

"Speaking of phones," said Jackie, who'd elbowed out Bernice for the plum seat at the head of the table. "Could I borrow yours?" She extended her hand toward me. "If wedding plans are being batted about in Oostende, I need to start making preparations now for my big debut. This is going to be *so* fabulous, darling! I'm going to be bigger than Vera Wang. Bigger than Carolina Herrera. Bigger than—"

"Oh, put a sock in it," groused Bernice. "If you get any bigger, you're going to look like a giant yard ornament."

"Spoilsport," sniffed Jackie as she palmed my phone. She stood up, all atwitter as she addressed the table. "I'm so fond of everyone here, I want you to be the first to know. I'm abandoning my life coaching career to pursue something I'm going to be really good at. Wedding planning! So if any of you are thinking about tying the knot in the near future, I'm your girl. And to show you that friendship has its benefits, I'll even offer exclusive senior discounts."

Nana's eyes lit up. "Do you take AARP?"

"AARP, Triple-A, library cards. Whatever you got, Mrs. S. Now, if you'll excuse me."

"Where's she going?" Bernice asked me as Jackie exited the dining area.

"She probably wants to find a private spot to make her call."

"How come she doesn't talk right here?"

I offered her a sublime smile, accompanied by a meaningful look. "Because she's trying to be polite."

Bernice, being Bernice, didn't give an inch. "You're so behind the times. Didn't you hear the conversation? Things are different now. Times have changed. No one cares about politeness anymore. Everyone *expects* us to be rude." Her face softened with an almost beatific look. "It's so comforting." And as a testament to her convictions, she pulled out her smartphone and powered it up.

"You have to do that right this very minute?" I reproved.

"Yup. I'm gonna purge all those Maine people from my friends list right now. They're all mental."

"You can't hold off until you get back to your room?"

"*Psssh*. I'll forget by then."

It was impossible to ignore her since she was sitting right beside me, so as she accessed her Facebook page, I angled my body in her direction, watching.

"Are you on Facebook?" she asked.

"Nope. I guard my privacy tenaciously."

"You're so nineteenth century."

A page blossomed on her screen, filled with a cartoon of cow heads, bushel baskets of vegetables, and a lot of pictures. I squinted at a number appearing in parentheses after the word "Friends." "Is that how many friends you have now?" I blinked to make sure I was seeing correctly.

A hush fell over the table as all eyes were riveted on Bernice.

"Yup. This trip helped me crack a thousand."

"That's impossible," argued Margi. "How could you add over three hundred friends since you left Iowa? It's only been three days. We haven't met that many people."

"Persistence. I won't have quite that many when I finish with my purge, but it'll be ten times more than the rest of you slackers." She isolated a photo and tapped her finger to the screen, causing the number in parentheses to decrease by one.

"Was that Margi's photo you just deleted?" I asked.

"Yup. I unfriended her."

"You what?" shrieked Margi.

Uh-oh. This wasn't good. The rest of the gang went for their phones like gunslingers going for their guns, lips compressed, eyes intent, thumbs at the ready.

"I thought you were going to purge the Maine people," I reminded Bernice.

"I am. That was just a little unfinished business."

"So how come so many of your photos are headshots of faceless people?" I asked.

"My friends aren't very photogenic."

Before she could zap another photo, the number indicating her friend count began dropping faster than Netflix stock after its price hike, leaving her with a sum total of—"Take *that!*" crowed Margi, as high-fives broke out all around the table—ten fewer friends.

In the space of two thousand years, our methods for fighting foes had switched from eliminating them from the face of the earth, to eliminating them from our computer screens. I don't know what the military-industrial complex had to say about the new methods, but funeral home directors were really taking a hit.

Ignoring her dinner companions, Bernice called up Mary Lou McManus's photo, touched the screen, and scrubbed her.

"Wait a minute." I stopped her as she prepared to go on. "Go back to that generic headshot. There. Mary Katherine Fruth. Mrs. Fruth. She was my first grade music teacher!"

"Imagine that," said Bernice, skipping ahead to another photo.

"But … why is Mrs. Fruth on your friends list? She died when I was ten."

Margi gasped so loudly, her new Belgian lace collar got sucked into her mouth. "*That's* why her count is so high. She's friending dead people!"

"Could I borrow that, please?" I asked Bernice as I snatched her phone out of her hand. "Who else do you have in here?"

"Give that back to—"

I shooed her hand away. "Here's another faceless headshot. H. J. Saterlie. Is H. J. merely unphotogenic or stone cold dead?"

"I used to know a H. J. Saterlie," Osmond recalled. "He ran the Esso station on the corner of First and Main. But he died about the time Prohibition ended, so I doubt it's the same fella."

"It's the same fella all right," accused Helen. "Bernice has finally hit an all-time low. She's having séances to call up the dead, and then she's communicating with them on Facebook!"

I stared at Helen, wondering if medical research would one day discover a link between the overuse of eyebrow pencils and a decline in cognitive thinking.

"Good news, good news," tittered Jackie as she strutted back to the table. "Wally suffered a very minor concussion, so he's going to remain in the hospital overnight, and then he and Beth Ann will take the train back to Amsterdam tomorrow. And what's even more fabulous, Beth Ann says that Wally is so grateful she's there with him, she thinks she's starting to hear wedding bells."

"I heard bells once," reminisced George, "but it turned out to be tinnitus."

Jackie flashed all thirty-two teeth as she snuggled back into her chair, her smile gradually fading as she absorbed the negative energy of her dinner companions. "What's wrong with you people? Did someone else die while I was gone?"

"I'm outta here," snarled Bernice, clambering out of her chair. "My water pill just kicked in."

I craned my neck to follow her progress, and when she'd exited the room, I gave the signal. "Okay, she's gone. Now you can talk about her. But cut her a little slack. That was a pretty clever way to game the system."

For the next ten minutes the conversation grew heated as the gang complained about how they'd been hoodwinked.

"I bet she drug up them dead folks and give 'em all fake accounts 'cuz she needed folks to play Farmville with her," reasoned Nana.

"What's Farmville?" I asked as I continued to pore over Bernice's Facebook page.

A collective gasp.

"You've never heard of Farmville?" marveled Tilly.

So while everyone explained how Facebookers could partake in the joys of growing fruits and vegetables on a computer screen rather than in an actual rain-soaked field, where they might have to face real mud, real bugs, and real odor from passing pig haulers, I checked out the rest of Bernice's online friends.

"Doesn't anyone want to hear about the exciting launch of my new business?" implored Jackie.

Even though a majority of Bernice's friends were dead, she'd still managed to snare a few live ones. Mike McManus, Beth Ann

Oliver, Gary Bouchard, Laura LaPierre, Chip Soucy, and some guests whose faces I recognized, but whose names I hadn't learned yet. I touched the headshot of a familiar face and was surprised when the screen changed to that person's page, complete with their personal profile and a column listing all *their* friends. *Uff-da.* I knew what Facebook was now. A pyramid scheme!

"I need a catchy name for my business," said Jackie. "Anyone have any ideas?"

I noted the person's current city, marital status, birthday, work information, educational background, and then I browsed through the photos of the people listed as friends, all ten of them. Doris Albert from Binghamton. William Albert from Binghamton. Tom Thum from Binghamton. Hey, Jackie's husband! Then I ran across two names that gave me pause.

"How's this for catchy?" asked Nana. "And the Bride Wore—"

"Omigod, Mrs. S. I love it!"

I studied the names—Matthew Albert and Sue Albert—but what really threw me was the city of residence: Bangor, Maine. *Hunh.* Beth Ann had never mentioned having any connection to Bangor.

"I thought you told us Wally and his girlfriend weren't coming back 'til tomorrow," crabbed Bernice as she skulked back to the table.

"I did," said Jackie. "They're taking the train."

"Then how come I just saw the girlfriend sneak up the stairs by the lobby restroom?"

Jackie pulled a look. "What?"

"OH, MY GOD!" I knocked my chair over in my rush to get up. I threw a desperate look at Jackie. "What's Beth Ann's room number?"

269

"Two-twenty-five. Why? Where are you going? Have you paid your bill yet?

"Gimme my phone back!" yelled Bernice as I raced out the door and through the lobby. The elevator was open, but remembering how slow it was, I pushed through the door to the stairwell and took the stairs instead. I could kick myself for being so gullible. I *hated* being duped. I *hated* being made to look the fool.

I pelted up the stairs and yanked opened the fire door. Running down the corridor, I found room 225 and pounded on the door. "I know you're in there," I yelled. "Bernice saw you head into the stairwell." I pressed my ear to the door.

Silence.

I squeezed Bernice's smartphone, holding it close to my chest. "I'm looking at your Facebook page right now and noticing that you have a couple of friends who live in Bangor, Maine. Their last name is Albert. Would they be any relation to the Mr. Albert who taught math at Francis Xavier? Because if they are, I'm thinking you might be related to him, too." I listened through the door again.

Nothing.

"Mr. Albert was your father, wasn't he, Beth?"

The floor creaked, as if she were creeping closer.

"I heard how shy your dad was. I can't imagine how difficult it must have been for him to face Paula Peavey and Pete Finnegan every day. Or to be insulted by dumb jocks like Ricky Hennessy. Or to have mean practical jokes played on him by the football team. He must have felt traumatized on a daily basis."

I could hear her breathing on the other side of the door.

"It's why you killed them, isn't it. To pay them back for what they did to your dad."

"They were so mean to him," she uttered in a small voice. "Paula humiliated him. Pete made him feel stupid. He didn't deserve that. He'd been such a dedicated teacher, and they ruined him. They turned him into a broken, nerve-riddled shell."

"Were you going to stop at two, or did you have more people targeted in your master plan?"

"I didn't really have a master plan. I just had to watch for opportunities and take advantage of them."

"Like running into Paula on your way back from the Red Light District? Or standing next to Pete in Anne Frank's house?"

"Or finding Wally on the stairs at the Atlantic Wall."

It took me a half-second to process that. "YOU PUSHED WALLY DOWN THE STAIRS?"

"No one's told you yet?"

"NO!"

"Damn."

"Why did you push Wally? What did he ever do to you other than want to get to know you better?"

"Because I made the mistake of showing him my Facebook page the night I helped him with his computer. If he asked to friend me, and he noticed the Bangor connection, he might have asked questions I wasn't prepared to answer."

"So your only option was to kill him?"

"That was the idea. Hey, I didn't want to take any chances. And then *you* go and *screw* things up by asking me to ride in the ambulance with him. Who do I look like to you? Freaking Florence Nightingale?"

I sucked in my breath. "Oh, my God. Did you lie to us about his condition?"

"Well, duh! I had to tell you something, or you would have gotten suspicious."

"Is Wally all right?"

"How should I know? Do you think I planned to hang around until he regained consciousness? Do you think I wanted to be there when he told his doctors he'd been pushed? He didn't see me, but why risk it?"

"You … you …"

"I didn't really want to hurt Wally. I would have preferred to push Ricky Hennessy or Gary Bouchard … or that annoying woman with the wiry hair who wouldn't stop hounding me until I became her Facebook friend. All three of them were next on my list. But they were never by themselves, so I had to settle on Wally."

Oh, my God. Bernice had been on her hit list? "I can't believe what you've done! And to think I believed your phony story about sucking up to Jackie because you wanted writing advice. What a cover story for you. What an alibi!"

"That wasn't a lie. I still want to be a writer. I'll even do e-books if I have to, but what I'd really like is—"

"Why did you come back here? When you ran away from the hospital, why didn't you just keep running?"

"I couldn't." I heard an irritated scuffing sound at the bottom of the door. "I forgot my passport in the room safe."

"A lot of good it's going to do you. I'm calling the police."

As I tried to figure out how to exit Facebook so I could make the call, the door suddenly opened and Beth Ann flew at me, driving me against the opposite wall with enough force to knock the wind from my lungs. My spine screamed in protest. My head slammed against the wall. Bernice's phone squirted out of my hand and fell to the floor, where it got crunched beneath Beth Ann's foot. I doubled over, gasping, agony exploding in my chest, while Beth Ann pounded down the corridor toward the stairwell.

Uff-da.

Inching upward, I sucked down gulps of air as I massaged my chest, kneaded my spine, and rubbed the back of my head. When I was able to breathe again without pain, I took off after Beth Ann at a half-run, picking up speed as I descended the stairs.

"You won't get away," I yelled down the stairwell.

I heard the ground-floor door open, then close.

I lunged recklessly over two and three stairs at a time. I hit the ground floor running, shot through the door and into the main lobby. I looked left and right.

She was heading for the revolving door.

"Stop her!" I shouted across the lobby, pointing in her direction. "Someone stop her!"

Officer Vanden Boogard raced into the lobby from the dining room.

"She's the killer!" I gesticulated as she swooped into the glass enclosure.

Officer Vanden Boogard gave chase, but she speeded up the door's revolutions by depressing the horizontal bar. Before Vanden Boogard could even cross the floor, she'd rushed onto the sidewalk and—

Screeeech. BAM. Thunk.

I winced at the sound before peering through the revolving door at the tire that was still spinning crazily in the air.

Oops. I guess she forgot to look both ways.

TWENTY-TWO

"TOM IS SO EMBARRASSED about his part in this," Jackie apologized the following day. "Can you imagine his guilt? Hooking me up with a serial killer. But she seemed so normal to him. I think it was a case of his being dazzled by her hair." She shot a look heavenward. "Men. They can be so dense." She fluttered her lashes at Wally and smiled. "No disrespect to you, of course."

We were gathered in my room, celebrating Wally's return. He'd broken bones in both arms in his fall, so he was sporting casts that we'd all signed with goofy get-well wishes. Beth Ann's lie about a slight concussion had turned out to be true, so he was battling a headache as well, but he seemed to be enjoying the attention we were heaping on him.

"That young woman is dang lucky to be alive after that bicycle run into her," said Nana.

Tilly shrugged. "She might not think so, Marion. She'll have to pay quite the penalty for what she's done."

"Did she ever talk to Tom about what happened to her dad?" I asked Jackie. "People probably dish more dirt in the styling chair than they do in the confessional."

"Well, word on the rumor mill is that her dad suffered a complete nervous breakdown after Paula Peavey's class graduated. One of Tom's stylists knows someone who knows Beth Ann's aunt, so we have this straight from the horse's mouth. He couldn't return to teaching, so he moved to Binghamton to be close to his brother, but the aunt says he was never quite the same. He performed menial jobs, married late in life, and fathered Beth Ann, but he went into a depression after his wife ran off, and his mental health got worse and worse as the years went by, and Beth Ann was left to deal with him. The aunt said that on his occasional good days, he'd work himself into a lather about the students back in Bangor, listing their transgressions and damning them all by name. I guess Beth Ann heard an earful growing up."

"And she vowed to get even," I lamented. "Somehow."

"Enter the age of the Internet," said Tilly, cradling her smartphone. "St. Francis Xavier High School creates a website that lists every student in every graduating class and posts the latest news about future reunions and who's signed up for them. So Beth Ann can obsess over her father's tormentors at length."

"Slam, bam, thank you, ma'am," said Jackie. "Beth Ann knew about this tour and was going to sign up for it no matter what. The way everything else came together was just plain bad luck."

I glanced at Wally, smiling gently. "Did you know it was Beth Ann who pushed you?"

He shook his head. "Not exactly. When I finally regained consciousness, I told my doctor I'd been pushed, so he quizzed me about what else I could recall. That's when I remembered smelling Beth Ann's perfume. Oil of Roses. I hate that stuff."

"Why did it take so long for the Amsterdam police to be contacted?" asked Jackie. "What was the holdup?"

Wally laughed. "Are you kidding me? With all the bureaucratic red tape between countries? That was pretty doggone fast."

"That nice young police officer wasn't none too happy about the delay," confided Nana. "When he come into the dinin' room lookin' for Beth Ann, he was complainin' about leavin' this place one minute, then havin' to turn around and come back the next."

"Our new tour director arrives bright and early tomorrow morning," I said, exchanging a look with Wally. "You're being relieved of duty so you can recuperate. I bet you'll be happy to leave this whacky crew of ours behind."

He lifted his shoulders in a slow roll, as if he were doing warm-ups for yoga exercises. "Mmm, not so much. In fact, I've been thinking that I might just tag along and finish out the tour with you guys. What else am I going to do?" He raised his plaster-casted forearms. "Play the harp?"

"Do you play the harp?" cooed Alice. "That's my very favorite stringed instrument."

"I prefer steel drums," said Dick Teig. "They're louder."

"Since when is a drum a stringed instrument?" asked Margi.

"Why does my favorite instrument have to have strings?" asked Dick.

"The steel drum is a tuned percussion instrument," advised Tilly, "as opposed to the triangle, which is nontuned."

"I'm fond of handbells," said Grace. "Do they count as an instrument?"

"I prefer a gong myself," admitted Osmond.

"You people are such morons," huffed Bernice. "Next up, Osmond will want to know how many of you think a glockenspiel should be classified as a wind instrument."

"What's a glockenspiel?" asked Margi.

Nana stuck out her bottom lip in thought. "I think it's some kinda gun."

Bernice groaned. "*Why* do I come on these trips with you people? I should have my head examined." She folded her arms across her chest, giving everyone a pinched look. "And before I sign up for the next one, someone had better buy me a replacement for the phone she smashed, or we'll be talking major litigation. I might even offer this one to Judge Judy."

As they continued to pick at each other in their nonsensical fashion, I leaned back in my chair and smiled, happy that everything was returning to normal.

A cellphone chimed nearby. Mine.

Digging it out of my shoulder bag, I left the affectionate anarchy of my hotel room and stepped out into the corridor. "Hi, sweetie! That was a pretty short fishing trip. How did it go? I've missed talking to you."

"Your parents took great delight showing me how exciting it is to sit in a shallow-bottomed boat, attaching worms to fish hooks. We sat for hours in the rain, waiting for the fish to bite, only to *throw* them back into the water once they did bite, so we could begin the process all over again—some mystifying practice called catch and release."

"Had the time of your life, huh?"

"Your parents did. In fact, they claimed they had such a wonderful time hanging out with me, they're anxious to do it again."

"I'll talk to them. Fear not. You'll never have to go fishing again."

"It's much worse than that, Emily. They've decided to sign up for the trip to Scotland."

"What?" My heart stopped dead in my chest. "You mean, *our* trip to Scotland?"

"They've already made a deposit. They're coming with us."

"TOGETHER? Not together. *Please*, tell me they're not coming together."

"Together."

Oh, God.

THE END

ACKNOWLEDGMENTS

When my Passport to Peril mystery series was canceled in 2007, I thought Emily, Nana, and the rest of the gang had been permanently grounded. So I began work on another project, which is when emails started trickling, then flooding, into my inbox. "When will the next adventure be published?" you asked. "Emily and Nana have become part of my own family," you confided. "Please don't let the series end." You were eloquent, passionate, giddily enthusiastic, and relentless. I never realized how many loyal fans I had until the books stopped being published.

Then, in 2009, in a turn of events I never saw coming, newly hired Midnight Ink acquisitions editor, Terri Bischoff, contacted me to ask if I'd like to resurrect the Passport to Peril series. It took me all of two seconds to realize the answer to that was YES! I was dying to reconnect with the Iowa gang, because sometime when I wasn't looking, they'd become an integral part of my own family, too, and I missed them.

So, thank you, Terri, for renewing the gang's passports and allowing them to travel again. Thank you to fellow writers Pam Johnson and Carrie Bebris for coming up with bankable ideas for me at our annual writers' retreat. Thank you to my literary agent, Irene Goodman, who backs my projects enthusiastically, no matter what they are. Thank you to my husband, Brian, who always makes sure I'm fed when I'm in a writing frenzy. But most of all, thank you to my fans, whose words of encouragement and unflagging good wishes bolstered me when I needed it. You make me feel a little like Tinkerbell, who came to life again after she heard the wondrous applause.

Thank you, dear fans, for clapping.

ABOUT THE AUTHOR

After experiencing disastrous vacations on three continents, Maddy Hunter decided to combine her love of humor, travel, and storytelling to fictionalize her misadventures. Inspired by her feisty aunt and by memories of her Irish grandmother, she created the nationally bestselling, Agatha Award-nominated Passport to Peril mystery series, where quirky seniors from Iowa get to relive everything that went wrong on Maddy's holiday. *Dutch Me Deadly* is the seventh book in the series. Maddy lives in Madison, Wisconsin, with her husband and a head full of imaginary characters who keep asking, "Are we there yet?"

Please visit her website at www.maddyhunter.com, or become a follower on her Maddy Hunter Facebook Fan Page.